MALCHUS

To order additional copies of *Malchus,* by Noni Beth Gibbs,
call 1-800-765-6955.

Visit us at www.reviewandherald.com for information on other
Review and Herald® products.

MALCHUS

Touched by Jesus

NONI BETH GIBBS

REVIEW AND HERALD® PUBLISHING ASSOCIATION
HAGERSTOWN, MD 21740

The author assumes full responsibility for the accuracy of all facts and quotations
as cited in this book.

This book was
Edited by Gerald Wheeler
Copyedited by James Cavil
Cover designed by Genesis Design
Cover illustration by Robert Hunt
Interior design by Candy Harvey
Electronic makeup by Shirley M. Bolivar
Typeset: Bembo 11.5/13.5

PRINTED IN U.S.A.

09 08 07 06 05   5 4 3 2 1

R&H Cataloging Service
Gibbs, Noni Beth, 1972-   .
     Malchus: touched by Jesus

     I. Title.

ISBN: 0-8280-1826-X

– DEDICATION –

To Jenilyn Drake Kahrs,
my dear sister-in-law,
whose encouragement
kept me going
from beginning to end.

– ACKNOWLEDGMENTS –

From my earliest years my parents, Don and Susan Kahrs, instilled in me a love of books. By the age of 5, I was strenuously protesting my father's unfairness in limiting me to four hours of reading a day. I am so grateful to both of them for everything they taught me and for not saying "I told you so" when I had to start wearing reading glasses.

My maternal grandparents, Ken and Marie Day, were both English teachers and introduced me to great literature. I will never forget my grandfather's dramatic renditions of the stories of John Colter, Hugh Glass, and other frontier favorites.

It was always such a treat to visit my grandmother Doris Kahrs. Her house was the springboard for exciting trips into the desert—experiences that I little knew at the time would influence my ideas of what it was like for Jesus in His temptation.

Eventually I hope to have written enough books to be able to thank all my teachers by name. I look up to all of you still and owe you an eternal debt for putting up with me for so many years. In this book I want to make special mention of my English teachers: Calvin Unterseher, of Lodi Academy; and William Agopsowics, from San Joaquin Delta College.

My knowledge of the events surrounding the trial of Jesus has been enriched by the information that attorney Lewis Walton presents in his tape series *Rediscovering Calvary*. My heart is touched anew every time I hear it and contemplate the sheer and utter torture that the sinless Lamb of God took upon Himself.

Thank you to the superb team of editors and designers that helped polish this book and bring it to fruition—I could never have done this without you.

My two brothers are fantastic. Thank you, David, for your helpful input and for bringing the aforementioned Jenilyn into the family. And Kenny, I appreciate more than I can say your extreme patience and tolerance in dressing up in all kinds of exotic costumes and posing for inspiring photos. Any of my readers who want a copy can e-mail me at . . . just kidding, Kenny!

Hey, Tina, you thought I had forgotten about you, didn't you? Your fountain of great ideas is invaluable. The time you spend helping me try to keep things orderly while I'm in the throes of creativity deserves a medal. You are just the sister I wanted, the best I could possibly have hoped for, which is fortunate since you're the only one I ever got.

Sweetheart, you've been my inspiration in more ways than you know. I appreciate all that you do, and thank you for encouraging my writing and music. I love you.

Damon, Christy, and Devon—my sweet children, my messy little angels—you are the next generation of bookworms. No more than four hours of reading per day!

– Principal Characters –

- **Allat**—a primary goddess of Nabataea.
- **Alona** *(strong as an oak)*—wife of Malchus.
- **Annas** *(one who answers; humble)*—father-in-law of Caiaphas and former high priest himself.
- **Aretas IV** *(virtuous)*—king of Nabataea during the time of Jesus.
- **Arnon** *(roaring stream)*—treasurer of Barabbas' rebel army.
- **Barabbas** *(son of his father)*—a robber, murderer, and self-proclaimed messiah.
- **Betzalel** *(in God's shadow)*—the paralytic at the Pool of Beth-zatha.
- **Caiaphas**—high priest of Israel.
- **Chaim** *(life)*—the infant son of Chaya, Safiya's friend.
- **Chaya** *(life)*—Safiya's friend; a resident of Bethlehem at the time of Jesus' birth.
- **Claudia**—wife of Pontius Pilate.
- **Deron** *(free)*—guardian of first Josu, then Malchus.
- **Dushara**—principal god of the Nabataeans.
- **Eben** *(rock)*—head of security in Barabbas' army.
- **Elan** *(tree)*—Barabbas' military advisor.
- **Elazar** *(God helps)*—a captain of the angelic host.
- **Elhanan** *(God is gracious)*—the father from Capernaum whose son was sick.
- **Erith** *(flower)*—Alona's maid and best friend.
- **Gabriel**—angel in charge of Jesus' safety
- **Gershom** *(exiled)*—Malchus' father; Safiya's husband.
- **Gurion** *(young lion)*—guardian of Safiya.
- **Herod Antipas**—son of Herod the Great; murderer of John the Baptist.
- **Herod Archelaus**—son of Herod the Great; the last true king of Israel.
- **Herodias**—illicit wife of Herod Antipas; former wife of his brother, Philip.
- **Herod the Great**—king of Israel; ordered the slaughter of the children of Bethlehem.
- **Husam** *(sword)*—Malchus' Nabataean cousin.
- **James** *(supplanter)*—member of the inner circle; John's brother; a son of thunder.
- **Jesus** *(salvation)*—the center of everything.
- **John** *(gift from God)*—member of the inner circle; James' brother; a son of thunder.
- **John the Baptist**—Jesus' cousin; chosen to prepare the way of the Messiah.

- **Jonas** *(dove)*—Chaya's husband; a resident of Bethlehem.
- **Jori-hod** *(descending-vigorous)*—Malchus' barely tolerated donkey.
- **Joseph of Arimathea**—a top member of the Sanhedrin.
- **Josias** *(God is salvation)*—Othniel's preferred alias.
- **Josu** *(God saves)*—Safiya's first son and Malchus' brother.
- **Judas Iscariot**—the treasurer of the inner circle.
- **Kivi** *(protected)*—Alona's cherished black mare.
- **Lazarus** *(God will help)*—one of Jesus' closest friends.
- **Malachi** *(messenger of God)*—Malchus' preferred alias.
- **Malchus** *(king)*—Caiaphas' chief servant; also the name of an ancient king of Nabataea.
- **Malthace**—wife of Herod the Great; mother of Herod Antipas and Herod Archelaus.
- **Marcus Aburius Geminus**—a Roman officer under Pilate.
- **Martha** *(lady, mistress)*—sister of Lazarus and Mary.
- **Mary** *(the beloved one)*—Jesus' mother.
- **Mary of Magdala**—sister of Martha and Lazarus.
- **Maryam** *(the beloved one)*—wife of Aretas IV; Malchus' grandmother.
- **Najiyah** *(safe)*—discarded wife of Herod Antipas; Safiya's half sister.
- **Nasir** *(the helpful one)*—guardian assigned to Gershom.
- **Nathaniel** *(gift of God)*—a scribe for Barabbas.
- **Nicodemus**—a respected member of the Sanhedrin and secret ally of Jesus.
- **Oded**—Alona's friend; a servant of her uncle.
- **Ornah** *(cedar tree)*—Oded's sister.
- **Othniel**—Malchus' cousin; also a servant of Caiaphas.
- **Pontius Pilate**—Roman governor of Judea whose cruelty often inflamed the Jews.
- **Ranon** *(joyful)*—Oded's nephew; son of Ornah.
- **Ronia** *(my joy)*—wife of Elhanan, the father from Capernaum.
- **Safiya** *(tranquil)*—daughter of Aretas and Maryam; Malchus' mother.
- **Salome**—daughter of Herodias.
- **Simeon** *(hearing)*—son of Malchus and Alona.
- **Simon Peter**—an impulsive fisherman and member of the inner circle.
- **Taavi** *(dearly loved)*—the little son of Elhanan and Ronia.
- **Valerius**—messenger for Pontius Pilate.
- **Vitellius**—superior of Pilate, and Syrian legate.
- **Yachne** *(kind)*—mother figure in the village of Nain.
- **Yagil** *(he will rejoice)*—Gershom's employer in Bethlehem.
- **Yasirah** *(lenient)*—a Samaritan woman.
- **Zacharias** *(remembered by God)*—father of John the Baptist.
- **Zarad** *(ambush)*—the mysterious colleague of Annas and Caiaphas.

– Prologue –

"Chaya! Oh, Chaya, let me see him," Safiya called as she shifted the small boy on her hip and hurried toward her friend. "Whatever are you doing out so early in the morning? Oh, you should have heard your Jonas go on when he stopped by to tell Gershom the good news. You would think no one had ever had a son before."

The other woman smiled as she drew back the wrapping from the small bundle she carried. A tiny brown face came into view, brow furrowed intently, and eyes crinkled shut. "I can hardly blame him when I feel just the same way," she said as the newborn reacted to the light. She rocked the infant gently, and his face relaxed. "Here he is, only nine days old, and already it seems as if we've always had him with us."

Safiya laughed, causing several passersby to glance curiously in her direction. "What did you name him? Is he Jonas, after his father and grandfather?"

Leaning a bit closer, Chaya whispered, "Jonas' father wanted him named so, but Jonas decided to name him after me. This is our little Chaim." Carefully she unwound a lock of dark hair wrapped around his fingers and brushed it back over her shoulder, saying whimsically, "See how he entangles himself in our lives." With a meaningful look at Safiya she added, "And it looks like it will not be too long until your family grows as well."

With the gesture so familiar to all mothers Safiya ran her hand over the swelling of her abdomen. As she looked at Chaya's glowing face, she wondered that she had ever thought her plain. "Yes, it's only a few more weeks until our new son makes his appearance. It might as well be a year, how I feel right now," she groaned, "but at least I know what to expect this time."

But Chaya had stopped listening and was peering over Safiya's shoulder. "Look," she breathed, "they are getting ready to leave already. Did you ever see anyone so rich?" Suddenly Safiya became aware that the marketplace was filling with noise and confusion. Camel after camel appeared, brilliant crimson tassels on their bridles and finely worked gold and bronze on their saddles. Through it all wove exotic servants in brightly colored garments. A few, obviously of high rank, had heavy gold chains looped about their necks.

"What? They just arrived yesterday, and I heard they had been traveling for more than a year," Safiya said, shifting her son, now heavy with sleep, to the other arm. "I can't believe they're going so soon. Have you heard what is going on?"

A toothless old woman near them in the crowd turned toward them. Her eyes gleamed brightly, and her crooked finger pointed straight at Safiya's nose. "I can tell you just what happened." The woman leaned in closer, savoring the bit of gossip she was about to share.

"A little more than a year ago, it was, during the counting. You remember how full our town was. Well, a young couple showed up, the wife just bursting with child." Fascinated, Safiya stared at the woman's wagging finger, then moved her gaze upward to the woman's face as the old one went on. "I heard as how they had been married only two or three months, and that night the baby was born. Early, I'll wager." She cackled scornfully. "But not six months early, I tell you. I leave you to draw your own conclusions."

"Remember the star," Deron whispered to Safiya. "Remember the star over Bethlehem." Veiled from her sight, he listened to her conversation with intense interest, wondering how to make her understand.

For a moment Safiya frowned in puzzlement, her lips moving as she counted silently. "But wasn't that—yes, it was a year last month since the star came. How did you know about all this?"

The woman picked at the sleeve of her faded blue robe. "My husband was the innkeeper who let them use his stable. He died a short while later. Anyway, that was the very same night the star first appeared."

Safiya's eyes widened. "It was, really? But what does that have to do with the kings?"

"That's what I keep trying to tell you," the old woman said. "The kings came to visit that same couple, the one from our inn. Of course they aren't staying with us anymore. I would never stand for that sort of woman under my roof, so as soon as my husband died, that was that!" She nodded emphatically.

Suddenly the crowd gasped and fell silent. A small group of men appeared, dressed in such glorious garments that even King Herod would have looked poor by comparison. Safiya and Chaya stared as the foreigners barked a few orders in an unfamiliar tongue, glanced around to make sure all the camels were properly loaded, and hastily climbed on their mounts. The beasts scrambled awkwardly to their feet, riders swaying wildly. Then the visitors led the procession out the city gates, their faces set and grim.

"Don't you notice anything different?" Deron asked. "The kings are leaving so quickly. Something must be wrong."

"I think something is wrong, Chaya," Safiya said. "Did you see them when they arrived yesterday? They acted as if they were on their way to a celebration. Now they look almost angry."

"I didn't see them yesterday," the other woman sighed, "This is my first day out of the house. But you're right—I think they do appear upset. I hope no one offended them. I'd hate for them to come back with an army."

Deron turned to the massive, glowing being beside him. He straightened his slighter frame and ran his fingers through his hair in a gesture of frustration. "What more can we do, Gurion? I've been trying for days, and I know you have too. Isn't there any way to save him?" His eyes filled with tears as he looked at his small sleeping charge.

"Ah, my friend," Gurion sighed, "you know our orders as well as I do. We may speak only to their hearts and try to awaken them to the danger."

"But time is so short," Deron countered. "There are only hours left until—"

"Don't lose hope yet. As you say, we still have some hours left. All we can do is keep trying." Gurion clapped his friend on the shoulder and tried to look encouraging.

The two young women found themselves swept along as the crowd followed the procession out the city gates. They ignored the cloud of dust that bathed both rich and poor alike. At first the camel train was a mass of churning confusion, but soon it straightened out in an orderly line on the road to Jerusalem.

Chaya turned to her friend. "I wonder if we'll ever know what that was all about."

Safiya shook her head. "I doubt it. From the looks on their faces, I think we've seen the last of them. We might as well go—everyone else is." Still chattering briskly, they entered the village.

One small boy, more curious than the rest, ran as fast as his short legs would carry him to the top of a nearby hill, hoping to watch the strange procession a little longer. At the crest he threw himself down on the grass, panting, to rest for a while. For some distance the caravan continued on straight, but when they were out of sight of Bethlehem, they slowed to a stop by a goat trail that led off to the left of the main road. The riders turned their beasts onto it, carefully picking their way in a wide circle around the town, and headed in the opposite direction from Jerusalem.

The boy puzzled over it for a moment, but then his stomach growled hungrily, and he hurriedly retraced his steps to Bethlehem. By the time he entered the town's narrow streets he had forgotten what he had seen.

＊　＊　＊

Safiya hummed to herself as she prepared the meal, her supple hands working the dough and carefully shaping it into small loaves.

"Here, Josu, would you like to make a loaf too?" The child squealed with laughter as the bread dough oozed through his tiny fingers. He squeezed it and patted it in careful imitation of what he had seen his mother do. His dark eyes sparkled with pride as he gave a small, deformed lump to her. "Very good, Josu. Wait until Abba sees it. He will think your loaf tastes the best of all!"

"Abba," repeated the toddler. "Abba, Abba!" He clapped his sticky hands in delight.

His mother chuckled. "That's right, your father will be home very soon, and you can show him all the things you have done today." She was busily about her tasks when suddenly two strong, rough hands closed over her eyes.

Wrenching free, she threw herself into the arms of a tall, wavy-haired man in a striped, dusty robe. "Gershom! I didn't think you would be home this early," she cried, giggling as he planted a whiskery kiss by her ear.

"I finished early, so I came home to spend some time with my wife and son." He swooped the child up in his arms, throwing him into the air again and again until they both were out of breath and Safiya was begging him to stop.

"Honestly, it's a wonder you don't drop him on his head," she scolded. "Oh, did you hear about those foreign visitors we had today?"

Instantly sober, Gershom nodded. "I heard quite a bit in the market-place. Yagil came by to check my work and said he had seen them this morning. He had heard from someone else that they came because of the star. What I don't understand is why they would travel all that way, then leave so soon. I hope no one here made them angry."

"Chaya said almost exactly the same thing," his wife commented. "Do you know what else I heard?" She told Gershom of her conversation with the old woman. "What do you think it means?"

"I don't know, but I wouldn't worry too much about it. Even if the dignitaries were angry about something, it would take years for them to go home, gather an army, and return here again." He reached over and picked up one of the cooling loaves. "And you think the star might have something to do with that couple? It's hardly likely anything would happen because an impure woman gave birth. She's just lucky she found someone to marry her before she was stoned."

"Oh, Gershom, you know we can't just stone people anymore—it's against the law." She buried her face in his chest, holding him close. Feeling a tug on her robe, she looked down. "Little man, are you feeling left out? Come up and see your abba." She picked the baby up, and they both stood there within the circle of Gershom's embrace.

"You must leave this place at once," Gurion whispered to her. "Go to your husband's family. There is no time to spare." He turned to another guardian nearby. "Nasir, you have been with Gershom all day. Were you able to get through to him at all?"

Nasir shook his head. "All the people of this town are so stubborn and pre-occupied with their lives, but it seems as if the men are the hardest to reach."

Gurion sighed. "Don't blame yourself. It is usually that way. They just don't trust the impressions we keep giving them. Even the women are barely listening to us. I don't know if anyone will choose to escape."

Deron covered his face with his hands. *"What about the Lord?"*

"Of course Gabriel has personal charge of His safety," Gurion assured him. *"And I think His parents are more responsive than those native to this city, but even they have not left yet. Still, I know that the Almighty would not have chosen them to care for Him if they were not loyal to Him."*

Once again Gurion spoke inaudibly to Safiya. *"Go quickly to your husband's parents. It is a matter of life and death."*

Stirred by a sudden unease, Safiya raised her head. "Your parents are not far away, and we haven't seen them for several months. Could we visit them?"

"When—after the baby is born?"

"No, husband, I mean now. Tonight. I can't explain why, but I really want to see them."

"Love, I think in your condition it would be better to wait. Besides, Yagil really needs my help tomorrow. I promised to finish the south field with him." She opened her mouth to protest, but Gershom interrupted: "Here is our little man. See? Notice how he can barely keep his eyes open. He needs his supper and bed. For that matter, I do too."

Although Safiya took her son willingly, her mind was still churning. *Oh, well,* she thought to herself, *Gershom is probably right. I'm just being silly because it's almost my time.* With a sigh she forced herself to concentrate on the work at hand.

— — —

"Captain Elazar, what news do you have?" Deron was the first to spot their commanding officer.

Elazar's face was solemn. He held his wings stiffly behind his back and stood tensely. *"In less than two hours Herod's spies will tell him of the foreign visitors' supposed trickery. Gabriel has asked me to pass the word that the guardians may now attempt to influence their charges through dreams."*

"But—" Gurion and Nasir both started to speak at once.

"No," the captain answered, knowing what each was about to ask, *"there is no other change to your orders. When the time comes, you are to watch. Nothing more."*

The three stood silent a moment as they watched their commanding officer stride to the next house. "Come," Deron said. "There is still hope. We must not give up. The life of my charge depends on it."

— — —

A giant sword hung in the sky over Bethlehem. Wielded by an unseen hand, it plunged into the ground in the center of the city. The earth shuddered and quaked as a fountain of blood rose where the blade pierced the soil. Quickly it became a raging torrent, a crimson flood that flung itself through the streets, sweeping the inhabitants along in its crest.

Safiya stood, frozen, on her doorstep. She felt a tug at her hand. Josu stood between her and Gershom, trying to pull them toward safety. As the flood hurtled at them she turned to run, but too late. A powerful force pulled her off her feet and into its lethal embrace. All became blackness.

With a shrill cry Safiya sat up in bed, drenched with sweat. Next to her was the sleeping form of her husband. Stirring a little, he rolled over, his breathing once again even and deep. She groped around in the dark until her searching hands located Josu. Laying a palm on his chest, she felt herself partly reassured by his strong, steady heartbeat, yet it still seemed as if a heavy weight bore down on her. As she had often done before, she pushed aside her blanket and felt her way to the stairs leading up onto the roof.

Many times during the previous months she had spent peaceful hours bathing herself in the light of Bethlehem's strange star. Its rainbow colors twinkled and danced, seemingly just beyond the reach of her outstretched arms. She had almost come to think of it as her own, a special talisman in the heavens.

As she stepped out onto the roof, a chill seized her, and she sank to the rooftop. Trembling and rubbing her hands across her eyes, she again looked up into the night sky. The star was gone. The sky was black.

Gershom awakened a few moments later as someone shook him and plucked at his covers. "Safiya, is that you?" he mumbled. "What's wrong?"

Her teeth were chattering so much she could hardly get the words out. "The star. It's gone. We have to go. Somewhere, anywhere."

He drew her into his arms, "Hush, love, all is well. Remember a few days ago when the star moved over toward Jerusalem? It came right back in a day or two. I'm sure it will return this time, too."

Tears trickled down her cheeks and onto her husband's chest. "Please, may we go? I don't care where, so long as it is far from here."

Gershom stroked her hair soothingly. "All right. If it means that much to you, we will go. First thing in the morning. A few more hours can make no difference."

For a long time Safiya lay there, eyes open wide. The sky was growing bright, and she was just about to drift off again when she heard an unfamiliar noise. At first it sounded like the distant beat of a drum, but crescendoed to a pounding roar. Then came the sound of many feet, all stepping in unison. The first scream was soon joined by another—and another.

Creeping to the door, she glanced out. Far down the street she could see a contingent of Roman soldiers, armor gleaming faintly in the first light. One of them entered a doorway, only to emerge carrying a small bundle. He tossed it into the street, and several spears thrust into it simultaneously. A new outcry came from that house, while the soldiers moved on to the next. A woman ran out clutching a small boy. One quick sword thrust, and both lay dying in the street.

Panicking, Safiya scrambled over to the sleeping mats, beating on Gershom with her fists, then roughly snatching up Josu. At his whimper of protest, she clamped one hand over his mouth. Gershom blinked dazedly. Safiya would wait no longer.

Without stopping for a cloak, she darted out her door, immediately turning down the small alley by the neighbor's house. Looking up and down the next street, she darted across into the nearest alley, trying to work her way to the gate. Josu clung to her but kept silent.

There, the gate was in sight, but a half dozen red-plumed soldiers, swords drawn, barred the way. "After her," barked the commanding officer when he spotted her. Instantly two of the soldiers broke off and ran toward her.

Ignoring the cramping of her belly, Safiya fled in total panic, her breath coming in great gasps. She could hear the men gaining on her, but dared not risk a glance back. The air parched her throat. She tasted bile, and in spite of herself felt her steps begin to slow. Slipping into another alley, seeking a hiding place, she found herself in a small, dim courtyard with no way out.

She turned to face her attackers, retreating until she felt the wall press her back. "Please," she choked out. "I'll give you anything. Just let him go." As she stood there, face flushed, eyes raised boldly to meet theirs, the younger soldier was touched with pity.

"Let her go," he said softly to the other man. "One babe can surely make no difference. None will ever know."

In answer, the first soldier, a gnarled veteran accustomed to following orders, raised his spear. "Give the boy to us, and you will not be hurt."

"Never," she spat at him, holding her child close. With no further hesitation the older soldier gripped the spear with both hands and thrust it, pinning mother and child to the wall. He had to push against the wall with one foot before he could free it. As he hurried to rejoin his troop, he did not even look back as Safiya slid down the wall and slumped to the ground, a gory smear marking her path. She still clutched the body of her young son, their blood mingling in the dust.

Deron and Gurion both stood by her, one on each side, as she faced the soldiers. Their faces were wracked with pain, knowing they could not interfere. The spear raised. Just before it plunged home, Deron stepped in front of his charge. The blow passed through him, and he did not deflect it, but with his arms around the small boy he took away the pain, the fear, and cradled him as he died.

Frantic, Gershom searched the streets around his home in an ever-widening circle. He heard a voice call his name. Glancing in the door of a narrow court, he saw a huge man with dark, curly hair and a white robe kneeling over the body of a woman. The man had fastened a cloth around her shoulder, holding it tight to stanch the flow of blood. As the stranger stood, Gershom's view shifted to the stone floor next to his wife. What he saw brought a strangled cry from his lips. Harsh sobs shook his frame as he picked up the tiny body of his son. Then he felt a gentle hand on his shoulder and heard the man say, "Safiya will live, but you must get help for her quickly. She has lost much blood." When Gershom, eyes blurred with tears, turned to thank the man for saving his wife, the little courtyard was empty.

All over the city it was the same. In some places the grieving families could hardly walk without slipping in blood as they went about the gruesome task of retrieving their beloved sons. Flies began to gather on the eyes and mouths of the dead. In the unnatural hush following the devastation all that could be heard was the ululating cry of mourning.

Hundreds of guardians knelt in the streets and houses of Bethlehem, Deron among them. Like glowing pools of light, they stayed next to their charges, unseen by human eyes. Unheard by human ears was the sound of many angels weeping.

Chapter 1

Near sunset a lone traveler in a dusty robe made his way along the path leading into the Wadi Musa, the Valley of Moses. Rose-colored, purple, and brown sandstone walls streaked with yellow and gray loomed hundreds of feet into the air on either side of him, pitted with tombs high up the cliff face. The path narrowed, and the paving became smoother, worn by countless feet. Clay pipes carrying drinking water ran a jagged course along the length of the Siq, one of only two ways into the city. Not far ahead, the caravan with which he had crossed the desert shifted to single file to pass through the space between the towering rocks. The entrance was a narrow crack in the cliff, guarded by four soldiers.

Slowing his pace, Malchus allowed the noise and confusion of the caravan to mask him as he slipped into the city. He kept to the right, head lowered submissively. Towering above him on the left stood the place of sacrifice. The priests appeared tiny as they carried out their rituals high above the city. At times the blood ran down the stones and into the channels designed to carry it to the foot of the high place. Carvings of Dushara and a host of other deities decorated walls and pillars.

The marketplace was, as he expected, a confusion of swirling colors mingling with the smell of bread, fruit, dried fish, and incense. Merchants and buyers almost drowned each other out as each tried to get the better of the other. "Greetings," he said in Aramaic to a man reclining on a cushion in a little booth full of spices. "Might I have a drink of water?" he added humbly.

"Of course," replied the man, handing him a water skin. "What business brings you to Petra?"

"I received word that my grandmother has become very ill,"

Malchus lied easily, "so naturally I came as quickly as I could."

"Yes, yes," the man nodded. "What is your grandmother's name? Perhaps I know her." The merchant took the skin Malchus handed back to him. "You look as if you have traveled far to reach her."

"Her name is Maryam, but I doubt one of your exalted stature is acquainted with her. She is a good woman, but very poor." He easily sidestepped the question of where he came from. "I need a place to stay for tonight only, as it is getting late, and I am not sure just where Grandmother is living now."

The merchant pursed his lips in thought. "I have a room. Perhaps you would be interested in it." The two men haggled over the price, at last reaching an agreement. The merchant held out his plump hand to receive the coins and climbed slowly to his feet, panting from exertion, and led the way to a small chamber.

"Blessings on you and your family for your hospitality," Malchus said, bowing slightly, his golden-brown eyes candidly meeting those of his host.

Once alone, he looked around the small room, noting that it appeared to be reasonably clean. He splashed water on his face from a small, cracked basin and used a rag to wipe as much dirt as possible from himself. It would have to do. Sinking to the sleeping mat, he pulled his robe tightly about him and fell immediately into a light sleep.

A few hours later he woke, listening into the darkness for any sound. Muted voices and laughter drifted through from the open windows of nearby homes, and crockery shattered as someone accidentally knocked a dish to the ground. The air was still hot, with only a languid breeze occasionally stirring through the room.

Slipping noiselessly from his bed, Malchus shed his robe, revealing a loose-fitting black garment. He checked the sealed pouch carefully strapped against the bare skin of his chest, then hung his sandals around his neck by the cords. Taking a deep breath, he crossed to the window and climbed out.

A soft hiss escaped his lips as his fingers and toes found cracks in the wall. About halfway down he let go, dropping into a crouch as he landed, then stepping quickly into the shadow of the building. A quick glance around the marketplace as he put on his sandals showed no sign of anyone watching.

Slipping from one well of blackness to the next, Malchus skirted the marketplace. Two streets over, he stood by the outside wall of the palace. About six paces away lounged a royal guard at the gate, unaware of his presence. "Friend," Malchus whispered, "I bid you to allow me entrance."

The guard concealed his start of surprise. "Who sent you?" he whispered back in a gruff, deep voice.

"As a lion cub of Judah, I bear tidings for the Great Winged Lion," he recited as he had been instructed.

The gate opened, and Malchus stepped inside the moonlit gardens of the royal palace. Without hesitation he entered the narrow pathway to the right, avoiding several large fountains and an oval-shaped pond full of exotic fish. The scent of blossoms and ripening fruit hung thickly in the air. His sandals made no sound on the grassy walkway.

Suddenly the path opened up into a clearing, and beyond rose the stately buildings of the king's harem. Statues of the various gods formed corridors leading into the women's quarters, with the goddess Allat dominating the center. Dwarfing every other piece in the garden, Allat stood with her arms outstretched, a huge base supporting her stone weight.

Malchus crept stealthily to its base and examined the intricate carving carefully, at last reaching to touch an inlaid altar surrounded by handmaidens of the goddess. A section of the base swung free, exposing a cavity underneath. Bending low, he stepped inside and pulled the cleverly designed handle to shut the door behind him.

Steps carved into the stone slanted steeply down, the passage so narrow he could touch it with both hands to guide himself down in the darkness, the smooth stone cool and dry under his palms. His nostrils recoiled from the fetid air in the tunnel.

At the bottom of the stairs the passage continued, veering off in the direction of the largest building. An eternity later the way ended in a solid wall. Groping on the left side, Malchus felt a strand of cloth and gave it a gentle tug. Soft chimes sounded somewhere far away. Footsteps; a latch releasing; then sweet air poured into the tunnel.

A small, elegantly robed woman stood with him in a shadowy corner of a large room. Giant draperies rich with red and gold hung on the stone walls, making them appear less stark. Bowls full of flowers decorated nearly every available surface. Their perfume blended with the smell of costly spikenard as the woman drew him out into the room.

"I have been expecting you," she said at last as he squinted in the light after the darkness. A long pause grew awkward as her eyes filled with tears, and Malchus found himself suddenly seized in a fierce embrace. At last she released him, holding him at arms' length. "You look so like her, you know. How handsome you are!"

He gazed down into her unlined face, beautiful and ageless. It was impossible to guess how old she really was. And though he had never met her, he felt an uncanny familiarity. "Grandmother?" he ventured.

She nodded slowly. "Your master said he would send you the next time he had information for the king. But come, you must be thirsty." She served him herself, bringing him cool water, dates, figs, and honey cakes, never taking her eyes off him as he ate. Unexpectedly Malchus laughed. "What is it?" she asked.

"Nothing important. Not really. I just realized that I accidentally told the innkeeper the truth. I told him I was here to visit my grandmother, Maryam, except I said she was poor."

She smiled. "I have a thousand questions to ask you, but business first. You brought the message?" In answer, Malchus reached beneath his robe and unfastened the pouch. "Good. Do you know what it contains?"

"Yes, mostly. So far the Romans are holding to their part of the peace agreement with the king, and my master has heard no word of a possible attack. Herod is another matter. He has been trying to raise another army to retaliate against your king, but so far without success. Other than that, it's just the news from Jerusalem." He handed his grandmother the entire packet.

Maryam took it without opening it, handing him a smaller pouch and a sealed letter in exchange. Discreetly squeezing the pouch as he fastened it underneath his garment, Malchus guessed it must contain several gemstones, and judging by the splendor of the women's quarters, probably of very high quality. His master would be pleased.

Unable to wait any longer, Maryam burst out, "Tell me, how are they? How is my little Safiya? Are you married? How many brothers and sisters do you have? Your master would tell me nothing, save that your parents are alive and that you were coming." Her eyes, bright and expectant, fixed on his face.

Malchus shifted uncomfortably, his features suddenly grim. "That is more than he told me. I had no idea you were even still alive, although my father has told me your name and said you lived in Arabia. He neglected to mention the palace." He stopped, cleared his throat. "You might as well know the worst of it first. I had an older brother who died just before I was born. Did you hear of Herod's slaughter?"

"Yes," his grandmother whispered. "How I prayed they would be safe." Her voice trailed off, and she waited for him to continue.

"His name was Josu. The same spear that killed him struck my mother in the shoulder, and she lost the use of her arm."

Maryam cupped her hand over her mouth to stifle any sound, and tears ran down her cheeks. "The next day, I was born," Malchus continued. "I don't know if it was the shock or something else, but my mother never spoke after that day. I have never heard her voice."

The woman began to sob. The old pain was for her as fresh as if it had just happened. "What of her now?" she managed at last. "What is she like? Is she happy?"

"I think she is—at times," he said, not altogether truthfully. Growing up, he had seldom seen any trace of a smile on her face, only an unspeakably sad, haunted gaze fixed on the past. On those few occasions his father had tried to bring her to the present, or mention the love of Elohim, she would turn her face toward the wall for hours. He remembered crawling into her lap many times as she sat there, patting her cheeks with his small hands, holding her tight in his little arms. Nothing he did could bring her out of her private nightmare.

Other times she would care for him deftly with her one good arm, cleaning him or giving him food. Never did she embrace him or kiss him, though, withholding her love as if it were a curse that would bring him death. His father had tried hard to fill the void, wrapping his son in affection, but Malchus had always felt something lacking.

"Do they need anything?" Maryam's words brought Malchus back to the present. "Any money? Physicians? Servants to help care for my Safiya? Whatever they need I will give you."

Malchus smiled faintly. "Thank you, no, Grandmother. My master pays very well. Enough to see to my own household and still ensure my parents' comfort. Enough to consult every doctor for miles, but they all say the same thing. There is nothing they can do for my mother."

"If only there were more I could do," Maryam said, wiping fresh tears. "I had always pictured her happily surrounded by her children. She is so far away, and all I can do is beg Elohim to be gracious to her."

"Elohim? Gracious?" Malchus gritted his teeth for a moment and lowered his voice, saying angrily, "If He is so loving and gracious, then why didn't He take care of her already? Elohim took away my brother and robbed me of my mother. If He even exists, He is worse than a murderer."

In spite of herself, Maryam shrank back slightly in the face of his open hatred. "No, no. He is not that way at all. He loves each one of us, and at one time your mother loved Him too. Even if we don't always understand His ways, we can always know that He loves us."

"What love is there to know? Elohim killed my mother. She has been dead all my life. Nothing remains but for her body to follow." Malchus turned away, hating the weakness that made him tremble before the force of such unaccustomed emotion. Trying to hide his reaction, he firmly gripped the table and started to rise.

His grandmother reached out shakily as if she would touch him, then drew her hand back. "I still know so little of you," she said, trying to find a safer subject. "Tell me about yourself."

"There's not much to tell." Malchus gratefully accepted the change of subject, reluctant to leave his grandmother so soon after finding her. "I began working for my present master a little more than 15 years ago. He needed my unique talents for a project, and I have been with him ever since. I am married to a beautiful woman named Alona. No children." A little bitterness crept into his voice.

"Alona. What a pretty name. What is she like?" his grandmother asked.

He smiled. "Alona is very, well, devout," he said wryly. "Still, she keeps a good household and seldom loses her temper, but when she does, watch out! Also she takes good care of my parents. She wanted them to come live with us in Jerusalem, but my mother refuses to leave the house I was born in for anything. Mother can be so stubborn sometimes."

Maryam laughed in relief. "She certainly can. Why, when she met your father, no one else would suit her. Not any prince or king from any country. As daughter of Aretas she could have been queen in her own right, but only Gershom, a poor Jewish boy, won her heart. I think she also wanted to marry someone who worshiped as she did, even though she is only half Jewish herself."

Malchus leaned forward, stunned. "How was she able to marry him? Surely the king did not approve of the match."

"No, he did not. In fact, she was to have made an even more brilliant marriage than her half sister, Najiyah." As Malchus' face went pale underneath his tan, his grandmother smiled ironically. "I can see that name is familiar to you."

"You mean," he stammered, "that all the while I was growing up, my aunt was a few miles away in the palace of the tetrarch?"

"Yes. But our time together is nearly at an end. Najiyah was only the daughter of a lesser wife, but as you know, Aretas was furious when Herod discarded her. You must stay away from Herod, for if ever he had a member of her family in his power, there's no telling what he might—" she broke off and listened intently. "Quickly, you must go back the same way you came. That is also how your mother left the palace for the last time. Give her this when you see her. It was her favorite." Malchus gripped the small toy she thrust into his hands, then bent and kissed the smooth cheek.

A quick turn of a torch handle on the wall, and Malchus found himself once again in the dank air of the tunnel. Carefully he felt his way along, remembering the path perfectly, though he had traveled it only once. Opening the door into the garden just a crack, he scanned the area, but just as he was about to step out, the sound of bare feet running made him pause. Three girls, laughing and giggling, played a childish game of chase through the garden, dodging in and out of the statuary, their wispy robes fluttering behind them. At last they collapsed in a heap, breathless from laughter. After a moment the tallest of the three jumped to her feet with a gleeful shout, and the other two raced after her, back in the direction from which they had come.

As fast as he could, Malchus slipped out and shut the door behind him. Creeping from shadow to shadow, he retraced his steps to the grassy path, but this time, rather than risk another encounter with the guard, he eased up to the wall in a different spot. Just as he was reaching to touch the bricks he heard a faint, metallic sound behind him, the hiss of an iron weapon being drawn from its scabbard.

In one motion he leaped away from the wall to face the sound, reaching to his waist for the long knife that usually hung there. As his questing fingers met only fabric he breathed an oath. Knowing that to be caught with a weapon on the palace grounds was certain death, he had left it in his room at the inn.

Bare hands open and relaxed, arms spread wide in readiness, he half crouched to await his attacker's first move. His attacker laughed softly, his eyes mocking in the dim light. "In less time than it takes you to blink thrice your lifeblood will be draining onto the ground. You might have a few moments to regret the first step you took onto my domain before you breathe no more." A reflection of starlight flashed the length of his blade.

Malchus said nothing, merely beckoning the man forward, an expression of unholy glee lighting his face. They circled each other like two desert jackals fighting for the same carcass. The other man gripped the handle of his knife tightly, lunged forward, and made a swift stab at Malchus' heart.

Instinctively Malchus dodged to one side, blocking the thrust away from his body with his right arm and gripping the attacker's elbow in his left. A numbing grip on his assailant's wrist forced him to drop the knife, which fell with a thud on the grass. With his opponent completely off-balance, it took Malchus the space of one heartbeat to lever him, facedown, to the earth. He knelt on the man's back, applied a light touch to a pressure point on his neck, and stood, his opponent lying crumpled at his feet.

As he bent to check that the man's breathing was still strong and steady, he once again saw a faint reflection of light from the honed blade. Picking it up, he hefted it in his hand. A slow hiss escaped his lips. It was no ordinary weapon. Jewels sparkled on its hilt, and it had been crafted and balanced by a master. He had never seen the like. Without further thought he unfastened its sheath from his opponent and slipped the whole beneath his robe.

One look at the lightening sky, the stars disappearing one by one, was all he needed to know he was nearly out of time. With desperate haste he slid up and over the wall, dropping lightly on the other side, and made his way back to his lodging. It took but a moment to slip out of his sandals and scale the wall with practiced ease.

In the safety of his room he at last had the chance to realize the significance of some comments of his grandmother. "Daughter of Aretas," "queen in her own right," she had said, but how could that be? It was impossible to reconcile the image of a beautiful princess, surrounded by all the glitter and ceremony of a royal court, with the frail, haggard, empty woman who had given him life.

Then an even more shocking thought struck him. *If my mother truly is the daughter of Aretas, then I am his grandson.* Anger welled up inside him. Why had no one told him? Then the realization: *My master knew. This is why he sent me—to discover the truth about my family.*

As he lay down and stared at the ceiling, unable to sleep, anger at last gave way to pity. Pity for his mother, who had left everything for a God who had apparently abandoned her. Pity for his father, burdened with secrets, tragedy, and the heavy responsibility of caring for an incapacitated wife and infant son.

For a long time he remained motionless. Finally, giving up all thought of sleep, he stood and gathered his belongings. His outer robe was travel-stained and stiff with dirt. Malchus suppressed a shudder as he slipped it on. Laying a coin on the mat, he stepped out quietly to avoid waking the curious innkeeper.

A few of the merchants were beginning to set up their booths as he strode up the hill toward the Siq. He glanced around to see if there were more soldiers than usual, but it seemed his gamble had paid off. Malchus counted on the pride and arrogance of the guard, or whoever he had been, to keep him silent. There, just as he had hoped, another large camel train was preparing to leave, and it took only a few minutes to arrange safe passage with them.

For a second he turned for a last glimpse of the city. The sun, still low in the east, made the rock appear almost blood-red. Ahead, just outside the range of mountains they were descending, lay the thin line of the desert. Already it was so hot that his robe was soaked with a fresh layer of sweat. Patting the bulk concealed at his chest, he resolutely continued on his way. Regret mixed with relief. He would never be king, but it was enough for him to be Malchus ben-Gershom, chief servant of Caiaphas, the high priest.

Chapter 2

High doors of smooth cedar opened into a private chamber. A guard, his imposing bulk nearly concealing the short sword that was his only weapon, bowed deferentially to Malchus as he passed by. No trace of the dirt-encrusted traveler was visible in the noble figure that strode into the room, inclining his head respectfully before the priest. Black hair waved neatly back from his forehead and curled about his shoulders, costly blue robes draped gracefully about him, the chain of his high office lay about his neck, his feet were shod in ornate sandals, and the aroma of expensive perfume enveloped him.

"Welcome, my son. How glad I am to see you in time for the Passover. I trust your mission met with success." Caiaphas regarded him affectionately from under bushy brows.

Malchus gripped his master's forearms. "It was all you hoped it would be. My contact sent you this." He held out the leather pouch and watched with interest as Caiaphas opened it. As a handful of fabulous stones spilled into the wrinkled palm, Malchus nearly gasped aloud. Some kinds even he had never seen before, and all were magnificent, glowing as if lit from within.

"And what of your contact?" Reflections of the gems flickered in the shrewd eyes that surveyed Malchus from head to foot, then Caiaphas motioned him to a nearby chair.

"My surprise was all you could have hoped for," his servant said with a chuckle, seating himself. "It's too bad you couldn't have been there. My grandmother is quite an interesting woman."

"She always has been. We have known each other all our lives, and when she was chosen to join the royal court in Petra we kept in touch, even when the tetrarch provoked war against them. Indeed, we have been very helpful to each other." A troubled expression settled on his face. "Eager as I am to hear of your journey, there is something pressing I must discuss with you."

"As always, I await your bidding," Malchus said. "Is the Baptist making trouble with the people again?"

"Yes, always, but this time it's even more than that. As you know, before you left, the people were listening to John in increasing numbers, which rather concerned me. But one day, shortly after you left, a man came to him to be baptized, apparently some distant relative."

"Surely there's nothing unusual in that?" Malchus asked with gentle sarcasm. "After all, that is why he's called the Baptist."

"True, but how many times have you seen John bow down to the earth in front of anyone who came asking to be baptized?"

Malchus pictured the man he had met several times: tall, rough, clad in simple garments woven from camel's hair, and standing straight and proud before the loftiest noble or priest who might come to him. "I admit I never have seen it, nor would I expect to. Are you implying that he did?"

Caiaphas grimaced. "Oh, yes, he did. Some of my men were there in the crowd and brought word. John also said something about needing to be baptized himself, which made no sense either. But the strangest part was that after the man was baptized, my agents said a brilliant light shone on him and thunder sounded out of a clear sky. A few people thought they had heard a voice, but you know how superstitious those peasants are."

"That does sound strange," Malchus mused. "There must be some rational explanation, though. I can guarantee that if I had been there you would not have heard any stories of magic or trickery."

"You still haven't heard the worst of it. John then pointed to the man he had just baptized and declared, 'Behold the Lamb of God, which takes away the sins of the world.' The crowd was huge that day, and word has been spreading throughout Israel that the Messiah has come."

"'Behold the Lamb of God,'" Malchus repeated thoughtfully. "I don't think any of the other so-called messiahs we got rid of used just that phrase. This one could be very dangerous if the people begin following after him. Especially if he works together with John. We both know how popular he is."

"Yes," Caiaphas said, "and after that incident more people than ever came to hear him preach. That's exactly why we were so careful in handling the problem. The Sanhedrin met several times to discuss it, since John has never asked permission to address the people. At first there was some question about our legal right to handle it, but we finally decided that as a public preacher he was under our jurisdiction."

"Very true." Malchus rubbed his chin with one knuckle. "What did you end up doing?"

Caiaphas smiled. "Why, we sent several senior members of the Sanhedrin to speak with him a little more than a month later. The crowd drew back in awe at their presence, even though I was not among them. They asked John who he was. Some of the peasants regard him as Elijah returned to us. We wanted to see what he would claim for himself."

"Did he tell them he was the son of Zacharias?" Malchus asked.

"No." A peculiar look crossed the face of the high priest as he fingered the sash at his waist. "He said, 'I am the voice of one crying in the wilderness, Make straight the way of the Lord.' Then they asked him why he baptized, and what he said next was even stranger."

"Everything the Baptist says is strange," Malchus commented with a grin. "He even looks strange."

He did not win an answering smile from his master. "John stared at them for a moment, as if he was about to answer. Suddenly he seemed to catch sight of someone in the crowd, someone he wanted very much to see. Instead of just answering their question, he said, 'I baptize with water, but Another comes after me. I am not even worthy to take off His shoes.' Clearly he was talking about the Messiah."

"But whom was he looking at? Surely your agents must have noticed something." Malchus found his interest caught in spite of himself.

"No one could tell for certain, but combined with the previous event, I think it could have been only this Jesus of Nazareth. And when you add the story of John's birth, this could be the start of something very dangerous to us and to our nation. The Romans are already stirred up enough by Barabbas and his kind. Remember, we need them to help us remain in power. They could easily find new allies."

Malchus' thoughts were still focused on something Caiaphas had said. "What do you mean about John's birth? It is common knowl-edge that he is the son of a priest. That might be embarras-sing, to be sure, but how could it add to the danger?" he asked in puzzlement.

The high priest's gaze seemed to withdraw within himself. "You would be too young to remember," he said slowly. "Indeed, only gray-beards like myself know the full story. It happened at Passover the year before John's birth." Caiaphas cleared his throat, his discomfort obvi-ous. "The only reason I tell you this is to help you understand the full extent of our jeopardy. I count on your discretion."

Malchus bowed slightly. "As I live, you may rely on my silence."

"Zacharias was chosen to perform the ceremony," the high priest continued, "and when he came out he was unable to speak. His face glowed like the sun." Caiaphas pinched the bridge of his nose, eyes shut for a moment, not liking the memory.

"When you say 'glowed like the sun,' you just mean he was very happy, right?" Malchus asked, afraid of the answer.

"Glowed. Shone. Emitted light like a lamp. I was there, and there were no tricks. He also was unable to speak. Not until the baby was named could he tell us what had happened. An angel came, he said, and told him the son of his old age would prepare the way for the Messiah. Most have forgotten this, but a few remember, and that is enough. Whomever John points to as the Messiah will not only have his own followers, but gain John's, too."

"And now John has pointed at this Jesus," Malchus said with sud-den comprehension. "Do you think there's any chance he could be right?"

The instantaneous rage on the high priest's face, the red blotches that appeared along his jawline and spread up into his face, shocked Malchus. "Do you think that Messiah would come to free our people without turning to God's appointed leaders? Without contacting me? I have been chosen by Jehovah as the shepherd of His flock, and you think His Messiah could pass me by?"

The long white beard on the older man's chin quivered as he shouted, flecks of spittle shooting from his mouth with each harsh con-sonant. Quickly Malchus sought to defuse the situation, saying sooth-ingly, "Of course the Messiah would never come without consulting you first. This Jesus must be investigated and dealt with quickly. John, too, if the opportunity presents itself. What did you have in mind for me to do?"

Deftly Malchus diverted Caiaphas' anger. Within seconds the high priest's color began to improve, although he still pressed the heel of one hand against the pain that sprang up in his chest. "The usual. Find him, follow him, and give me a full report of his activities." The aging priest took a deep breath and let it out as the spasm in his chest relaxed. "Also his associates. Give me a full report on each. They were last said to be leaving Cana. I'm ashamed even to tell you the superstitious nonsense my agents, including Othniel, brought back from that place. I trust you to sort it all out for me."

Malchus bowed low. "As always, my pleasure is to serve you, sir. Don't fear; I refuse to be led astray by whatever tricks this charlatan has dreamed up. A pleasant feast to you." Once again the two men gripped each other's forearms, and Malchus slowly exited the chamber, deep in thought.

As he walked down the long corridor toward the Temple court, he could hear the familiar sounds of oxen, sheep, doves, and other livestock bleating nervously as Levites led them to the sacrifice. Even at this distance a faint hint of the stable assailed his nostrils. A continuous clinking reverberated from the marble walls of the Temple courtyard as coins changed hands in a never-ending stream. Malchus smiled. It was a good sound. The priests had an arrangement with the moneychangers that brought a flood of wealth to all involved. Most important of all, it paid his generous salary.

All who came to the Temple from afar off had to exchange their money for Tyrian shekels in order to purchase their sacrifice. The rate of exchange was rather one-sided, in favor of the Temple, of course, and the price of animals for sacrifice was exorbitant, but Malchus had no complaints.

At first he thought he had suddenly gone deaf. But no, he could still hear his footsteps echoing in the colonnaded walkway. Puzzled, he stopped. Yes, all was silent. He stamped one foot. The sound echoed hollowly down between the pillars. For a moment he stood hesitantly, unsure what to do, then began to run at top speed for the Temple court.

Skidding to a stop around a blindingly white pillar, he looked across the courtyard. It was as if a magician had cast a spell, freezing each living being in their place. Goats and sheep huddled together in clumps, seeking security in numbers. Large numbers of men, visitors to Jerusalem, stood as if turned to stone. Row upon row of moneychangers sat, some with hands outstretched to give the Temple coin, others with palms turned upward to receive the Roman or other currency. But none moved. None blinked.

Everyone seemed to be looking in the same direction, and Malchus followed their gaze until one man caught his attention. Dressed in a plain homespun garment, he stood holding a cord of whips picked up from one of the merchants now cowering at his feet. As Malchus caught sight of his face, he too froze. His chest suddenly felt hollow. Beads of sweat broke out all over his body, trickling down his back. It seemed, somehow, as if those eyes, terrible and solemn, read every secret of his heart.

He tried to draw his robes more tightly around him, covering his vulnerability, but it was no use. His mind urged him to find someplace to hide from that searching look, but his feet refused to move. The man raised his whip high over his head, and his voice cracked across the assembly. "Take these things away from here! This is my Father's house, not a marketplace."

Unhindered, the man moved to the tables of the moneychangers and began to upend them one by one. As the first crashed to the marble tiles, sending a cascade of coins rolling here and there, panic seized the crowd. Pushing and shoving, they clawed their way to the gates and poured through. Their flight roughly knocked down and trampled several men, but they too staggered to their feet and limped away in terror.

A mindless, unreasoning fear filled Malchus. At last his feet responded, and he raced as far and as fast as he could from the man with the eyes of God. Down countless flights of stairs, half stumbling, and still he fled. Somehow he found a side entrance and gained the city street. Quickly he outstripped the priests, the crowd, and even the fleetest runners in front. On and on his panic drove him, until a cramp in his side forced him to slow and finally stop. Leaning up against the wall of a house, hands on his knees, he gasped for breath. A few passersby stared curiously, but most pretended not to see him.

As his terror ebbed, Malchus grew angry with himself. "I can't believe I just did that," he muttered, grinding the heel of his hand into his forehead. "He's only one man. I must be getting soft." He laughed. "Well, Caiaphas told me to find him, and I guess I did." Malchus had no doubt that the man in the Temple was Jesus of Nazareth. Still cursing his unexpected cowardice, he strode the long way back to the Temple Mount.

Once he was at the gate a chill grated up his spine, but taking himself firmly in hand, he continued on. A strange sight met him. Not everyone had run away. Those who were poor, or blind, or sick—they had stayed behind with Jesus. No visible trace of anything supernatural clung to the man who sat there surrounded by the dregs of society. A blind beggar crept close, groping with trembling fingers toward the sound of that kind voice. Jesus took his hand, drew him close, and touched his eyes. "I can see! I can see! Praise God!" the man suddenly shouted, gazing in awe around him before kneeling at the feet of his healer. "Master, I give my whole life into Your service. Thank You, thank You." Then he darted away, still shouting the glad news of his restoration.

A paralyzed child brought near on a pallet and lifted to his feet began to run and jump for the first time. A woman that Malchus assumed must be a widow lurking at the edges of the group shyly approached when Jesus beckoned to her. Just a few words whispered in her ear turned her expression of sorrow to joy. One after another people came to Him and went away healed or comforted. The children sang an exuberant song of praise to God, one of hope, deliverance, and the promised Messiah.

As he stared, transfixed, Malchus felt a nudge at his side. A priest that he knew by sight only stood by him, hate written all across his face. "What do you think of this so-called messiah?" he asked Malchus.

Feigning a yawn, Malchus replied, "Messiahs come and messiahs go. The Romans get stirred up and make our lives more miserable, and Caiaphas assigns me to rid the world of them. This will be no different."

"Do you realize this one must be in league with Satan himself?" the priest continued. "Otherwise, how else could he do all these things? There must be some vulnerability we can turn against him." Just then a new outburst reached their ears as yet another sufferer was made whole. The priest's eyes blazed. "Excuse me; I just remembered something I need to do."

Malchus watched as he gathered two other priests and bustled toward the happy gathering. The lead priest cleared his throat loudly to catch Jesus' attention. "Ahem. I have noticed you doing some rather, well, unnatural things on Temple property. You must show us some sign that your power comes from God and not from the evil one, or we will have to ask you to leave these sacred precincts." Folding his arms triumphantly, he stood back and waited.

Jesus stood. He looked sad as He spoke. "Destroy this temple," He said, hands outstretched, "and in three days I will raise it up." Immediately everyone who heard gawked up at the towering structures around them. The marble blocks dazzled every eye with their brilliance. The Temple complex seemed as permanent as the mountain it stood upon.

"We have heard enough," the priest intoned. "You must leave this place at once. Take this rabble with You." Jesus did not appear to have heard. He had already turned back to the needy pressed close by His side. A word here, a touch there, and peace spread in His wake. The priests found themselves left standing alone, looking rather foolish, until they made a hasty retreat.

The whole incident left Malchus puzzled, and judging by the faces of many who had returned from their earlier flight, he was not the only one. "The Temple has so far taken 46 years to build," he heard someone say, "and He thinks He can rebuild it in three days? The man is surely mad, or possessed by demons."

Insane indeed. Malchus had never heard such a wild boast. At least it would be easy to keep track of Him, here in the city. Motioning to one of Caiaphas' spies—the high priest preferred to call them messengers—Malchus instructed him to track Jesus' movements and to notify him if Jesus appeared to be leaving the city. Bowing and stammering, the young man agreed, overwhelmed by the personal notice of one so superior. Then for the second time that day, Malchus displayed uncharacteristic cowardice. Instead of reporting immediately to his master, he simply went home.

- - -

Alone in his audience chamber, the most influential man in the nation of Israel sat caressing the small heap of jewels held delicately in his palm. He selected first one, then another, holding each up to the light, the reflected colors dancing across his lined face. At a timid knock he scowled, snapping his hand shut around the gems. "What is it?" he asked gruffly. One of the priests opened the door and slipped in. A slender, studious sort, he stood there pale and trembling. "Come on, man, speak up. You are wasting my time."

Hesitantly the man did, managing only a few words before he had to shrink back at Caiaphas' shriek of rage. The high priest drew back his hand, hurling the precious stones across the room. One nicked the hapless messenger on the cheek, another on the arm he held up in defense. Turning, he fled.

Caiaphas paced the length and breadth of the room. "How dare that pretender come into my Temple?" he shouted, knocking over several small tables and chairs and throwing unlit lampstands against the wall until the room lay in shambles. "This is my house! These are my people! That is my money! I will kill him. I will kill him. I will kill him."

CHAPTER 3

Alona sat in a sunny courtyard reading the scroll spread out across her lap. As she reclined on the bench her long, straight black hair spilled over her shoulders. A stray strand tickled her cheek. Absorbed in the story of Deborah the prophet, she brushed the strand away from her face.

Her fine linen robe was dyed a light green, and she wore a belt of darker green double-looped around her small waist. Her bare feet peeped from under the hem of her garment, and sandals with spiderweb straps sat neatly on the floor in front of her. A pile of scrolls lay within easy reach, and servants bustled back and forth just outside the door, careful not to disturb their mistress.

At the sound of a familiar voice in the entryway, she quickly set her scroll down with the others, slid on her sandals, and straightened her skirt as she crossed to the doorway. "Oh, Malchus, I'm so glad you're home," she said, smiling a welcome. "I've just been reading the most interesting thing."

"Let me alone," Malchus said, waving her away. He brushed past her without a glance, entering the next room. Alona heard the bar slide inside, locking the door. A few steps, a scraping, and the connecting door between their rooms was barred as well. Tears stung the corners of her eyes, and she blinked rapidly to fight them back. Retreating into her own room, she stood before the closed door. With one hand she leaned against it, feeling its solid warmth. Turning again, her chin at a defiant angle, she marched off to see to the evening meal.

— ～ ~

At breakfast Malchus reappeared as if nothing had happened. Deep shadows lurked under his eyes, but other than that, he was his usual jaunty self. He pretended not to notice when Alona stared at him reproachfully. "Good morning, love. I trust you slept well," he said finally.

"Very," she said through compressed lips. "And you?"

"Oh, fine. Just fine," he said around a mouthful of bread, avoiding her eyes. "I may have to depart again at any time. Perhaps later today or tomorrow."

"Are you jesting? You just got home!" Hurt and anger showed on her face. "You have been gone for months, leaving me to take care of everything by myself, and then just when you get home you decide to go again?"

"You have done a fine job with the household," Malchus said. "Everywhere I look I can see that. I have no fears leaving it in your capable hands again. You know that when Caiaphas commands me I must go. I'm sorry, but it's what I do. It's who I am."

"It's what you want to do—who you choose to be." She sighed in resignation. "How long will you be gone this time?"

"I don't know. You know I can't discuss the details of my orders, but it's no secret that Caiaphas wants more information about this latest messiah. We all are afraid it could mean more trouble with Rome, the way the people flock to him. It seems he is even winning over many followers of the Baptist." He stopped; and then that crafty look she so despised crept over his face. "Yes, followers. H'mmm. Anyway,

I could be gone a few days or weeks. It's impossible to tell right now."

"I'm sorry; I'm just disappointed." She touched her husband's hand gently, then returned to her chores. *Maybe if I had given him a son he would stay with me,* she thought. *Maybe he would want me then.*

A son was the farthest thing from Malchus' mind as he sat mulling over the idea he had come up with. Many of the Baptist's followers were intensely loyal to him, and it seemed logical that at least some of them might be jealous of anyone who tried to undermine their leader's position or authority. Surely that could be put to good use.

— — —

The summons came that evening. A ragged boy of about 8 years stood, palm out, waiting for the expected coin. His eyes widened as he saw the generosity of the master of the house. The piece of papyrus he handed over was a bit crumpled and grubby, but the message was plain enough. Malchus swore, and the urchin scampered away, tightly clutching his windfall.

"Our assignment has vanished," he read the laborious lettering. "I last glimpsed him this morning, and a beggar may have seen him on the north road to Samaria. I would have contacted you sooner, but I wanted to have some information for you."

Malchus ground his teeth together. "He lost track of Jesus this morning and didn't tell me until after dark because he wanted more *information?*" He crumpled the bit of crude paper into a tight ball and threw it into the fire. "I have some information for him. He is the most incompetent, incoherent, illogical excuse for a spy that I have ever seen in my life."

One or two more comments on his underling's ancestry, and his wrath dwindled. "I will be prepared to leave the changing house by dawn," he muttered. "The man has, at most, only a day's start ahead of me. He should be easy to locate."

Alona found him in his room gathering a few items together. "Are you going now?" She tried to hide her worry.

"Yes; that fool I had working for me has botched things already. I must leave within the hour." Out of the corner of his eye he saw her hand swiftly dab her cheek. "What's this, not tears for me?" She half turned, hiding her face from him. Malchus was genuinely surprised. They had a comfortable enough marriage, he supposed, but he never would have thought that she had any deeper feelings for him.

Still keeping her face averted, Alona threw her arms around him, pressing a kiss into his neck. "Go with Elohim, and may He watch over you," she whispered.

Malchus kissed her hair lightly. "I will take your kiss with me instead. It, at least, is real." He pushed her gently from him. "Never fear, I know how to take care of myself. And besides, now I have this." He patted his side.

Curious, she asked, "What do you mean?" In answer, he reached through a slit in his robe and pulled out the large knife. Its perfect balance and deadly sheen amazed him even yet. Alona's eyes widened. "Where did that come from? It looks very valuable. Are these real?" With one finger she traced the shapes on the hilt, exploring the texture of the gemstones. The hilt had two hawks soaring back to back, their wings outstretched. Upon their shoulders they bore the moon, a gleaming silver orb, carrying it on its journey across the heavens.

"As far as I can tell the jewels are genuine." He paused. "A Nabataean gave it to me during my last assignment," he told her.

His face was so full of mischief that she felt compelled to ask, "Willingly?" At the chuckle that erupted from her husband, she laughed shakily herself. "No, of course not. Malchus, you are incorrigible!"

He only laughed harder, taking a swift kiss as his prize. "You look so pretty when you use big words. There now, I have made you smile. See, I have given you the proof that I can keep myself safe, much safer than your Elohim can."

His wife looked nervously over her shoulder. "I wish you wouldn't talk like that. He might hear you."

"Who, Elohim?"

She nodded. "I am afraid He would be angered against you if He heard the things you always say about Him. After all, remember the story of Korah, Dathan, and Abiram, straight from the history of our people."

"You mean the ones who showed disrespect to Elohim and were swallowed by the earth? Even if that were true, it was a very long time ago. If Elohim were really listening, He would hear the cries of our people under the Roman lash, and He would send His Messiah to

loosen the yoke of our oppression. But what does He do? Nothing!"
Malchus fastened the drawstring of his bag and slung it abruptly over
his shoulder. "But this is no time for theology. I must go quickly." A
quick caress of her face with his hand, and he departed. Alona stood
staring after him, one hand held to the place where he had touched.

— ◆ —

The changing house had been built far outside the city walls. To
the passerby it looked like an average household of moderate means,
with several buildings, a herd of sheep and cattle, and fields planted with
various crops. The crew of servants that maintained the tranquil appearance were all trustworthy and sworn to secrecy. The family portion of
the house contained a hidden room full of costumes, disguises, and
makeup. A concealed door led into the stable; thus a well-dressed man
like Malchus could walk in the front door, and a wizened, filthy vagrant
stagger out of the stable door, with no apparent connection between
the two. The servants would even go out of their way to invite traveling beggars to stay the night, in order to further confuse anyone who
might be watching.

There was no hurry this time, as Malchus could not leave until
dawn, so he lay down for a much-needed rest. His sleep was fitful and
haunted by vague, disturbing images. Each time he awoke, he could
still see that dreadful gaze directed right at him. The body of a man—
the eyes of God. Someday, maybe, he would forget.

About two hours before sunrise he left his pallet to bathe, probably
his last chance for quite a while. He dried thoroughly, relishing his last
few moments of cleanliness, then entered the hidden room.

Clothing of all kinds lined the narrow walls. On the left were the
shabby, filthy garments, and on the right the robes of priests and princes
and even the uniforms of Roman soldiers. The matching undergar-
ments hung on a peg underneath. Many of the costumes had a hand-
lettered sign above them reading "Malchus Only." Wigs of every
description hung at each end, and a wooden table with boxes full of
cosmetics had a bronze mirror and a lamp.

With a shudder of revulsion Malchus chose a familiar robe from a
nearby hook on the left and slid its scratchy roughness over his moist,

clean skin. Seating himself in front of the mirror, he bent under the table. He saw three or four buckets, each containing a different type of earth, reached into one, and began carefully applying it to every exposed part of his body.

Then Malchus took a pinch of spice and rubbed it lightly into his teeth, giving them a yellowish cast. Some black wax daubed here and there produced the effect of the rotting teeth of a poor man. As soon as his hair dried, he dusted it with a white powder, a bit of dust, and combed olive oil through it. It was not an elaborate disguise, but Malchus had found through experience that when it came to longer assignments, simple disguises were far better. Besides, the largest part of any disguise was not the clothes, the cosmetics, or even the hair—it was the change in mannerisms, facial expressions, and walk.

At last he was ready. The cock was just calling a greeting to the new day when Malchus slid a tattered bag over his shoulder, picked up a crude staff, and stepped out the door into the stable. The yard was already a bustle of activity in the dim light. Servants milked goats, fed the cattle, watered the sheep, and lined up the plows, pointing them toward the fields. Malchus sought out the head servant, saying in a high-pitched whine, "Thanks to you, kind sir, for a warm place to stay. The blessing of Elohim be upon you."

The servant drew himself up to his full height. "And upon you, good man. You are welcome in our stable at any time." His face remained impassive, but a thick eyelid closed in a quick wink.

Malchus couldn't help the twitch at the corners of his mouth. The servants enjoyed the game as much as he did. Once in a while he was even able to fool them. He grinned as he walked along the path leading toward the north road and Samaria.

— — —

The afternoon sun beat down hard on the solitary traveler, his long legs still moving rhythmically in a mile-eating stride. The carefully applied dirt on his arms and legs had long since been covered over by dust rising up from the well-traveled road. Darker streaks in the light dust showed where sweat had beaded and run down. Up ahead a clump of fig trees promised respite from the heat. Eight men had already taken advantage of the sheltering branches. As Malchus drew near, he noted their simple manner of dress and their courteous way of speaking. Good. "Greetings, brothers. Where are you from?"

The oldest man, who seemed to be the leader of the group, answered him. "We are followers of John the Baptizer. He has baptized each of us and bid us rise out of the water to live a new life."

"I too am a follower of John," Malchus replied. "I left my life of ease and plenty because of his preaching." That, at least, was true enough.

"We have also left much," the older man said, "but the peace in our hearts has filled us too full to miss what we left behind."

Malchus nodded understandingly. "What brings you so far from John? Can it be you have the same questions as I do? I have heard much of a new teacher who is taking away support from our beloved master."

"Yes, yes," the man said. "That is just why we are here. We have heard of this new teaching and wish to see for ourselves if it is true. Some even say this man is the Messiah."

"Many men are foolish," Malchus said intensely. "We all know that when the true Messiah comes, He will do much more than just talk. It is John I am most worried about right now. You know Herod Antipas is against him, but has been unable to act because the hearts of the people are toward John, and the tetrarch fears that."

All the men voiced their agreement, some glancing around quickly to make sure no one was listening to talk that bordered on treason. A younger man with an honest, sincere face broke in. "I agree with all John has said about Herod and his whore Herodias, but he ought not to have said it to Herod. I fear it may yet cost him his life."

"Friend, I think you might be right," Malchus said, appearing to grow thoughtful. "And if you are, then John is put in even more terrible danger by this other man. If too many of us leave to follow this Jesus, even for a short while, John could find himself in trouble. Besides," his voice rose with indignation, "John was here first. It is most unfair for someone else to come along and undo all the hard work our brother has accomplished in trying to bring some much-needed reforms to Israel."

"He's right," the leader of the group agreed. "We must warn John of what is happening. It is not right for us to allow him to be trampled under like this. Our place is with John." He stood abruptly. "Who is with me?"

The other men also stood, all except for Malchus. As one they turned to look at him. "I am in full agreement, brothers, but have traveled far. I must rest a short while longer before going on. Go ahead, and I will rejoin you shortly."

"May Elohim bless you for showing us our duty," the leader said, facing south toward Jerusalem.

"May He cause His face to shine upon you," Malchus replied politely. He laughed outright as the group grew smaller in the distance, until all that was visible was a tiny cloud of white dust. It had been so easy.

His conversations with other followers of John had gone much the same way. Each had responded in indignation at the injustice being done to their master. Malchus stretched and yawned. Time to go. Jesus may have had a full day's start, but Malchus was confident he would soon catch up with Him in spite of the extra time it had taken to stir jealousy between the disciples of John and Jesus. Once again he faced north and resumed his swinging stride in pursuit of the new teacher.

— — —

The Valley of Shechem was a place of unrivaled beauty. Well endowed with trees and shrubs, it had green grass spreading lushly underfoot, fruit of all kinds to be had for the picking, and wells of water spaced close together for the refreshment of the weary traveler. At the entrance to the valley stood Jacob's Well, a place revered by Jew and Samaritan alike. Both peoples lovingly tended it, so the water remained as clear and pure, and the rock wall surrounding it just as strong and sturdy, as when their ancestor Jacob must have built it so many years before.

As the woman approached the well from the nearby Samaritan village, a strange sight greeted her eyes. A dirty, disheveled man lay flat on his stomach on the rock wall, his feet hanging out into empty space. His head and shoulders were hidden from view as he leaned as far as possible into the well. She could hear a faint, repetitive splashing noise coming from inside the well, and a muffled curse echoing hollowly. The woman covered her mouth with one hand to hide her amusement, and her eyes danced merrily. Obviously some of the local boys had played a prank and removed the public pitcher that was to remain tied to a stake by the rock wall.

Deliberately the woman tripped on a rock, sending it flying to clink against the retaining wall. The stranger, startled by the noise, nearly fell headfirst into the well. Scrabbling and kicking his legs wildly, he managed to slide to the ground without letting go of his belt, which he had tied to his water skin. His eyes widened as he saw the Samaritan woman, and he hastily jumped to his feet, pulling his robe tightly down around his knees as he did so.

Then he stood haughtily off to one side, nose in the air, apparently taking no notice that anyone was there. The woman, though well past youth, was attractive. Her fair skin gleamed in the sunlight. Mischief sparked in her eyes as she approached the stranger. "Excuse me," she said respectfully. "Would you like a drink?"

Her words startled Malchus. He would sooner have expected the sun to fall from the sky than for this woman to speak to him, let alone offer him a drink. Giving water to a thirsty traveler was a sacred duty in all cultures of that region, but the animosity between Israel and Samaria had grown so deep that neither would offer this courtesy to the other. They were not so hardened as to withhold the gift of water if asked, but the pride of each was so great that neither would stoop to beg a favor.

Malchus stood there stunned, his mouth gaping open, showing yellowed, rotten-looking teeth. He tried to speak, but nothing came out. "I didn't quite hear you," the woman said. "Did you want a drink?"

Finally Malchus managed a nod, and she took his water skin from unresisting fingers. Quickly she lowered her jug into the well, its weight pulling it easily below the surface of the water. The pitcher kept sinking until all that was visible was a small terra cotta circle just below the surface.

Hand over hand the woman drew up her brimming jug, filled Malchus' goatskin, and handed it to him. He tilted it back and drank deeply, great gulps of the cool water washing and soothing his dry throat. At last he paused, looked at the woman again in puzzlement, and said, "Thank you." It came out as almost more of a question.

The woman smiled, her whole face radiating joy. "My name is Yasirah. I know you're wondering why I am helping you. Only yesterday I would have felt just as you do, but then I met Him."

"Met who?"

She laughed. "It's kind of silly, but I don't even know His name, only that He was from Israel. I came at my usual time to draw water, and He was sitting here alone, obviously thirsty. I had no thought to offer Him a drink, but He asked me anyway, and how could I refuse? He said that He had water for me, too, living water, and that if I drank it I would never be thirsty again. I took Him for a madman at first."

Malchus sat straighter, his attention caught. "What did this man look like? Medium height, slender build, strange eyes, and leading a group of men?"

"It's funny you should mention His eyes. They were strange, and I felt they saw everything about me. Then He told me all that I ever did." Her eyes lowered in embarrassment. "I have been married five times, and until yesterday I was living with a man who was not my husband. He couldn't possibly have known. I certainly didn't tell Him. But somehow He did, and still He looked at me with such love that I couldn't help being drawn to Him."

Puzzled, Malchus thought for several moments. "Did He say anything else?"

"Yes, but being a Jew, you probably won't like it. I asked Him which mount we should worship at, Jerusalem or Gerizim, and He said the time was coming when we wouldn't worship on either one, but would all worship the Father in spirit and truth, whatever that means. I still haven't figured it out. One mountain or the other must be the right one."

"That does sound strange," Malchus agreed. "Go on."

"Well, I didn't understand what He meant, so I said, 'Someday the Messiah will come and explain all this to us,' and He said He was the one." An expression of amazement filled her face. "When that man said He was the Messiah, suddenly I knew in my heart it had to be true. I raced back to the village to tell them He was here, and they came back with me to listen."

Malchus stiffened. "Did this man you spoke with actually say He was the Messiah?" he carefully asked.

"Well, just as I said, I mentioned the Messiah that was to come, and He said He was the one. It seemed clear enough to me. He spoke with such love and kindness as none of us had ever heard before, even from our priests—or yours." Yasirah met Malchus' gaze. "Our whole village is a different place after spending just a few short hours with Him. My heart is different since I met Him."

"Which way did He go? I would like to meet Him." Malchus told the truth whenever possible.

"He went north, and I think I heard one of the men with Him saying they were going to Galilee. Maybe He has friends or family there." Yasirah carried her water jar to the well and filled it again. "Perhaps I will see you again." With a wave she was gone, balancing the heavy jug on her shoulder.

Malchus shook his head in disbelief. Were it not for his bulging water skin, he would think the whole experience had been merely a vivid dream. Indeed, who would believe that he had just conversed at length with a member of his people's despised enemy—and a woman at that? His thoughts turned to what she had said. If she was correct, then Jesus was actually claiming to be the Messiah. Well, the sooner he could find Him and evaluate the potential danger, the better.

"Living water," Malchus said scornfully to himself as he resumed his journey.

Just past Shechem the road divided, the right branch leading directly to the southern tip of the Lake of Galilee. The left branch went to the heart of the province of Galilee. Malchus pondered a moment and started to the left, deciding that most likely Jesus had gone to visit His old home, Nazareth.

— — —

Had he only been there to see it, Malchus would have been very pleased with the results of his work. The Baptist, though noting the shrinking numbers who came to see him, was still hard at work preaching and baptizing when a group of more than 100 men approached him, all trying to speak at once. He held up his hands to silence them. "You," he pointed to an older man in front, "please explain what this is about."

"Teacher, the one you baptized earlier—you remember, the time there was thunder?" The man swallowed hard. "Well, He is now having baptisms too, and everyone is going to hear Him preach. We—we came straight here to warn you that He is trying to steal your followers."

But Malchus would not have been at all pleased at what happened next. In the tone of a father instructing a selfish child, John patiently explained to his followers, "How many more times must I tell you that I am not the Christ. I was simply sent before Him, to prepare His way." The Baptist smiled at them. "You could not have brought me better news. It means I have accomplished what I was sent to do. He must increase, and I must decrease. That has always been the plan of Elohim." A trifle shamefaced, the men drifted away.

CHAPTER 4

The place that had been Jesus' home for so many years was small and remote, surrounded by orchards and fields of wheat. The city itself was built on a rise, with a gentle slope overlooking a fertile plain on one side and a steep cliff on the other.

As Malchus sat on first one street corner, then another, listening for word of Jesus, he heard a great deal of talk about the events at Passover. *How quickly the news has spread, even here,* he mused. When some hours passed with no mention of where Jesus might be, Malchus began to wonder if he had perhaps passed Him on the way, or maybe even taken the wrong road. At last when a full hour at the well brought no new information, he bought a loaf of bread and a handful of cheese, joining the beggar camp he had noticed just outside the city.

It was growing dark, and as little fires bloomed here and there, ragged men and women, even a few children, huddled close to them. Battered clay pots hung over the fires of those lucky enough to have something to cook. As Malchus entered the encampment, the stench of stale urine and unwashed bodies was nearly overpowering.

After scanning the crude shelters and sleeping pallets spread out under the open sky, he decided to try his luck at a fire where a solitary beggar sat with nothing to cook. The man looked much older than he must have been. His gray hair hung matted and uncombed, his face was hard and lined, and his fingernails dirty and jagged. Bony knees protruded from under what might once have been a robe. His breath was sour with wine, but he had not yet fallen into a stupor.

Malchus squatted at arm's length. "Good evening, friend. Are you hungry?" The man only grunted, but his eyes gleamed with interest. Malchus popped some bread and cheese into his mouth and, observing how his companion's mouth watered, handed some of each to him. "Been here long?" he asked. Again, the man only grunted. "I just came from the Passover in Jerusalem. I have heard many people here talk of it, but I saw it with my own eyes."

"You saw Jesus?" The man's tongue at last loosened.

"Yes, and I am looking for him now. I thought he might come here, since this was his home." Noting the man still greedily eyeing his food, Malchus divided the remainder in two equal parts. "If you can help me, I will gladly share."

"All right, I'll help." The man reached out for the food, but Malchus held it back.

"Not that I don't trust you, but I'd rather hear what you have to say first." Cross-legged and with his arms folded expectantly, Malchus sat with the morsels displayed temptingly on his lap.

"He lived here most of His life," the man said, slurring his words slightly. "I knew Him some. His father owned a carpenter's shop. Jesus was a nice, quiet fellow, but a bit strange."

"What about now?" Malchus interrupted. "Has he been here?"

The man shrugged. "Everyone thought He would come. We all heard wild stories about what happened in Jerusalem, and Him performing miracles and stuff, so we thought if He could really do those things He would come show us. Some even said He claimed to be the Messiah."

"And you?"

The old drunkard cackled. "Don't be ridiculous! I watched him grow up. So did everybody else in these parts. I don't know what he is, but he's no Messiah. Ask anyone." His owllike eyes were dilated, unblinking.

"Then where is he?"

"How should I know? Cana, maybe. He has some relations living up that way. More than that I can't tell you. Now gimme my food." At the frown darkening Malchus' brow he hastily added, "Please."

Malchus tossed the bread and cheese into the man's lap. Falling on it, the beggar began to devour it, washing it down with gulps of cheap wine. Malchus sat motionless until the man slipped into oblivion, a dribble of saliva trailing down his grizzled beard. The beggar's attitude toward Jesus didn't really surprise him. There would be no mystery about him in his hometown. No one would mistake his forceful personality for anything divine. In fact, these were about the most sensible people Malchus had met thus far. They refused to be fooled by the superstitions of the ignorant.

Malchus rested his head and arms on his knees, dozing occasionally, trying not to think of his own encounter with Jesus in the Temple. At first light he rose before anyone else and again began walking, stiff at first from sleeping in such an uncomfortable position. It was not far to Cana, and he reached it in time for the noon meal.

The city gates opened into a small marketplace studded with trees and flowering shrubs. It took only a moment to toss a coin to a seller of bread sitting on a pad of blankets, his crudely made crutches beside him, and scoop up a loaf. At the far end of the square, under the spreading shade of a large tree, sat what must have been nearly every person in the town. The crowd was too thick to see just what had attracted their interest, but Malchus smiled with satisfaction. Obviously he had come to the right place.

Even before he elbowed his way through those standing around the edge of the crowd he knew just what he would see. The familiar figure was seated on a smooth rock placed at the base of the tree. His homespun clothes were dustier, more worn, and His sandals showed the effects of many miles walked, but there was no mistaking the rich, full voice or the authority in the way He conducted Himself. Those nearest to Him pressed still closer, eager to hear and touch Him. He did not draw back from even the dirtiest of them, but gave to each a kind word, a gentle caress.

The children clamored for a story, and Jesus began, "There was once a wise man. A wise man, and a foolish man, and each decided to build a house. The wise man chose to build his house on a—"

"Rock!" all the children chorused in unison.

"That's right," He responded with a laugh. "The wise man built his house on a rock, but the foolish man built his house on the . . ."

As Jesus hesitated, feigning forgetfulness, the little ones shrieked with laughter and shouted, "Sand! He built it on the sand!"

Jesus laughed again with them and bent low. "Yes indeed. All of you know this story so well. Now, after their houses were all finished, a terrible storm came." His sweeping gestures drew the tempest in midair for the spellbound children. As Jesus repeated the story they so loved to hear Him tell, Malchus tried to shift position to catch a glimpse of His face. Finally Jesus turned His head toward one of His small listeners, rewarding Malchus with a full view of His features. Caiaphas' servant caught his breath in surprise. He saw no trace of the stern judge who had rebuked those at the Temple—only love, peace, and such joy. When He smiled, Malchus felt blinded by it.

He hardly knew the story was over until a middle-aged man in drab clothing twisted his awkward way over to Jesus, a rude crutch in each hand. Malchus recognized the man who had just sold him the bread. The man half knelt, half collapsed at Jesus' feet. "Master," he said humbly, "I have heard You speak, and I believe in You. I know You are able to help me, but could it be that You are also willing?"

The hand he reached out in desperation Jesus clasped gently. "I am willing," He said softly. "Just get up and walk." The bread seller let go of his crutches and stood, wobbly at first, and took a hesitant step, then another. In moments he was running madly about, tears streaming down his cheeks, shouting his gratitude to the heavens. "You're welcome," Jesus called after him with a chuckle.

A burly fisherman, one of Jesus' disciples, walked slowly back and forth, examining each face in the crowd. When he saw Malchus, he frowned, a trace of suspicion crossing his features. Instinctively Malchus slid down farther, trying to be inconspicuous. It worked, although once or twice after that the disciple's gaze lingered on him.

As at the Temple, a never-ending stream of despairing humanity came to Jesus by turn, each receiving the blessing their hearts cried for. Malchus felt himself drawn in spite of himself, and had to take a firm grip on his emotions. "It must be false," he tried to tell himself. "This is all some kind of trick, and I will find how he does it and expose him for the fraud he is." Somehow his words seemed hollow.

A man, well dressed and in his early 20s, came before Jesus to present his request, but was weeping almost too hard to speak. "My son, my only son, is sick," he at last gasped out. "He is not quite 4, and he means everything to me. I'll do anything, even believe that You are the Messiah, if You will only come and heal him."

No one quite expected what happened next. The smile left Jesus' face, and He said to the young father rather sadly, "Unless you see miracles, you won't believe." The words hung heavy in the air, and no one moved as His eyes met and held those of the petitioner.

Horror crossed the young father's face. "Dear God, what have I done? I believe! No matter what, I believe!" He shuddered, nerving himself to ask again. "Please come and heal my son. If You don't, he will die."

Jesus gripped the man's shoulder as he broke down sobbing. Tears lurked in His eyes, but the smile was once more on His lips as He said, "Don't worry. Your son is already well."

"Thank You, Master," the father managed to say. "I will serve You always, I and my family." Then, to the amazement of all, he seated himself near Jesus' feet to listen, fully trusting the Teacher's word that his son was healed. All the rest of the day he sat, never displaying the slightest impatience to return home.

It took Malchus but a few moments to realize this was the opportunity for which he had been waiting. All the other so-called miracles had taken place immediately and in front of a crowd, and it would have been easy to hire a few people to pretend to be sick or lame. This time, all Malchus had to do was follow the man to his home and see that the little boy had died, thus proving Jesus false. Settling himself on the ground in view of the father, Malchus waited just as patiently, mentally preparing the report he would bring to his master.

— — —

The day was far spent when at last the father from Capernaum recalled how far he had to travel to reach home. With many more thanks he left the village, Malchus following at a discreet distance. At sunset the man turned off the road to make his bed on the soft grasses, his arms for a pillow. Malchus walked right on by, pretending not to notice, and a short distance away concealed himself in a thicket a few feet from the road.

It was far from the worst night he had spent, but he did not sleep so soundly that he missed the sound of footsteps near his head long before first light. As soon as the sound died away he again followed cautiously.

The man, unaware of anything behind him, hurried onward, never looking back. He did not even stop to drink, but poured the water into his mouth from his water skin without missing a stride. A stranger he overtook on the road received only a brief salute.

As Malchus approached the other traveler, he prepared to walk by quickly without calling a greeting. Then he froze as a friendly voice asked, "Malchus, is that you? Whatever are you doing in that outfit?"

Denial springing to his lips, Malchus turned, only to be stopped short at the sight of a slightly familiar face filled with mischief, dark-brown eyes laughing at him, and a white robe whipping about in the breeze. Malchus had met the man only a few times before, but he was the kind of person it was difficult to forget. "Deron! What are you doing here?" Malchus gripped the man's shoulder, amazed. "You've caught me fairly enough—just don't tell anyone you've seen me."

"Of course not," Deron assured him. "You ought to know me better than that."

"Walk with me a while, as long as you recognized me. Is my disguise really so poor?" Malchus asked anxiously.

Deron laughed at his crestfallen expression. "No, your disguise is fine. I just have a knack for faces, I guess. Can you tell me why you are here? Whatever it is, it probably has something to do with Jesus, doesn't it?"

Malchus looked startled. "Right as always. My master wants to know more about him." The high priest's servant shook his head. "If it weren't him, it would be some other troublemaker. I lost count long ago of how many power-hungry lunatics I have investigated for Caiaphas."

"Is that how you see Jesus—a troublemaker or lunatic?"

"Definitely a troublemaker, and I'll know soon whether he's a lunatic." Malchus snorted. "You act as if you believe him."

"I do," Deron replied soberly. "I have—all my life."

Malchus threw up his hands in a gesture of surrender. "All right; I'm sorry. I meant no offense. But what attracted you to him? You have always seemed so sensible. I don't understand."

"Truly you don't," Deron mused, more to himself than to Malchus. "Have you read the words of the prophets telling of the Messiah?"

"Of course," Malchus replied, a bit defensively. "I hear them read nearly every week either at the synagogue or the Temple."

"Yes, but have you really read them for yourself? It's not the same thing at all." Deron did not let on that he knew just how rarely the high priest's servant even glanced at one of the sacred scrolls.

"My wife reads them more often than I do," Malchus admitted, "but I still don't see what that has to do with this."

"It has everything to do with it," Deron insisted. "Micah even tells the very city in which the Messiah would be born."

"And where is that?" Malchus asked, interested in spite of himself.

"'But you, Bethlehem Ephratah,'" Deron quoted, "'though you are little among the thousands of Judah, yet out of you shall come forth to me the one to be ruler in Israel.'"

"I was born in Bethlehem," Malchus replied casually. "So was King David. Perhaps Micah meant one of us."

"'The one to be ruler in Israel, whose goings forth are from of old, from everlasting,'" Deron finished. "My friend, that could not be you. Nor could it be King David. Did you know that the Sacred Scriptures foretold even Herod's slaughter?"

Malchus stared at him. "How could that have been? Surely it wouldn't have happened if there had been a warning," he said skeptically.

Deron's voice rose and fell in the cadence of words hundreds of years old, yet steeped in a pain that was ever fresh. "'A voice was heard in Ramah, lamentation and bitter weeping, Rachel weeping for her children, refusing to be comforted for her children, because they are no more.'"

The bleakness on the other man's face surprised Malchus. "I had an older brother who died then," he said after a pause. "At least you and I have been spared any memory of it."

"Were we?" Deron asked ironically. "Perhaps. Anyway, Jesus was the only infant to escape that night."

"Next I suppose you're going to tell me how Elohim could be fair and loving and still let something like that happen." Anger seeped into Malchus' voice. "You don't know what my life has been like as a result of that massacre."

Deron stopped in the middle of the road and faced Malchus. "I know much more than you think. I also know that Elohim is filled with love. He *is* love. And Jesus is His Son."

The man's bold claim startled Malchus. Deron was obviously sincere, but just as obviously he was wrong. The idea that the common, dusty, homeless man he had seen only the day before could be the Son of the Highest was laughable. Still, he found Deron's vehemence disturbing. "That is not possible. I have met him, and I assure you, he is just a man."

"In the Temple?" Deron asked, a hint of a smile on his lips. "Besides, you forgot one of the most important pieces of information. When pronouncing a blessing on his sons, Father Israel said, 'The scepter shall not depart from Judah, nor a lawgiver from between his feet, until Shiloh comes.' Herod's son Archelaus was Judah's last true king. The moment the Roman emperor appointed a governor, the scepter departed from Judah." Deron paused, giving emphasis to each syllable. "By the sure word of prophecy, the Messiah is already here."

Malchus just stood gaping. The idea had never occurred to him before. "How can we know for sure?" he finally asked.

"Read the prophecies yourself and ask Elohim to guide you into His truth." Deron's eyes twinkled. "Here is where we part, friend. We are nearly to Capernaum, and that man is leaving you far behind."

With a start Malchus saw that it was true. The road had been skirting the Sea of Galilee for some time, and a small town was just visible in the distance. The person he was following was just a speck, growing smaller each instant. "Even if we never agree, it was good seeing you again," Deron said. "May your journey meet with success."

"Yours also," Malchus replied, but Deron was gone. An observant traveler walking along the road after them would have noticed with puzzlement a pair of footprints, side by side for miles, until one continued on into the town, and the other ended abruptly in the middle of the road.

— — —

Malchus had to abandon any attempt at stealth and run as fast as he could to catch up with the man he had been following, but he need not have worried. Someone who had not looked back once on his whole journey was not about to start now. His attention seemed to be focused on a sprawling dwelling at the edge of town, so near the shore that the waves almost lapped at his doorstep.

When someone noticed his approach, a glad cry went up inside the house, and a crowd of people gathered around him. Family and servants alike all talked so loud and so fast that none could be understood. The man laughingly held up his hands for silence, but the excited babble only increased in volume.

"Elhanan!" From the doorway a woman who must have been his wife called his name. Hardly more than a girl, she held in her arms a toddler in the bloom of health. The little boy wiggled out of his mother's arms and ran joyfully to his beloved abba. At last the noise died away, except for a few furtive sniffles.

"My Taavi, my Taavi. Here you are, as well as ever." Elhanan scooped the child up, holding him close. The child squeezed his father in return, his tiny hands gently patting the father's broad back. "For a while Abba thought he might not see you anymore, but Jesus made you well—yes, He did." Tears streamed down his cheeks, and his lips moved in a silent prayer of thanks.

A tug on his cloak called his attention to the young woman at his side. "What happened, Elhanan? How did He do it?"

He looked down lovingly at his wife clutching his elbow. "First, Ronia, I have a question for you. What time yesterday did Taavi get well?"

"It was the most amazing thing. His fever was so high that no amount of water would cool it, and his skin was bright red at first, but then it turned kind of gray. He was barely breathing. Once or twice he even stopped, and I had to shake him a bit to get him to draw another breath." She reached up and caressed her son's cheek. "I thought he would die at any moment. Suddenly he opened his eyes, sat up, and said, 'Mama feed me.' I had given up all hope, and then to hear him say that—" Overwhelmed by a flood of tears, she stopped.

"But what time did that happen?" her husband asked insistently.

"At the seventh hour," she said, and the others all nodded in agreement.

"But that," Elhanan exclaimed, "was the very moment I spoke to Jesus—when He said my son was already well." The courtyard exploded in excitement. Father and son led the procession into the house, where no doubt the rest of the family would demand a full account of all that had happened.

Malchus stared into the now-empty courtyard. Bits of conversation tumbled themselves around in his head, assembling into a pattern he did not like. At the seventh hour. Yes, that was just when Jesus had spoken the words of healing. Could the incident have possibly been faked? No, without an audience to be fooled, there could be no reason for a deception of this magnitude. Surely no one had noticed him watching. At last he found himself forced to accept that some unknown power at Jesus' command had healed the boy.

"That's it!" Malchus said, grasping at straws. "The priest was right—he is in league with the devil." It seemed odd to say it. Malchus had never given much credence to stories about an actual Satan, but it seemed preferable to believing that Jesus was working for God. "I must go to Caiaphas at once. Israel must be warned!"

Springing to his feet, he immediately began the long trek back to Jerusalem. All the way he had to fight to keep from his mind the sight of father and son tightly holding each other. He ached as he tried not to wonder what it would feel like to have a son of his own, a child's chubby arms clasped about his neck.

CHAPTER 5

It was perhaps the most pitiful sight in Jerusalem, though the place itself was attractive. The pool consisted of two sections separated by a dam, or causeway. Four porticoes surrounded the pools, and a fifth occupied the causeway. Even from a distance one could hear the moans and cries of the sick and injured, but up close the commotion was deafening.

Tradition held that the sporadic bubbling upsurge of current from the base of the pools resulted from an angel stirring the water, and that each time, the first sufferer to cast their wasted body into the spring would be cured of whatever ailed them. The fortunate ones had family or friends to help them down the stairs, or to make room for them at the very edge of the pool, where they might be able to roll themselves in quickly enough to be healed.

Each story was tragic, but Betzalel most of all. Thirty-eight years before, at the age of 10, he had crept into the house of a local merchant, intent on stealing some of his wares. When the merchant discovered him, he beat him mercilessly and left him for dead. Even since, Betzalel had been paralyzed.

His family carried him to Jerusalem and left him near the Sheep Gate, at the Pool of Beth-zatha. There he became a beggar. As the long years passed, he bitterly regretted the choices that had brought him to such a place. Hourly he cried out to God for forgiveness, never truly expecting help, but not quite giving up hope.

The early-morning sun peeped above the surrounding buildings, its light inching across the floor to where Betzalel lay shivering on his mat. At last it reached him, and he closed his eyes, soaking up the warmth. Suddenly a shadow fell across his face. Startled, he opened his eyes and rose up on one elbow, using the other arm to shade his face.

A man stooped over him, His face hidden in shadow. The sun lit Him from behind, as if He were glowing. A flash of white teeth revealed a friendly smile. The stranger's voice, vibrant with new energy, asked him the strangest question. "Do you want to be healed?"

— — —

"Are you almost ready? I don't want to be late." Malchus poked his head through the door adjoining the two bedchambers. Alona held her mirror of polished brass, hastily looping a belt around her slim waist and smoothing an imaginary wrinkle in the white skirt of her robe.

"There, I'm ready, and just on time," she returned laughingly as the ram's horn sounded nearby, calling the people to worship. Cheeks flushed with excitement, she took her husband's arm, happily aware that the blue sash draped around her neck set off her fair skin to perfection, and that she and Malchus made a most handsome couple.

Amused, Malchus listened as his wife chattered on and on, catching him up on all that had happened while he was gone. Abruptly he broke away from her in midsentence and crossed the street, leaving Alona standing by herself. After a moment she recovered from her surprise and followed him.

Malchus approached a priest who was angrily questioning a man.

That was not so remarkable in and of itself, but it was the Sabbath, and the man was carrying his sleeping mat. According to the teachings of the Pharisees, this was a grave offense, as they considered that to bear any burden, large or small, was to work on the day of rest. "What seems to be the trouble?" Malchus interrupted.

The two men turned to him, the priest with irritation and the offender with obvious relief. "As you can surely see," the priest's voice quivered with outrage, "this man is carrying his bed—on the Sabbath!"

The servant of the high priest looked inquiringly at the man. Despite the serious charges that could be brought against him, the accused individual seemed happy, almost as if he couldn't help himself. It was growing to be a familiar expression, and Malchus had a nagging suspicion that he knew what had produced it. "What is your name, and what excuse do you have for breaking the law?" Malchus spoke calmly and understandingly to put the man at ease, hoping he would respond more freely.

"I am Betzalel," the man replied, "and I was unable to walk for almost 40 years." Malchus nodded encouragingly. "This morning I was at the Pool of Beth-zatha, just as always, when a man came and told me to pick up my bed and walk. I was never more surprised in my life, but I did it—and now I can walk!"

Suddenly sure he was telling the truth, Malchus scanned the man from the top of his scraggly head to his bare feet. "Who healed you?" he asked offhandedly, as if the answer was of no particular importance. "What was his name?"

"But that's just it," the man answered, bewildered. "I don't know. I didn't even get a good look at His face."

"I'll tell you what," Malchus said, holding up one hand to silence the priest, who was trying to interrupt. "I will take you to my house. You certainly can't go to the Temple looking like that, and if you walk any farther with your burden you might be arrested." He thought for a moment. "I know the family who lives in that house"—he pointed to a dwelling two doors down—"and they will keep your bed until after the Sabbath. As long as you've already carried it this far, a few extra feet won't matter much. And I know someone who will be very interested in your story."

The man thanked him and hurried to do as he was bid. Malchus turned to Alona. "Go on without me. I will catch up as quickly as I can. And you," he addressed the priest, "take a message to Caiaphas. Tell him that I will be a few minutes late, but that it is urgent that he meet with me. His audience chamber will do fine." Without giving either of them a chance to argue, he and Betzalel departed, moving with a speed unseemly for the Sabbath.

Malchus worked so fast that it was yet a few minutes before services started when he and a transformed Betzalel arrived, a bit out of breath, in the audience chamber. Caiaphas stood waiting for them, his stance a mixture of curiosity and irritation. "Malchus, I trust you have a very good reason for this." He eyed the unfamiliar man with his servant, the robe a few sizes too big, hair and beard neatly combed. The man was now clean—at least everywhere that showed.

Bowing at the waist, Malchus signaled Betzalel to do the same and said to the high priest, "I apologize for the intrusion at this late time, so I will come straight to the point. This man," gesturing to Betzalel, "was paralyzed. He was healed this morning by a man he did not know or recognize, although I trust his benefactor is not unknown to us." He raised an eyebrow. "The man instructed him to carry away his bed, and, caught up in the excitement, he did."

Caiaphas' eyes gleamed. "Don't worry about that," he reassured Betzalel. "If you see the man who did this, point Him out to me. I would enjoy talking to him."

Unsuspecting, Betzalel stammered, "Yes, sir, I would be glad to. Thank you, sir."

"Ah, but it is I who thank you. Quickly now, else we are late to the service." Caiaphas swept past, leaving the two men to follow.

"Is there anything else you need?" Malchus asked Betzalel. The man turned red under his tan, looking shamefaced at the floor. "What is it?" Malchus urged. "You have been a great help to us today, and I am sure you will be even more help when you find the man who healed you."

Shyly the man met Malchus' eyes. "It's only that you've done so much already, but yes, there is one thing." He nerved himself to speak, and the words came out in a rush. "I would like to give a thank offering and a sin offering."

Malchus smiled. "Both? I'm not surprised. Consider it done." His gamble paid off. Just a little more than an hour later Betzalel was back at his side, leading two lambs.

"There He is," he whispered excitedly. "That man right over there."

Malchus looked in the direction he pointed. "Just as I thought; I know who that is. His name is Jesus."

"Jesus," the man repeated. "'Our salvation.' Do you think it could be? He knew all about me, even the sin that paralyzed me."

"What do you mean?"

"I was taking my offerings to be sacrificed when He came up to me. I recognized Him by His voice, and He told me, 'Don't fall into the same sins as before, or an even worse thing might happen.' I had always told anyone who asked that I had been accidentally run down by a freight wagon. Even my own parents didn't know the truth."

"He seems to have that effect on people. No secret is safe from Him," Malchus muttered. "Thank you again." Pushing his way through the crowd, he looked for Caiaphas. Soon Malchus watched from a distance as several members of the Temple police intruded on the little group, telling Jesus, "You'll have to come with us."

"Of course," Jesus said politely, "but may I ask why?"

"Ask the high priest when you see him." At the Temple guard's curt tone, several burly disciples took a step forward, but Jesus motioned them back. Then He walked peaceably into the Temple complex, a serene expression on His face.

Later at the evening meal Malchus found himself being thoroughly questioned by his curious wife. "Why did they take Jesus away? I heard a few of the things He said today, and they all made perfect sense. I can see why so many people follow Him."

"You know as well as I do that he broke our law and must face the Sanhedrin." Malchus tried not to sound defensive.

"He broke the regulations of the Pharisees, but I don't believe He broke any law of Moses—or of God." Alona set her mouth in the way she always did when she was going to be stubborn about something.

"We'll know tomorrow," Malchus told her. "Of course they couldn't do anything on the Sabbath, but I'm sure the Sanhedrin will meet at first light." He attacked his supper doggedly, hoping to avoid further questions.

Alona leaned toward him. "I have heard many saying He must be the Messiah. If even half the stories I've heard are true, He probably is."

Holding his head, Malchus groaned, "Not you, too. Please forget this foolishness and tend to your household."

Her face darkened with anger. "Malchus ben-Gershom, that was unfair. When have you ever known me to neglect the household for any reason? And as for calling it foolishness, I can show you any number of the prophets of Elohim who would disagree with you." She glared at him across the table.

His laughter at her statement infuriated her still more. "You can say whatever you want, my dove. There is no denying the man has a certain appeal, but his power comes from below."

Losing her temper, Alona slammed her fist on the table. "How dare you!" she shouted. "You think that just because you sneak around spying you know everything about Him, but you don't! Your mind is closed to any opinion except the one your precious master gives you!"

Her husband eyed her thoughtfully. "I may be closed-minded and stupid, but if this is any example of what his followers are like, I want no part of him."

"Oh, Malchus," she cried out, "I didn't mean it. I am so sorry I let my wretched temper get the better of me. Please don't judge Jesus or His followers by my poor example."

He only rolled his eyes. "Whatever you say, my dove." Her words had stung him more than he cared to admit.

"Please, Malchus, you must know by now that I love you, and I would do anything to take back what I just said." She stretched her hand toward him.

Ignoring it, he replied only, "I must say, you have made a reasonably good wife. I have even grown accustomed to having you around, and you are certainly entitled to your opinions." Then he turned his attention again to his plate, ignoring her pleading eyes.

Alona had hardly dared to hope that her affections would be fully returned, but the coldness of his reaction stunned her, and her eyes filled with tears. "You won't be able to provoke me again," she said, rising, "because the more I see of Jesus, the more I want to be like Him." In the doorway she paused and turned back. "Remember, I do love you."

With a shrug Malchus kept eating, his thoughts fixed on the trial that would commence in the morning. It was probable that Jesus would be found guilty of Sabbathbreaking, but then what? The Sanhedrin no longer had the power of life and death over its prisoners, and the Roman governor would be reluctant to execute someone who had broken no Roman laws. However, it was their best chance yet to rid the nation of this latest threat, and he was sure Caiaphas would make the most of it.

⸺ ⸺ ⸺

Well before dawn on that moonless night Malchus crossed the bridge on the west side of the Temple compound, passing through the double arches to stand at the corner of the sacred precinct. He turned left into the first doorway, unworried by the sign proclaiming death to any Gentile who stepped inside, and climbed the stairs leading to the entrance into the Court of Israel. The priests were already busy preparing for the day's sacrifices, and inside the court the lamps and torches had been lit as the Sanhedrin prepared to hear their case. Malchus slipped his own torch into an empty wall bracket and glanced around. Storage rooms lined the perimeter of the courtyard and the Hall of Hewn Stone, where the Sanhedrin always met.

As he expected, Caiaphas was already inside the large chamber with its decorative wood panels lit by flickering lamps. Highlights of gold gleamed on the walls. Marble pillars stretched from floor to ceiling in the front of the room, where the high priest presided over the council. An open circle of cushions, 71 in all, skirted three sides of the room, and in the center was a wide area to hold the accused and any witnesses.

Next to Caiaphas stood a man of rather haughty bearing. His thin brows were raised in an arrogant expression, and his closely trimmed beard scarcely moved as he talked. Far above average in height, he towered over the high priest. The way Caiaphas seemed almost to grovel before the man puzzled Malchus. It was as if the visitor were master to the high priest and not the other way around.

Malchus had to cough twice before Caiaphas noticed his presence. "Ah, Malchus. Come and meet Zarad, a colleague of my father-in-law, Annas. He has given me some excellent advice regarding today's trial. Zarad, this is Malchus, my most trusted servant."

Stepping forward, Malchus bowed to the men. "A pleasure, sir. Good morning, my master." As he stood, his eyes met those of Zarad full on. For a moment he thought his heart had stopped. Never before had he credited the stories of people possessed by demons, but then never before had he looked into a face so full of hate. Zarad's eyes, glittering black stones of obsidian, seemed like pools of hate. Angry with himself but having no choice, Malchus dropped his gaze to the floor.

The visitor turned to the high priest. "Just gain a conviction against that impostor. If you can get the council to sentence Him to death, I will clear the way with the governor." Caiaphas raised his eyebrows slightly in disbelief. "I know his every weakness," Zarad continued. "Leave Pilate to me." With a flourish he strode from the hall.

Just as the sun was about to rise, the other 70 members of the Sanhedrin filed into the chamber to join the high priest. All of them were older men, married, had children, and ideally should have been known for their wisdom. In practice, many gained their seats through political pressure rather than merit, but it was still an imposing group that prepared to sit in judgment that day. Malchus heard the hum of their voices talking in hushed tones as he sat in the third row of novices. Caiaphas thought it would be helpful if he heard for himself how Jesus responded to the charges brought against him, just in case this first effort to put him to death failed.

According to the laws governing the Sanhedrin, the council could conduct a trial involving a capital offense only during hours of daylight and after the morning sacrifice. So it was that just after the first rays of light illuminated the roof of the Temple that the Temple police led the prisoner to stand among the council. Just as He had the day before, Jesus walked calmly between the two guards, making no struggle or attempt to escape. He faced Caiaphas unafraid as a scribe read the dual charges of Sabbathbreaking: healing on the Sabbath and commanding someone to bear a burden on the sacred rest day.

"Do you wish to answer these accusations?" Caiaphas asked. "After all, many witnesses can testify as to what happened."

Jesus paused for a moment before answering. "My Father has been working without stopping, and so have I. Would you have My Father stop the sun in the sky on the Sabbath day? Or perhaps the flowers should cease in their growing, and the trees produce no fruit. Should

My Father halt the waves at the shore of the sea one day each week?"

An unwilling and nervous laugh broke out around the room. Caiaphas' face flushed a mottled red. "Do you call yourself equal with God? That is blasphemy." He held his arms wide, addressing the entire council. "You see what a danger this man is. He calls God his Father."

Before he could say more, Jesus interrupted. "My Father will show you greater works"—He placed a subtle emphasis on the word "works"—"than what you have already seen. My Father gives life to the dead, and in just the same way, His Son will give life to whomever He chooses." Instantly a raging argument broke out between the Pharisees, who believed in the resurrection of the dead, and the Sadducees, who held that no life existed beyond the grave.

Caiaphas cut through the uproar with a strident and angry voice. "Your own testimony condemns you. You are a Sabbathbreaker and blasphemer. According to the law of Moses, you should be stoned to death. Do you think to accuse us and escape blameless?"

Jesus remained unruffled. "I do not accuse you before God." The members of the council listened silently to His words. "However, there is a man who does. It is Moses."

A shocked gasp spread through the assembly. The traditions of their nation had long spoken of Moses being raised to life three days after his death, but no one had ever dared confirm it with such authority. "What do you mean?" the high priest asked irritably. "We all have believed Moses from our birth."

"You say you trust the writings of Moses, but that is not true," Jesus answered pointedly. "Moses wrote about Me, and you do not accept what he says, so will you then accept what I say?"

"We follow the law of Moses," Caiaphas retorted, "which you stand accused of breaking."

"Show me from the Scriptures just which law I have broken." Silence filled the chamber. "I have broken nothing except human tradition," Jesus then said, "which has been laid on the people of Israel like a heavy yoke. The Sabbath should be a delight, never a burden."

Here and there most members of the Sanhedrin murmured their agreement. Caiaphas saw that having lost their support, he was beaten. Humiliated and defeated by the unanswerable logic of an itinerant preacher from Nazareth, he held his hands up in surrender. "Release him," he snapped, and retreated to his palace.

Malchus shifted his aching muscles and tried hard not to laugh aloud. As much affection as he held for his master, he still recognized that Caiaphas was a hard man whose pride had just suffered a huge blow. "That will teach him to think that I exaggerate in my reports," he chuckled softly. Never again would the high priest underestimate the former carpenter from Galilee.

Later that day Malchus received written orders from Caiaphas to send messengers to every part of the land, warning them of the pretender to the throne of Israel. Malchus himself was to organize a network of spies to document every word and act of Jesus and report them to Jerusalem. One thing was certain now. Caiaphas would never rest until Jesus was dead.

CHAPTER 6

The spies did their work well. Though the public defeat in the Sanhedrin left a bitter taste in Caiaphas' mouth, he continued to work feverishly to discredit Jesus. At first his efforts seemed to produce few results, but gradually Jesus' popularity began to diminish. When John the Baptist became Herod's prisoner in the fortress of Machaerus east of the Dead Sea, the people of Judea made a mad scramble to distance themselves from the Teacher of Galilee. At last He found Himself forced to retire in obscurity to the northern provinces of Israel.

For Malchus life had settled into a monotonous routine. He had Caiaphas' daily business to attend to and the periodic reports of the spies and messengers to sort through. Because Jesus was keeping a lowered profile, most of the high priest's agents had been reassigned to other tasks, and the daily reports had stretched to weekly.

Just when he thought he couldn't endure the tedium another second, Malchus received a summons from the high priest. "Dear boy," Caiaphas greeted him, "not that it hasn't been nice having you around for so long, but I want you to see what's happening in Galilee. Things have been almost too peaceful, and I would value your assessment of the situation."

Malchus eagerly leaned forward. "Right now?"

"Tonight will be soon enough. You have been so restless lately. Go, before you drive me insane with your pacing."

"Thank you, Master," Malchus said over his shoulder, departing with unseemly haste.

All the way home he pondered what he would say to Alona. She had seemed to enjoy having him at home, greeting him enthusiastically at the end of each day and arranging to have all his favorite dishes served each evening meal. When he could spare the time, he even allowed her to read to him from her scrolls, listening to the prophecies of Messiah's coming with an unwilling, yet growing, interest.

At the doorstep his feet slowed, and he entered the house silently. He could hear the servants working in the courtyard kitchen, and the tempting smells made his mouth water. Tiptoeing down the hallway, he looked in Alona's open door. She sat on a low bench holding the scroll of Psalms, reading aloud to a girl at her feet. Not wanting to disrupt the scene with the news of his departure, he stood quietly, wanting to postpone the inevitable as long as possible. Alona's voice rose and fell with the cadence of the words.

> "Then they cried to the lord in their trouble,
> and he saved them from their distress.
> He sent forth his word and healed them;
> he rescued them from the grave.
> Let them give thanks to the Lord for his unfailing love
> And his wonderful deeds for men.
> Let them sacrifice thank offerings
> And tell of his works with songs of joy."

Alona turned to her maid, Erith, who listened with wide-eyed interest. "Doesn't that sound just like what Jesus is doing? And though I haven't heard of Him rescuing anyone from the grave yet, if He did it would be clear evidence that He is really the Messiah. Listen to this part, too." She found her place in the scroll.

"Others went out on the sea in ships;
  they were merchants on the mighty waters.
They saw the works of the Lord,
  his wonderful deeds in the deep.
For he spoke and stirred up a tempest
  that lifted high the waves.
They mounted up to the heavens and went down to the
    depths;
  in their peril their courage melted away.
They reeled and staggered like drunken men;
  they were at their wit's end.
Then they cried out to the Lord in their trouble,
  and he brought them out of their distress.
He stilled the storm to a whisper;
  the waves of the sea were hushed.
They were glad when it grew calm,
  and he guided them to their desired haven."

The servant girl let out a long breath. "What do you think it means?"

"I'm not entirely sure," Alona admitted, "but isn't it fascinating?" She unrolled the next section just as her husband cleared his throat. Alona looked up with a start. "Malchus! How long have you been standing there?" Jumping up, she ran to him. Erith ducked her head shyly as she slipped past, returning to her work.

As Malchus opened his arms to her he was still trying to think what to say. A few seconds later she drew back, examining his face. "You're going away, aren't you?" she accused.

He sighed and nodded. "Caiaphas just told me. I don't know how long I'll be gone."

Her eyes narrowed. "Where are you going?"

"I can't tell you that." Malchus couldn't meet her gaze.

"I don't know why you bother to answer like that. You are going after Jesus—I can see it on your face. He is in Galilee; therefore, you are going to Galilee. Now, why didn't you just say that in the first place?"

Defeated, he shook his head. "Maybe you should be working for Caiaphas instead of me. I'm sorry. I know how you feel about Jesus, but you just don't understand how dangerous he is in these times of unrest. I'm trying to prevent Pilate from committing another massacre. Can't you see that?"

She studied him before replying. "Oh, I think you're sincere about what you're doing. Sincerely wrong. Everything I have read in Scripture points to just one thing: Jesus is the Messiah. I had hoped you would eventually understand that." A thoughtful, almost sly look crept over her face. "But I'm not going to stand here and argue with you. Go get ready to leave, or whatever you're going to do. I have things to attend to." With a toss of her head, she walked briskly away.

Malchus massaged his temples and stretched his neck to each side. He felt regret for hurting her, but frustration too. Why couldn't she see that he was just trying to shelter her from harm, and to protect their people? With a shrug he forced himself to go and pack. The ways of women were beyond him.

As soon as Malchus disappeared into his chamber, Alona ran in search of Erith, not wanting to call for her aloud. She found the girl on the roof, watering the plants Alona had brought from the hills around Jerusalem.

"You have to help me," she said urgently, taking one last glance down the stairs to make sure that no one could hear her. "Malchus is getting himself in a lot of trouble, and I have to do something." Drawing near her servant, she whispered into the girl's ear.

Erith had always been more of a friend than a servant, and she didn't hesitate to express her opinion. "You're insane!"

Alona's expression grew more determined. "If you won't help me, I'll do this alone. I've made up my mind, and nothing you say will make any difference."

The girl threw up her hands in surrender. "All right, all right. Of course I'll help you."

"Good." She hugged her fiercely. "How soon can you be ready?"

— — —

It was a fine, crisp early morning, and Malchus was enjoying every minute of it. He much liked his role as Malachi, the moderately wealthy and moderately portly Hebrew. It was a far cry from the beggars he had impersonated, and best of all, he was mounted. Caiaphas had kept to his word, allowing Malchus to choose a fine donkey from his stables. The shaggy gray creature was large enough that he didn't look overly comical riding the beast, though his feet hung rather near the ground. A striped wool blanket kept most of the animal's sweat from staining his clothing.

True, it had taken Malchus several minutes to convince his new donkey to move in a forward direction—or even any direction, for that matter—but he fancied himself a fine figure of a rider as he trotted majestically along the north road. Before long he passed a small camp, with two women and a man sitting by a low fire. A fine ebony mare grazed quietly nearby.

Malchus raised one hand in greeting, and the man returned the salute. The women lowered their heads shyly, just as custom required they should. For a moment he thought of his wife, who had not even told him goodbye. She must have been furious that he was leaving again with no warning, and in pursuit of her favorite teacher, besides. He hadn't realized how much her loving nature had come to mean to him. Now he hoped she wouldn't stay angry long.

⌐ ⌐ ⌐

"Is he gone yet?" Alona whispered.

Erith, Alona's maid and best friend since childhood, peeked out from under the scarf she held tightly beneath her chin. "I think so." She giggled. "Are you sure that was him? He looked almost, well, fat!"

Relaxing, Alona laughed aloud. "Of course I'm sure. I would know my husband anywhere. I'm just glad I kept Kivi at Uncle's house, or he might have recognized her. Quickly now, let's go." It took only two or three minutes to roll their bedding, fasten it to the horse's back, and smother their fire with earth. They set a brisk pace, but watched carefully lest they should overtake their quarry unawares. When several miles passed with no sight of him, the third member of the party spoke at last.

"The way he's moving, he'll be lucky to stop before he lands in the Great Sea." The man's sun-bronzed face was solemn, unreadable.

"But we are traveling north," Alona protested, frowning in puzzlement. "He would not reach the Great Sea until far into the land of the Phoenicians."

"That is just what I mean," their companion said, his face creasing into a smile. "That little donkey looks as if it goes much better than it stops."

"Oded, I never know if you are teasing or not." Alona grinned. "I don't know why my uncle has kept you around all these years."

"It's only because he has a way with any four-footed beast," Erith said. "Otherwise I'm sure he would have been sent packing long ago."

"I always said that whichever man wed you would be led a merry chase, Little Mistress," Oded said fondly. "Now I know for sure I was right."

Erith leaped to Alona's defense. "Any woman worth her salt would have done just the same thing," she retorted.

"Enough, you two," Alona said. "You know I dare not take sides." Then more seriously: "Thank you both for coming with me. I would have gone by myself if I had to, but it's much nicer with company."

"Safer, too," Oded grumbled.

"As if we would let you make your journey alone," Erith protested.

"Still, you have my thanks."

Against her wishes, Erith was riding, with Alona and Oded walking alongside. Both servants had at first been horrified at the thought of their beloved mistress enduring such hardship in walking so great a distance, but at last they bowed to her insistence that she was much less likely to be recognized if posing as a servant herself. Oded had jokingly proposed that both women act as his wives, walking meekly behind him while he rode in state ahead. It dissolved the tension, and Oded held up his hands in mock fear at the sight of their faces. Their lighthearted banter continued as they journeyed, making the time pass quickly and helping Alona to forget her aching feet.

It was just as well for Malchus that none of his three pursuers ever knew how nearly true was Oded's comment about the donkey. Thankfully, no one was around when he finally decided to bring it to a stop for the first time. When Malchus pulled on its bridle, the donkey only tossed its head, never breaking its stride. As its rider became more insistent, it danced sideways a bit, but kept right on going, now increasing its pace. They started up a small hill, and the blanket began to slip a bit on the creature's back. Malchus dug his knees into its furry sides, trying to keep his balance. The donkey began to gallop.

"Stop!" Malchus shouted. "You misbegotten offspring of a camel, stop at once!" His mount brayed insolently in response. As they crested the hill, Malchus immediately realized that a gallop downhill was going to be very different from one going uphill. The donkey sawed back and forth, its hooves pounding the rocky path.

In a last desperate attempt to halt the fleeing beast, Malchus pulled harder on the reins, but it only angered the animal. When it lowered its head, the reins slipped from his fingers, passed over the long gray ears, and trailed in the dust, beyond all hope of recovery.

Most travelers along that stretch of the north road would have considered that particular hill to have had a reasonably gentle slope, but to Malchus, inching his way inexorably along the donkey's back, it appeared nothing less than a precipice. Clinging to the rough mane, he tried to regain his balance. It was no use. The majestic rider of a short time before now straddled the donkey's shoulders, his legs wrapped tightly around its neck and his hands desperately tangled in its mane, trying to push himself back up. It seemed as if his head were aimed squarely down at the stony trail.

At the bottom of the hill the road leveled out. The donkey thrashed its head about, but was unable to dislodge Malchus. By the time his weight at last forced the stubborn animal to slow and then stop, it would have been hard to say who was more tired. The donkey stood head down, flanks heaving, foam trailing from its mouth. Malchus lay where he had dropped on his back in the middle of the road, having just enough presence of mind to grasp the reins in trembling fingers.

Finally the man sat up. "An extraordinary donkey should have an extraordinary name," he said conversationally to his still-panting companion. "I think I will call you Jori-hod, because you descend so swiftly." He shook his head to clear it. "At least now I know why Caiaphas' stablemaster laughed when I chose you." Staggering to his feet, he reached for his water skin and discovered it empty. "Come on, Jori; let's find something to drink." Much subdued, the animal walked docilely beside his new master.

The donkey was well behaved the rest of the day, even when Malchus remounted and rode at a walk toward Samaria. The next morning Malchus discovered to his dismay that Jori's reformation had been exceedingly short, and the scene of the previous day repeated itself in bone-jarring detail. Fortunately, his natural creativity came to his aid, and after several failed experiments Malchus finally discovered a way to bring the creature to a halt. He would start Jori at a trot and keep a steady pace until the donkey slowed to a walk on its own. When Malchus was ready to stop completely, he found a long, straight stretch, took a firm grip on the reins, and jumped swiftly to the ground. Trotting alongside, he guided Jori into a circle that grew smaller and smaller until the donkey had no choice but to stop in the center. It was awkward but effective.

Upon reaching the region of Galilee, Malchus began his inquiry into the whereabouts of Jesus. Learning that a crowd was following the Teacher to His own town of Nazareth, Malchus decided to give Him a homecoming that He would never forget.

— ⸺ —

"What on this fair green earth is that man doing?" Oded drawled. "He's going to make that poor donkey dizzy." Alona tried to answer, but could only laugh helplessly. Several times they had been close enough to her husband to watch him as he straddled his donkey, but this was the first time they had seen him dismount.

Concealed by a grove of trees on a small rise, the three had an excellent view of the tightening spiral as Malchus ran alongside his donkey. "Has he been doing that this whole trip?" Alona finally gasped. "I thought he looked a bit tired, but I never would have guessed why!"

"It's no wonder he decided to get off here," Oded commented dryly. "If the donkey started to run up that hill, it might miss Nazareth altogether and fall from the cliffs just on the other side of the city."

Alona sobered a little, but couldn't help a little chuckle as Malchus finally drew his animal to a stop and, panting, rested both arms on its back. "My husband would never be so careless. He is the most cautious person I know, always talking about the safest way to do something."

"Speaking of safest, you shouldn't go to the synagogue tomorrow."

Erith couldn't resist the chance to bring up their ongoing argument. "With so few people around, you run a great risk of being recognized."

"Malchus will not be looking for me way up here," she said with supreme confidence. "I have never missed synagogue services for as long as I can remember, and I'm not going to start now. Besides, there may be more people than you think."

Alona was right—the town was packed with people who had heard that Jesus would be there. Only with difficulty did they even find lodging space. It was close to sunset before they were settled.

When the sun was slivered on the horizon, Alona lit the oil lamps she had brought with her and gathered Oded and Erith. Together they joined their voices in the plaintive melody, a hymn of welcome for the Sabbath. *"Baruch atah, Adonai. Eloheinu melech ha-olam. . . . Shel Shabbat."* All over the city others sang too, adding their voices to the chorus. *"Blessed be the name of the Lord."*

━ ━ ━

Malchus wasted no time. The whole town buzzed with talk about Jesus. Some were curious, but others were downright resentful because He had not come sooner. "I think He will speak tomorrow," Malchus would interject into the conversation whenever he could. "He's probably just here to show off and make the rest of us look bad." Or "He has been here all day and hasn't performed one miracle yet. You would think that if the stories of what He has done in the Gentile countries were true, He would help the people in His own town."

Such seeds of doubt found fertile soil in the hearts of the Nazarenes, and it was a dissatisfied, seething crowd that assembled in the synagogue the next morning. The people sat either on the tiered benches along the walls or on mats in the center of the room. Malchus sat with the men on one side of the room, while the women and children occupied the other. A stray breeze drifted through the open doors, lightly lifting the head covering of the local synagogue leader as he rose to speak, gray beard bobbing with each word.

"This morning we have in our midst a special guest—yet not a guest. Jesus bar-Joseph, you know our custom about visiting teachers. Would you give the Scripture reading this morning?"

With a nod Jesus walked to the front and accepted the scroll from the man He had known since His youth. When He turned and faced the gathering, the room was totally silent. Jesus opened the scroll and began to read, every eye fixed on Him.

> "'The Spirit of the Lord God is upon Me,
>   Because the Lord has anointed Me
>   To preach good tidings to the poor;
>   He has sent Me to heal the brokenhearted,
>   To proclaim liberty to the captives,
>   And the opening of the prison to those who are bound;
>   To proclaim the acceptable year of the Lord.'"

Then rolling the scroll back up, He handed it back to the leader's assistant. Everyone waited with interest to see what He might do or say next. Taking a seat, the traditional posture for teaching, He began, "Our people have waited for the Messiah for hundreds of years. Since Adam fell captive to sin, each generation has watched and waited, wondering when the Lord's Anointed would appear to set His people free."

The congregation, much surprised and enthralled by the authority in His voice, scarcely breathed. "All of you young mothers," he addressed the women's side of the synagogue with a twinkle in His eye, "have spent—don't try to deny it—hours wondering, 'Will I be the one to give birth to the Messiah?'" A few hushed giggles came from the women, and knowing chuckles from the men.

"The prophets have told us much about the Promised One, often at the expense of their own lives. Isaiah was no exception, but with what beauty he reveals the purposes of the Messiah! The Holy One would be called to share the good news of our loving Father with the poor, the neglected, and those trapped by sin."

The congregation, caught up in His words, responded with a loud "Amen!" Even Malchus found himself drawn by Jesus' power and had to remind himself again and again that this teacher had allied himself with the kingdom of darkness. But his own words were beginning to ring hollow in his mind despite all their repetition.

"I tell you truly," Jesus went on, "that the prison doors are being opened. Every soul mired in wickedness can be freed if they desire.

Those whose hearts are broken with sadness can be made whole." He paused to let His words sink in. "Isaiah said the Messiah would proclaim the acceptable year of the Lord, and today this scripture has been fulfilled in your hearing."

In the stunned, frozen moment that followed, only Jesus moved, calmly returning to His place in the congregation. Malchus glanced at the man on his left. "It is blasphemy," he whispered. "You have known him all his life. Do something!" To the man on his right he said softly, "His whole family is here, where he grew up. What right does he have to say that we are wicked and need to be set free?"

The whispers in the room grew to loud, ugly murmurs until Malchus shouted out, "Kill him!" He sat back, greatly pleased as tempers exploded all over the room.

No one but Alona ever knew for sure who had started it, and in her horror she abandoned all attempt at secrecy and screamed, "No! Leave Him alone!" Her husband would surely have discovered her identity had not most of the townspeople leaped to their feet then, all shouting and gesturing violently.

In the center of the commotion stood Jesus, an oasis of peace in a raging storm. Men grabbed Him, ripping His clothes and bruising His flesh with their rough handling. "The cliff! Take Him to the cliff!" a cry spread through the synagogue. Several men and a woman were nearly trampled in the rush for the door. Holding Jesus firmly to give Him no chance of escape, the mob raced through the city streets. Malchus kept a little way back from the front of the crowd but just close enough to be able to provide Caiaphas a good account of the defeat of their enemy.

About 300 paces outside Nazareth stretched a long, jutting overhang. Scraggly trees clung here and there to the sheer face, and boulders littered the base. It was here that the rioting crowd bore the former inhabitant of their town.

Wanting to get a better view when the teacher plunged over the side, Malchus worked his way to the edge of the mob. As more and more people pressed into the back of the crowd, it swung closer and closer to the precipice. Suddenly Malchus found himself right on the brink, a solid wall of raving humanity blocking his way to safety.

He hammered with his fists, he shouted, he clung to the robes of the men forcing him ever nearer to death, but to no avail. The men around him were also panic-stricken and in just as much danger. They paid him no heed. Relentlessly Malchus found himself driven closer until his heels hung over the precipice. A shower of debris plummeting to the ground below testified to his attempts to find a foothold.

The two men nearest him shoved and hit at him, afraid that when he fell he would drag them down as well. Once he almost lost his grip on their clothing, and one foot dangled into empty space while they beat him on the head and shoulders, cursing him with each blow.

Malchus looked into their eyes, knowing he would die yet unwilling just to let go. His gaze dropped to the rough cloth he gripped in hands like talons, veins and tendons bulging, as the fabric above his right hand started to rip. He braced himself for the fall, the sudden impact at the base of the cliff. The fabric tore farther. An image of Alona came to his mind, the thought that he would not see her again. Then the last strip of material gave way.

A strong hand held to his wrist in a numbing grip. "Deron!" his lips shaped the name. "Help me!" Somehow his friend created an opening in the mob and drew Malchus into it. He didn't stop or slow down until both had reached a grassy spot well clear of the crowd, now milling around in confusion.

"Thank you," Malchus managed at last, greatly shaken. "I can't believe I was so careless."

Deron gripped Malchus' shoulder, his face stern. "You should not have done that. You were more careless than you know." He straightened. "Go to Capernaum. You will find what you seek there." It took Malchus several minutes to catch his breath, and when he looked for Deron to thank him again, the man was nowhere to be found.

━ ━ ━

Fear shook Alona as she stood inside the synagogue. Never in all her sheltered life had she experienced such raw violence. She turned to Erith, whose face mirrored her own shock. Without a word the two women lifted their long skirts and began to run.

They met Oded at the city gate. "You must stay here. Don't go near them," the older servant commanded.

"My husband is in there. I am going," Alona gasped, and sped toward the left side of the cliff, just far enough from the melee to be relatively safe. Oded did not argue further, but remained at her side.

As she sighted along its length, Alona spotted the bright-blue robes her husband had worn to the morning service. It took but a moment to grasp his grave peril, and she would have gone to him, but muscular arms held her back. Screaming, biting, her arms and legs flailing, she sobbed and begged Oded to let her go, but he would not.

The crush of the mob knocked several townspeople from the brow of the cliff, and they fell, arms clawing empty air and mouths opened in horrendous screams drowned out by the angry shouts of the rest of the crowd. Gently Oded drew Alona away from the scene, holding her until she quieted in his arms. "Hush, Little Mistress," he soothed. "There's nothing you can do. Nothing you can do."

With tears blinding her, Alona didn't at first notice the tall, muscular man dragging her husband from the deadly embrace of the crowd. When she did, she joyously shrieked his name, but Oded clamped his hand over her mouth. "Shhhh," he warned. "You know he's safe. Do you really want him to discover that you're here?"

Alona shook her head as a fresh outbreak of weeping shook her. Erith took her from Oded, supporting her slight frame. "You go and get her mare and our things, and we will meet you at the far gate of the city."

Oded nodded. "It is good that we leave this place. Go around the town, not through it. With all that has happened, no one will wonder why you both seem bowed with sorrow."

The two women walked slowly away, but Oded did not at first return to Nazareth. He stood, arms folded across his chest, and watched the people milling back and forth. Apparently no longer filled with anger, rather they seemed puzzled.

When the way was clear, Oded looked over the precipice. Three bodies lay crumpled at the base of the hill, but none were the Teacher. When he glanced around, he saw no sign of Jesus anywhere. He shrugged.

Alona calmed as she walked with Erith and soon remembered to offer a prayer of thanks that her husband had escaped death or injury. The two women reached the other side of Nazareth and continued on farther to a deserted area outside the city, knowing Oded would still find them. A boulder marked the crossroads leading to Capernaum, and the two women sat, leaning their backs against its sun-warmed surface. No human sound broke the stillness until suddenly a voice close by startled them, and they turned around.

Jesus stood just a short distance away. Alona and Erith caught their breath, filled with joy at His amazing escape. Though He stood alone, Jesus seemed to be talking animatedly to someone. "Where did He come from? I didn't hear any footsteps. Can you hear what He is saying?" Erith whispered, eyes wide with wonder.

"Hush," Alona whispered back gently. "I'm trying to listen."

But at that moment Jesus started in the direction of Capernaum. The two women stared speechless behind Him.

CHAPTER 7

Seated on his thronelike chair, Caiaphas' fingers scrabbled on the smooth papyrus roll in his haste to break the wax seal. A smile dented his full white beard as he read the florid salutation. With Malchus it was never the same twice.

"Noble and Honorable Master, Greatest of All Noble and Honorable Masters," the letter began. "Doubtless you have received other reports of the incident in Nazareth, where I very nearly succeeded in accomplishing our purpose. We were thwarted when some of the teacher's followers spirited him away just before the mob could throw him over the cliff. It was all done so cleverly that many thought he actually disappeared.

"None of your other agents were immediately able to track Jesus to Capernaum, which seems to be his new base of operations. As you know, it is one of the major crossroads for caravans and travelers. At this time, support runs high for the new teaching, largely because of the influence of the nobleman whose son was healed some months ago. Any direct attack would be quickly put down by his enthusiastic followers. If we hope to succeed against him, it must be on our own ground.

"Jesus seems to be gathering about him a small group of the most unlikely men. Many are fishermen, and the most recent addition is a tax collector, if you can imagine it! Hardly an elite group. The tax collector was nearly the undoing of the whole group when he and several other members of Jesus' inner circle gathered and ate grain on the Sabbath. I prepared the priests very carefully for their role, but even with the double accusation of harvesting and threshing on the Sabbath, they still botched everything. Jesus turned their arguments around on them, making them look like fools. He even said that the Son of man was also the Lord of the Sabbath. Clearly He applied 'Son of man' to himself—it was not the first time I have heard him use that term—but even with this near blasphemy the priests were too afraid to convict the man of anything.

"The very next week Jesus again showed his defiance toward the same priests by healing a man on the Sabbath. While that was bad enough, he had the gall to do it inside the local synagogue! I saw it for myself. A man with a withered hand asked Jesus for healing. Instead of asking the man to come back after the sacred hours ended, Jesus told him to stretch out his hand. When the man did, his hand became like new. I marveled to see such evil power unleashed inside the very doors of a place of worship.

"The wickedness of that man is almost unlimited. I have seen him heal lepers and send them before the priests to be checked, as if he actually valued the law of Moses. Another time I saw him heal a paralyzed man after first claiming to forgive the man's sins. That time it was straight blasphemy, no question about it, but by then the priests didn't dare say a single word of protest.

"I have saved the worst for last. Jesus is not only a blasphemer and possessed by demons; he is also a traitor to our people. A Roman centurion sent for help for his servant. Jesus met with him, healed the servant from a distance, and praised the Gentile above all the people of our nation. I am sure you can see clearly the danger if even the Roman oppressors start to follow the new teaching. Our tenuous truce with Rome has been hard-won, and this lone man must not be allowed to jeopardize it.

"Until my next report, I remain your faithful servant,

"Malchus"

Caiaphas gripped his forehead with one hand, holding the note out blindly with the other. "This man is forever a thorn piercing my flesh," he groaned. "Every report seems worse than the ones before it."

"Try not to worry so much—yet," Zarad said as he took the scroll and scanned it. "The confrontation will come in its time, and when it does our victory will be swift." He lifted his gaze, dark eyes blazing. "In the meantime, this is what we will do." His voice dropped to a low murmur, its cadences rising and falling in counterharmony with those of the high priest. Zarad paced restlessly as he spoke, laying his ideas before Caiaphas as Malchus had so often done before.

— ◆ —

Alona shielded her eyes with one hand as she rode, scanning the road ahead and each clump of bushes or clearing to the sides. Several times she looked back over her shoulder, growing increasingly impatient and nervous.

"Mistress," Erith interrupted her, "we must have passed them somehow."

With a frown Alona glanced behind her again. "I'm sure you're right, but it makes me so nervous to have him where I can't see him."

The servant woman grinned, not asking which "him" her mistress meant. "Me too. He walks so quietly that I can never hear him coming. It's as if he just appears by magic."

"That's always been one of his favorite tricks," Alona replied. "I hope he doesn't try it now."

"Look," Erith interrupted, "we're coming to a village. Do you know which one it is?"

"Nain," Oded replied, breaking his long silence.

Alona looked down at him in surprise. "Have you been here before?"

"Not for a long time," he answered. "My sister lives here."

"Your sister?" Alona exclaimed. "I never knew you had a sister. Tell me about her."

He shrugged. "There's not much to tell. She's a number of years younger than I am, widowed, with a son."

"You men are all alike," Alona said, exasperated. "You haven't told me anything. What is her name? What does she look like? What is *she* like?"

Oded's face crinkled in a smile. "Would you like to find out for yourself?"

Once in Nain he led them unerringly down the dark, narrow streets where the poorer houses leaned heavily on each other, as if for support. Dirty children in tattered clothing played happily or ran errands for their parents. The harvest that year had been plentiful, and they all seemed relatively well fed.

Stopping in front of one of the doorways, Oded called a greeting. No answer. He leaned partway inside, his hand on the doorframe. "Ornah?" he repeated. Suddenly, without a glance back at his companions, he leaped into the house. Alona and Erith exchanged a look of alarm and hurried to follow.

The sour stench of a longstanding sickness assaulted their nostrils. Alona gathered her skirts more closely around her, not wanting to risk contamination from the filth on the floor. Erith did the same. From somewhere farther inside came an eerie sound, almost as if some large animal were snoring.

As their eyes adjusted to the dimness Alona reluctantly took a few more steps into the dwelling, looking for Oded. A light flashed in the far corner as the servant lit a clay lamp. The scene it illuminated was so pitiful that Alona had to press both hands tightly against her mouth and swallow hard to keep from being sick. A young man, perhaps in his teens, lay on a soiled sleeping mat, his wasted body soaked in feverish sweat. His ribs stood out starkly, flaring with each tortured attempt to breathe. "Ranon, wake up," Oded begged, his voice rasping as he fought back tears. "It's Uncle Oded. Please wake up." Those sunken eyes never flickered, never opened.

"How long has he been like this?" Oded asked someone.

As he shifted position, Alona saw another figure at the bedside, a wraithlike woman with dark shadows under her eyes, deep hollows under her high cheekbones, and a look of total despair on her face. She was obviously in the last stages of exhaustion, and though her lips moved, the reply was too faint for Alona to hear.

Her brother glanced up at them. "Will you please take care of my sister?" he said over his shoulder, looking at Erith and Alona. His eyes were pleading. Almost as an afterthought he added, "Her name is Ornah."

Swallowing hard, Alona approached them. "Hello, Ornah. I am

Alona. I'm so sorry." She took the woman gently by the elbow and supported her away from the sickbed. Erith took the other arm, and together they helped her to a sleeping mat that was on the other side of the room.

Ornah's eyes filled with tears. "Thank you," she whispered, then stared around the room in horror. "The mess—I'm sorry—it's not usually like this."

"Don't worry about that," Erith reassured her. "Just rest for a while."

The woman slumped against the mat, her eyes closing against her will. "Thank you." A quick burst of fear propelled her onto one elbow, eyes wide. "Call me when—" She was unable to finish.

Alona patted her shoulder. "We'll call you if there is any change." The relief on the woman's face was obvious, and she was asleep, or unconscious, before her head touched the mat.

Standing, Alona began briskly rolling up her long sleeves and fastening her light-brown homespun skirts tightly out of the way. "Oded, what do you need first?"

"Water. Fire. Food. I don't know." The man looked as if he had aged 10 years in the few minutes since he first stepped inside his sister's hovel.

"I'll get the water," Alona volunteered quickly. Snatching up the waterpot just inside the door, she lifted it to one shoulder and walked hastily toward where she had seen the town's well. Once outside, she took deep, cleansing breaths of untainted air, shivering despite the warm sun on her skin.

Few took notice of her as she filled the jug and made her way back to the little home where tragedy was playing itself out. Erith already had a small fire burning in the courtyard and was preparing a stew of lentils over it. Four mounds of dough on a flat stone were half ready to bake. Ornah had not moved from her original position on the mat, and Oded still tried to spoon a bit of water between the clenched teeth of his only nephew.

When Erith saw that her mistress had returned with the water, she wordlessly picked up a basin and a cloth. Pouring some water into the basin, she grimly set about scrubbing every surface of the long-neglected dwelling and helping Oded change the bed linens on the sleeping mat, rolling the inert form of the sufferer to and fro. Though she had very little experience at scrubbing, Alona did her best to help.

Whenever Oded called her she would take the strips of cloth from him, soak them in fresh water, and watch as he laid them on the dying boy, trying desperately to quench his fever.

After two or perhaps three hours something changed. The boy's breathing became even louder and faster, and sounded as if he were bubbling inside. When Oded propped him up, it seemed to help a little, but the young boy's mouth gaped open from the effort to find air. Oded looked bleakly up at his companions and nodded to the far corner. "It's time to wake her."

His sister jumped, startled, when Erith touched her shoulder. For a second she looked around wildly, about to ask if her son still lived, then she heard the rattling noise coming from his bed. Even one who had never before watched death creep in to steal a life breath by breath would have known that it was lurking there, only minutes from dragging its prey into complete darkness. She scrambled over to her son's bed and held on to his limp hand, weeping bitterly.

Oded put his arms around her as if to share his strength. Tears streamed down his own cheeks as well. "If only Jesus were here," he said, almost to himself. "I know He could make him well. Please, Elohim, send Him in time, and I will believe He is Your Promised One. Please, just send us Jesus."

Ronan grew paler. The skin stretched tight across his face like a mask. His lips pulled back slightly to reveal his teeth, and his head jerked with each breath. With every inhalation his chest would suck inward, downward, then pop up with a rush as he dragged in just a little more air. Oded reached over with a corner of the cloth to moisten the dry mouth and give some small measure of comfort in the last few moments of his nephew's life.

Suddenly there was silence. All of them unconsciously held their own breath, willing the boy to live. With a wrenching gasp he took another breath, then another, and they began to breathe, too.

"Oh, Jesus, come quickly. Please hurry. I know You can heal him." Again and again Oded said the words, watching with an agony of suspense as Ronan's chest continued to rise and fall.

Once more the breathing slowed, stopped, and started again. The third time it stopped, a bit of pink foam trickled from between the bluish lips, and Oded numbly wiped it away. He placed his hand on the motionless chest and felt a tiny flutter, like a small bird turning around in its nest, and then nothing.

Ornah gave a half scream and bowed her head, leaning her cheek against the lifeless hand still clutched in hers. Then she pulled herself erect, took a deep breath, and again and again wailed the shrill mourning cry of her people.

Sympathetic neighbors soon joined in. Alona and Erith, feeling very much out of place, stood against the wall, crying quietly. *Why didn't Jesus come?* Alona wondered. *Doesn't He want Oded to believe in Him? I have seen Him heal so many people. Why not this boy?*

An aged woman, obviously used to having her own way, swept into the house and held up her hands for silence. "I see I got back just in time. In this warm weather we don't have any time to waste. It's almost noon already, and if we don't hurry this will have to wait till tomorrow, and we don't want that." She pointed to several sturdy men in the crowd that surrounded her. "Go get your tools and begin preparing a burial site. You women, help me prepare the body. Quickly now!" When Ornah opened her mouth to protest, the old woman cut her off. "You go bathe. I can see you have neglected yourself terribly." As she scolded and harangued, everyone hurried to do her bidding.

"Who is that woman?" Alona whispered to Ornah as she helped her prepare the water to clean herself.

Though still dazed from the shock of her loss, Ornah replied, "Her name is Yachne. She is the town mother. I don't know just how else to describe it. Although she is a shameless busybody, under her gruffness she is really quite kind." She closed her eyes for a moment. "Truly I am glad she is here to help. This is a task I have dreaded for days, and it is a relief to lay it on her capable shoulders." Alona smiled in understanding and held up a blanket to allow as much privacy as possible for Ornah in the crowded house.

In less time than anyone could have imagined they had finished taking care of the body, and many of the townspeople milled around, waiting to join the procession. Inside the house the four men who would carry the body to the gravesite had just set down the stretcher next to the bed. Ornah stood nearby, clean and in a borrowed robe. As soon as Yachne had realized how long it had been since Ornah had been able to wash the few clothes she had, she sent someone scurrying to find something she could wear in the meantime.

As two of the men took their places at the head and foot of the body, Ornah clung to Oded's arm. One man reached under the boy's arms while the other took his ankles. Together they lifted him from the pallet onto the stretcher. They tried to be gentle, but the body, just starting to stiffen, sprawled awkwardly, its limbs jutting at odd angles. Ornah cried out and hid her face against Oded's chest. He tried in his own way to soothe her, but without success. She only gripped him more tightly and wailed louder. The other women echoed her grief in a primitive chant.

The men lifted the stretcher, its burden now wrapped in a sheet. Oded set his sister gently aside, seized the nearest man by his outstretched forearm, and said hoarsely, "Let me carry him. It's all I can do now."

Alona and Erith slipped beside Ornah, supporting her fragile frame as she stumbled along next to her dead son. Alona couldn't help feeling jealous of the woman, for as heartbreaking as this moment was, she had shared 14 wondrous years with her own son. That was a joy Alona had never experienced, and by now never expected to.

Ornah and Ronan, though poor, had been well liked by the inhabitants of Nain, and it seemed as if nearly everyone in the village came to join the funeral procession. Oded and the others bearing the stretcher led the way out of the town, Ornah beside them. If not for the assistance of the two women, she would not have been able to make the trip in her weakened condition. The rest followed, a cloud of dust marking their progress to the cemetery.

Her eyes blurred by tears, Alona did not at first notice the second cloud of dust in the distance. She continued on toward the burial ground with head lowered, concentrating on keeping her footing as she supported Ranon's near-fainting mother.

Without warning, Oded and the other men came to a stop, though Alona stumbled on a few steps farther. When she looked up, she found herself facing Jesus and a column of followers stretching far back along the road. Reacting instantly, she turned to Ornah and hid her face as if in grief, hoping the Master had not recognized her.

Oded stood frozen, his features reflecting warring sadness and joy, despair and hope, disbelief and faith. As Jesus approached, the crowd surged in about Him. When those closest caught sight of the dead boy, most of them glanced at him matter-of-factly, with just a touch of curiosity at what Jesus would do. They did not have long to wait. Reaching the stretcher, He lifted the sheet and folded it neatly back to the boy's waist. One glimpse of the bony corpse, its mouth open despite all efforts to close it, and none had any doubt that he was indeed dead.

Jesus stood next to Oded and looked at Ranon for what seemed like a very long time. Tears glistened in His eyes as He picked up the wasted arm where it had spilled off the stretcher and laid it once again upon the bier. Turning to Ornah, He said, "Don't cry," then returned His gaze to the stretcher and said in a low voice, "Young man, get up."

Instantly color rushed into the faded skin, the flesh swelled and grew to the plumpness of health, and the jaw that moments before had gaped open closed with a snap as great shining eyes flew open. Blinking in puzzlement at the crowd around him, Ranon sat up. "Mother," he said, catching sight of a familiar face, "what am I doing here?"

Ornah remained rooted to the spot, her mind unable to believe what her senses were telling her. "He's alive!" Alona shrieked, shaking the woman joyously. "Do you see? Jesus raised him. He's alive!" Belatedly recalling her surroundings, she quickly shrank back, pulling her scarf tight about her face, trying to blend in again with the crowd.

Ranon swung his legs off the edge of the stretcher and stood, which was fortunate since mere seconds later it slipped from eight nerveless hands and fell to the ground to be trampled, unheeded, under scores of feet. He walked over to his mother, who stood trembling, both hands pressed to her mouth, tears streaming down her face. "Mother, what's wrong? Did someone die?" Looking down at the loose bindings that clung to his lower half, comprehension dawned. "Did I die?"

Hesitantly she reached out both hands to touch his face, then pulled him into her arms. "Thank You, thank You, thank You," she kept repeating.

"Thank who, Mother?" Ranon asked.

Suddenly remembering all that had happened, Ornah looked around until she saw Him. He was with His closest followers, smiling and laughing with delight, sharing in her joy. She led Ranon by the hand and bowed at Jesus' feet. "O Lord," she said humbly, "I can never thank You enough for what You have done. The hardest thing in the world for a mother is to have to stand by and watch her child suffer and die and be powerless to save him. But You have given him back to me, and we will always serve You." Meeting His eyes, she was surprised to see a look of such infinite sorrow that she felt she would drown in it.

Wanting to comfort whatever troubled her Master, she reached up and took His hand. He drew her to her feet, smiled once more, and said, "My dear woman, nothing you could give Me would please Me more."

Ranon looked at the ground and said shyly, "Me too. That is, er, thank You." The tips of his ears turned bright red. The flush spread to his collarbone when his mother once again embraced him in front of the multitude.

Oded, who had remained silent till now, caught Jesus' eye and said, "I'm sorry."

Jesus had no need to ask what he meant. "I forgive you," He said, then addressed the assembly. "Genuine faith does not come just from signs and wonders. The Word of the Lord leads into all truth, and truth alone can provide a foundation." He began walking again in the direction of Nain, telling those around Him a story to illustrate His lesson.

Ranon walked along too, his mother and uncle on each side. Partway Oded suddenly exclaimed, "Ornah, what happened? You look as young as a girl. The lines in your face are gone. Why, you don't even look tired!"

"It's true, Mother," Ranon chimed in. "You do look different."

Ornah thought for a moment and said, "It must have happened when I touched Jesus." She hugged her son again, still amazed to see him standing alive beside her.

Alona pulled Erith to the edge of the crowd, and they gradually began to lag behind. "If my husband is in the crowd, he won't rest until he has investigated this happening fully. We'll have to stay away for now."

The servant made a face. "You're right, of course, but oh, how I want to be there to see whatever happens next."

"So do I," Alona grinned impishly, "but you can bet that whatever it is, it won't be nearly as exciting as what we've just seen. Imagine, we have just witnessed with our own eyes proof that the Sadducees are wrong."

"Oh, when they say there is no resurrection? Will they ever be angry!"

Alona sobered. "I'm sure they will be. But wait until they find out that the resurrection is not just an event anymore. That—that it is a Person."

Erith stared at her, not sure what she meant. Then the two of them continued on their way, filled with awe at all they had seen.

Chapter 8

Malchus sat close to the outer edge of the crowd, the late-afternoon sun beating down on his back and shimmering across the deep-blue waters of Gennesaret. With his head bowed, fingers plunged into his wavy hair, twisting the strands between them, he somehow no longer resembled the man who had set out on his journey. At every turn he had found his efforts to discredit Jesus thwarted, and many of the common people had begun to talk about crowning the Teacher king of Judah. Malchus dreaded sending that piece of information to his volatile master. But those daily, even hourly, aggravations were not the main cause of his dejection.

His wife's face was ever before him, distracting his thoughts and cluttering his mind with the kinds of emotions he had always determined to avoid. Till now Alona had always seemed more of a convenience, a luxury that came as part of his elevated station. He had been gone from her longer than this many times during the course of their marriage, and it had never made much difference whether he spent time with her or not. Now his fertile imagination saw her everywhere. At times he even thought he heard her voice. Malchus stifled a groan, fearing for his sanity.

"The kingdom of heaven is like the grain of a mustard seed," Jesus said, shielding His eyes from the lowering sun. "Though it looks smaller than all the rest of the seeds, when it is placed in the heart of the earth it will grow and flourish. Its branches provide shelter, and the birds of the air find safety in its shadow."

While Jesus told several more stories, Malchus pictured what Alona would be doing right then: laying aside her scrolls and bustling to oversee the preparations for the evening meal. Perhaps she would be entertaining important guests, or had even invited a poor family to join her. She was extremely tenderhearted.

With a start Malchus realized that Jesus had quit speaking and had now stepped into a boat. The men of His inner circle had lined up to follow Him. Most of the people were now standing up and stretching, gathering their belongings, and drifting away in little groups.

Malchus scanned the shoreline. A handful of fishing boats were accepting passengers to cross the lake. One minute and a few coins later found Malchus settling himself gingerly onto a plank that served as one of the seats, his feet splashing slightly in the wooden bottom of the boat.

"Are you following Jesus too?" asked a friendly voice.

Malchus turned to the passenger next to him, a young man with a thin, patchy beard. "I guess I am," he said with a wry smile.

That was all the encouragement the young man needed. "I could listen to His stories all day long without growing tired of them, couldn't you?" Without waiting for a response, he went on: "And to think that I would see such miracles with my very own eyes! I have heard that He has even raised the dead to life."

"He has," Malchus said unwillingly.

"Were you there? Did you see it? Oh, tell me what happened!" The young man's eyes shone with excitement.

Malchus wished he hadn't said anything. Two more people crowded into the little vessel, and it scraped its hull against a black basalt boulder as the sailors pushed it from the shallow water to where it floated freely. Malchus glanced around to find every eye fixed expectantly on him and sighed resignedly.

"We were just coming up to the city of Nain when we met a funeral procession headed out toward the burial ground," he began. One sailor held the steering oar while another unfurled the thick cloth sail. The boat creaked softly as it rocked to and fro. A splash sounded close by as a silvery fish breached the surface and then vanished into the depths.

"Keep us as close as you can to the boat with Jesus in it," a woman in the vessel urged.

"Go on, go on," the young man told Malchus.

"At the head of the procession was a widow being half carried by some friends. Her son had apparently been sick for a long time." One of the women clucked in sympathy. "I was close enough to see the body," Malchus continued, "and the boy was certainly dead." Even now he felt chills as he remembered the event.

"What did Jesus do?" the young man prompted.

Malchus lowered his eyes and rushed the words out. "He just spoke, and the boy came back to life."

"Just like that?" The young man snapped his fingers, amid gasps of astonishment.

Reluctantly Malchus nodded his head. "Just like that."

The other passengers began to relate other miracles and clever sayings of Jesus. With their attention diverted, Malchus slumped, fists under his chin and elbows on his knees, staring back at the last red slice of sun as it disappeared over the mountains surrounding the lake. That moment, when Jesus had raised the boy to life and he had heard Alona's voice as clearly as if she were standing there with him, was the first time Malchus thought he might truly be going insane.

"I'll have to go home," he muttered. "Get this out of my system for good."

"What was that?" his companion asked, turning his attention back to Malchus.

"Nothing," Malchus said briefly, a dull flush coloring his cheekbones.

The boy shrugged and turned to his seatmate on the left, talking all the while. Malchus sat quietly watching the dusk turn to darkness as the shore faded into invisibility. The sailors lit oil lanterns, hanging them on hooks that dangled from the ends of the boats. A night breeze lifted his hair, cooling the back of his neck with soothing prickles. The other boats were close enough for him to catch stray bits of conversation and laughter. As the moon came up to leave its sparkling trail on the water the fishing vessels became dim forms, visible only as darker patches on the shadowy waters.

Expertly the sailors trimmed the sail, laying aside their oars at last. Malchus watched the steersman lean on the steering oar, anticipating each movement of the men adjusting the sail. They worked smoothly together, and it seemed as if no time at all before the steersman announced, "We're halfway there, with smooth sailing ahead."

No sooner had the words left his mouth when a huge blast of air came out of nowhere and sent the boat skimming out of control across the suddenly choppy water, the passengers flailing and staggering like drunks as they desperately tried to hold on. Though there were no clouds in the sky, lightning flashed all around them out of the clear sky. The moon still shone in the sky above, remote and unreachable. Frantically the sailors lowered the shredded sail, grabbed for the oars, and tried to regain control of the craft. Two men now sat at the steering oar, combining their strength to hold it steady.

A raging wind tore at them from another direction, and with a long flash of lightning they saw they were perilously close to the other boats. The waves, lashed under the scourge of the wind, rose and fell and sloshed over the side of the small vessels. Malchus felt the stirrings of fear as the cold water engulfed his feet. Moments later they were all drenched by the spray from the towering waves.

"Bail! Bail!" one of the sailors shouted. Malchus and the other passengers obeyed, scooping the water with buckets or bare hands. By now the lightning cracked across the sky almost continuously, and when by its light he saw abject terror on the faces of experienced sailors, he knew he would die. Still he bailed as fast as he could, determined not to perish without a struggle.

The wooden boat groaned each time a giant wave lifted it, rising higher and higher, only to plunge sickeningly into the trough and rise again. The wind howled around them like the voices of a thousand demons. Some sobbed, their wails of grief torn away by the roaring of the storm. Most prayed.

In horror Malchus looked up from his bailing to see that the whole fleet of boats was only a few feet apart on the angry sea. Each wave struck the forward boats and whirled around them, tossing the little vessels about like a flotilla of autumn leaves.

In the boat nearest him Malchus saw the desperate passengers as clearly as if it were day. One woman in particular caught his attention. She clung to the side of the boat with every fiber of her being, face raised, searching. Her great dark eyes turned toward the heavens, the scarf fallen, soggy, from her long black hair. For a moment their eyes met.

Malchus' heart felt as if it would stop. She looked so much like his Alona that he wanted to weep. "Elohim!" he cried out in desperation. "Elohim—" But he could get no further.

Looking around, the woman saw something and reached out one hand imploringly. Her lips formed one word over and over. Malchus followed her gaze and saw a sleeping form in the back of one of the boats. It was Jesus. His disciples bent over Him, frantically trying to awaken Him. But He slept on, heedless of their peril. Malchus felt that Jesus was a fit symbol of Elohim just then—slumbering, uncaring, deaf to the cries of His people.

Rage shook Malchus such as he had never known. He raised his fists in the air and screamed out his defiance. The wind whirled faster and faster around the boats, violently crashing them against each other. Water towered over them on every side. Suddenly the eyes of every passenger on every boat were drawn irresistibly to the place where Jesus had lain asleep. Now He stood, arms upraised, seeming to shimmer from within. When He spoke, His voice rolled and echoed throughout that corner of creation, easily heard above the shriek of the storm. *"Peace! Be still!"*

The silence came so suddenly that it was almost painful. Instantly the boats floated on a glassy sea, lit by the gentle light of the moon. Uncounted stars twinkled in the velvety sky, and Jesus calmly sat down. They all heard Him lovingly chide His disciples, "Why were you afraid, when I was with you?"

"What kind of man is that?" one of the sailors asked wonderingly. "Even the winds and the water obey Him."

In the sudden stillness Malchus remembered Alona the day he had last seen her, holding her beloved scrolls. Again he heard her voice as she read. "He stilled the storm to a whisper; the waves of the sea were hushed. They were glad when it grew calm, and he guided them to their desired haven."

An unexpected and unwelcome thought flashed into Malchus' mind: *In the Scriptures only Elohim Himself could rebuke the sea. Jesus has just done something only God should have the right or power to do. Could He be . . . ?* Angrily Malchus shook his head. No, it wasn't possible!

- - -

Alona turned her back to the spot she had last seen Malchus, and with shaking hands wrung the water out of her clothing. With her head covering drawn tightly about her face she felt more secure. The sight of Jesus still sitting in the nearby boat reminded her that she owed Him her gratitude, and she bowed her head. Erith put her arm around her mistress. "I thank Him too," she whispered.

"He saw me," Alona said, clasping and unclasping her hands nervously, "Malchus looked right at me and saw me."

Erith's eyes grew wide. "Did he recognize you?"

"I don't know," Alona said, then giggled. "I look half-drowned, and he's never seen me like this before."

"Still, we should keep our distance when we reach land. You don't want to take any more chances."

"I'm ready to go home now."

Her servant turned to her in amazement. "What?"

"I'm ready to go home now," Alona repeated.

"Why? Did what just happened discourage you? I thought you had a stronger spirit than that," Erith exclaimed, surprised.

"Just the opposite. The main reason I came, besides wanting a little adventure," she smiled to herself, "was to watch over Malchus and try to protect him. I know that sounds foolish, but it's what I thought." When Erith opened her mouth to protest, Alona held up her hand. "After tonight I can see that he is far safer being with Jesus than being with me. I am ready to trust him to Jesus and to Elohim."

The servant woman blinked. "I guess I never thought of it that way before. Still, I hate the thought of being so far away from Jesus."

"I do too, but how will our families and friends at home find out what we have learned if we don't tell them?"

"You're right," Erith sighed, "but you forgot just one thing. How do we tell them without letting them know where we've been?"

"Oh, I'll think of something," Alona said carelessly. "I always do."

"That's what I was afraid of," the other woman muttered.

"What? I didn't quite hear that."

"Nothing. Look!" she said, pointing, trying to divert Alona's attention. "We're getting ready to land."

"Thank Elohim for that," they heard a deep voice declare from behind them.

Alona looked over her shoulder. "Oded, I almost forgot you were with us. You were so quiet!"

He smiled faintly. "I've been speechless for hours. Tell me—is my hair the same color? It feels as if it's been scared white. I'm an old man now."

Mindful of her previous lapses, Alona stifled her laughter at his teasing. Carefully she set her bundle of belongings in her lap so that she would forget nothing. She wanted to be able to disembark as quickly as possible.

As soon as the boat scraped against the shoreline, Alona gathered her skirts and pushed her way to the front. Then she stepped over the side in water up to her knees and waded ashore on wobbly legs. Breathing hard from the exertion, she walked rapidly up the beach away from the boats, trusting Oded and Erith to follow.

———

In the early gray dawn the shore was just a dark line growing steadily larger. As he drifted nearer it, Malchus could make out some details: the rugged hills dotted with patches of trees, jutting boulders, and a general air of desolation. It was a wild, lonely country, and Malchus could see why Jesus would come here to get away from the crowds.

His boat ground ashore right next to the one carrying Jesus and the members of His inner circle, now 12 in number. Right away Malchus saw that the notorious sons of thunder had joined the group, and he turned his head away for fear of being recognized. John, one of the two brothers, had seen Malchus around the Temple. Jesus was deep in conversation with them, and Malchus strained his ears to catch each word.

"We must take full advantage of this little respite," Jesus was saying. "In just a few days I will send you out two by two to spread the good news of the heavenly Father's great love through the whole land of Palestine."

"Just like the animals into the ark," laughed a large rough fisherman Malchus recognized as Peter.

"What I actually have in mind is for you to be more like Noah," Jesus said. "If you have faith, your message will be even greater than his." He sobered. "Because you have Me with you for such a short time, you must learn to depend on the Father and not only on Me."

Caiaphas must hear of this at once was Malchus' first thought. *Six groups instead of only one—how long will it take for that to double, and triple? Never has the danger been so great.* He decided to accompany them to the nearest town, replace his soggy provisions, and return quickly to Jerusalem.

As he stepped into the shallow water, Malchus thought of the woman he had seen on the other boat. Instinctively he turned to look for her. She was already walking along the shore with her two friends. Malchus recognized them as regular members of the crowd following Jesus. Try though he might, Malchus had never been able to find out what that woman looked like.

Jesus started in the direction the trio was taking, and everyone else followed along. Unsure why it was suddenly so important, Malchus walked faster, determined to see the woman's face. Under his robe the padding he wore to make himself appear fatter, bounced heavily, now soaked with water. As he passed by Jesus, just ahead he spotted the mysterious woman with her friends.

A few quick steps and he caught up behind her, ready to reach out to stop her and turn her to face him. But without warning shrieks rent the air, seeming to come from everywhere and nowhere. Malchus jumped back, his hand flashing to his dagger as he tried to determine the direction of the danger so he could confront it.

The sounds now resembled weird, evil laughter and grew louder. The crash of rocks sliding down the hill to the right betrayed the position of the mysterious attackers. With a mad rush the creatures leaped from concealment and charged at those on the beach.

They were men—or at least they had been once. Naked, with long, matted hair, they had gashes all over their bodies, some half healed, others still fresh and oozing. Fetters encircled their wrists and ankles, the broken chains dragging behind them. The larger of the two men brandished his wrist chains and swung them menacingly in a circle.

Malchus pushed his way in front of the two women, dagger held ready. "Get the women out of here," he barked, dropping to a half crouch. "Take them to the boats." Apparently the man complied, because Malchus was dimly aware of a stifled protest from one of the women.

As the wild men approached, he cautiously edged backward. He hoped to keep them at bay long enough for the women to reach the boats. Risking a quick look behind him, he saw that the beach was deserted except for Jesus, who even now was walking purposefully toward him. Malchus continued his retreat as Jesus passed him, reflecting grimly that if the maniacs succeeded in tearing the teacher limb from limb, it would solve a lot of his and his master's problems.

"Jesus, Son of God most high," cried one of the man-demons, his wail like the sound of many different voices woven together.

"Leave us alone," screeched the other. "What do You want from us?" His voice had that same eerie quality.

Some of the boats had pushed off into deeper water already and were making good time in the direction of the western shore. Malchus stood in front of the three that remained just offshore, motioning for them to wait. Though badly frightened, their crews were still very curious about what would happen and confident that if the worst occurred they were far enough out of danger to reach deep water in time.

As Jesus walked right up to the two wild men they fell on their knees before him. Jesus seemed to be talking to them, and the men gestured as if pleading for something. Moments later a frenzied squealing broke out as a herd of swine stampeded over the edge of a nearby cliff, tumbling end over end into the water below. Their legs churned the water into foam as they lashed out, striking and biting at each other in panic.

Aghast, the youthful swineherds watched with horror from above as the thrashing slowly quieted. Soon the corpses of the animals bobbed across the surface of the lake. When the herders saw Jesus down on the shore talking peacefully with the two men who had terrorized the countryside for years, it was too much for them. They shot away as fast as their short legs could carry them.

By the time a delegation from the village arrived on the scene, the two men were decently clothed in borrowed robes, sitting at Jesus' feet. Intently they listened to every word He said. Some of the braver individuals from the boats had crept back to shore and stood nearby. Out in the water the offshore current had begun to scatter the bodies of the pigs, drifting them toward the distant shore.

The headman of the village was a nervous sort, his left eye twitching as he spoke. "You have killed all our pigs," he accused Jesus in a rising whine. "Look, you have destroyed our livelihood." The others with him began to murmur angrily and edge toward Jesus.

The two former demon-possessed men now interrupted, both stammering out their incredible tale, their words tripping over each other. The excited fishermen told the story of their escape from the storm only a short time before.

It made no difference to the Gentile villagers. "It has taken us years to build up our herds of swine, and in one moment you have ruined everything!" The headman gestured toward the bobbing carcasses. "You must leave us at once before anything worse happens!" The people from the village chorused their agreement, making superstitious signs to ward off the forces of evil.

Sadness flashed across Jesus' face, but He replied, "We will go." He started to leave.

"Wait!" the two healed demoniacs protested. "We want to go with You." Their faces, once hate-filled, now reflected peace and calm.

"I have a work for you to do here," He told them. "Go and tell what has been done for you." Then He walked slowly back to the boats, the townspeople of Gergesa following behind Him to make sure He departed. Everyone else was already waiting in the boats, afraid of being left behind.

As Jesus stepped into the lapping waves the two men bowed once more and begged, "Please, let us go too."

"What if the demons come back?" one of them asked.

Jesus smiled. "Encourage each other and rely on the heavenly Father. Go and tell everyone what the Lord has done." Quietly, so the townspeople couldn't hear, He added, "I will come back here again soon."

As the boats began the return trip to the western shore several of the dead pigs bumped against their hulls. Malchus had to stifle the desire to recoil from the ritually unclean bodies. He might question God and His ways, but he was still steeped in the customs of his people. At last the wind distanced them from the dead creatures. Malchus' stomach growled loudly. He was hungry. They were all hungry. The people of Gergesa had chased them away without any breakfast.

Malchus pondered the irony of a servant of Satan casting out demons, for that was what he had surely just seen. But the alternative was unthinkable. And yet, what was it that the demonic voices had called Him? "Jesus, Son of God most high," they had said. Surely Caiaphas, high priest and the most important man in Israel, couldn't be wrong and the demons on that distant shore be right. But the words continued to echo in his thoughts. *Jesus, Son of God most high.*

CHAPTER 9

Weary beyond belief, her feet aching and every muscle in her body sore, Alona plodded along next to Kivi, her cherished black mare. The faithful animal had been pathetically glad to see her mistress, whickering in delight when she returned to the stable on the western shore of Galilee. It was Erith's turn to ride, and Oded strode alongside, steady and tireless as always.

"We're almost home," Erith said. "I can't believe it's over already."

"What's over?" Oded asked.

"The adventure, the excitement, everything!" The servant woman slumped dejectedly. "You'll go back to the farm, Alona will return to her studies, and I'll be washing clothes and cooking."

Alona laughed tiredly. "Really, the adventure is just beginning. I mean, think of it. Our fathers, our grandfathers, our great-grandfathers, all the way back to Father Adam, have been waiting, watching, hoping, praying for the Messiah, and we have seen Him! With our very own eyes we have seen the new King of Israel. Our time of deliverance must be near."

"It can't come too soon for me," Erith sighed. "Our people have lived long enough with Roman feet on our necks, forcing us to serve them. You're right—it will be exciting to witness the Messiah break the yoke of oppression."

Oded said nothing, but walked close by Erith and glanced often in her direction. It was his keen eyes that first spotted Jerusalem in the distance and a donkey close to the gates running in a wide circle, a man tugging on its head. "Wait, isn't that—how did he get ahead of us?" he asked, one finger vaguely indicating what he had noticed.

As Alona looked where he pointed, a quick intake of breath betraying her surprise and near panic. "Hurry, get down," she said, almost pulling Erith bodily off the horse's back. Oded boosted her up, and she urged Kivi to a full-out gallop, abandoning all attempts at secrecy. A cloud of dust billowed in her wake as she thundered toward the city.

— — —

Malchus pulled with all his strength on Jori's bridle, trying to bring the stubborn little beast to a standstill. The donkey had not been exactly pleased to see him when Malchus redeemed him from the stable in northern Galilee. The animal had laid back its ears and brayed its defiance, baring long, yellow teeth. Its disposition had not improved any on the journey south. Now, just outside the gates of Jerusalem, it was making a terrible fuss, kicking up its heels and tugging against Malchus' hand on its bridle.

The pounding of hooves along the main road caught Malchus' attention. He looked up just in time to see a black horse flash by, the small rider slung low on its back. Although he craned his neck to see the individual's face, it was hidden in the horse's flying mane. "Some people let their children do anything these days!" he muttered to himself.

He coughed as the cloud of dust enveloped him. The sweat pouring down his face and arms made little rivulets of mud. Jori took advantage of the moment and broke free, trotting steadily back toward Samaria. Malchus girded up his garments and gave chase, cursing all four-legged creatures with hooves.

More than an hour had passed when the servants of the household spread the news of his return in excited whispers. With scurries and furtive, faintly guilty glances they went about their business, but Malchus failed to notice their discomfort. He walked rapidly through the downstairs rooms, scanning each one for his wife, and then took the stairs to the roof.

There he found her, digging happily among the plants on her rooftop garden. She hummed softly as she worked, the afternoon sun caressing her golden skin. Her hair hung loose down her back, still damp as if she had just taken a bath. Malchus crossed over to her, and at the sound of his footsteps she looked up. Joy lit her face, and in a moment she was in his arms, uncaring of the dirt that still caked him.

"Malchus, you're a mess," she exclaimed finally. "What have you been doing?"

Still holding her close, he scowled. "I was almost into the city when some maniac rode by on a horse, showering me with dirt." Alona's eyes grew wide, and she struggled to hold in her laughter. "As if that wasn't bad enough," he continued, "my good-for-nothing donkey got away and made a run for the north country. It took me nearly forever to catch him."

Alona could hold back no longer and shook with helpless laughter. Her amusement was contagious, and Malchus smiled in spite of himself. "Oh, husband," she gasped at last, "what is this generation coming to? What a thoughtless, heedless youth." Overcome, she leaned against him, laughing till the tears came.

"What of you?" Malchus asked, suddenly intent. "What have you been doing in the time I've been gone?"

Sensing he was actually interested, Alona blushed lightly. "Oh, different things. Charitable works, mostly. Caring for the sick and such."

Malchus held her hands, turning them over to look at the palms. "You have calluses, and your nails are cracked and broken, not to mention very dirty." She opened her mouth to protest, but he went on. "My poor love, you have been working much too hard. You need to take some time for yourself once in a while."

"Yes, of course," she murmured, eyes lowered demurely. "I'm very glad you're home."

"I am too," he said in a surprised tone of voice. Then more slowly, "I am too."

The days that followed blurred together in a haze of happiness as husband and wife grew to know each other for the first time. Malchus received a brief reprieve from his duties, and the two spent nearly all their time together. Still, Alona did manage to find opportunities to share with the faithful household servants the story of her experiences with Jesus and to thank them for making her journey possible.

Malchus felt as carefree as a boy. "Let's go visit my parents," he suggested one day. "We haven't seen them for a long time."

Alona hid her surprise very well. It had been many months since he had gone to see them, and unwillingly at that. "That would be nice. Didn't you once mention that you have something to give your mother?"

"Yes,"he sighed. "I should have taken it to her a long time ago." The wrapped bundle still lay in his room, untouched since he had put it there upon his return from Arabia.

"Never mind," Alona said soothingly, laying a hand on his arm. "I understand."

Early the next morning they were just about to leave when a messenger from Caiaphas approached at a run. Panting, he handed over a scrap of parchment bearing a curt summons to the Temple without delay. Malchus looked apologetically at Alona and shrugged. "What can I do? I'm sorry to ruin our plans."

She rolled her eyes. "How does that man always know when it's the most inconvenient? He does this every time."

"My master does have a certain talent that way," her husband laughed. "Will you still go?"

Alona thought for a moment. "I suppose I could just take one of the servants. It won't be the same, though." She glanced at him shyly.

Malchus kissed her cheek. "We'll go somewhere together later. Will you give this to my mother?" He took the package out of his bag and handed it to her.

"Of course," she said, holding out her hands to receive it. "I'll see you tomorrow evening."

"Thank you," Malchus said, then kissed her again right in front of the messenger. "Take two or three servants with you—it will be safer." He turned to go.

"I love you," Alona called after him as always. He flashed a grin over his shoulder, waving an acknowledgment as he ran off, his traveling bag still bumping against his side. Alona turned back into the house to choose her escort.

The sun was near its zenith when she reached Bethlehem. Her father-in-law sat in the shade by the city gates with the other elders. He jumped to his feet when he saw Alona, brushing the dust from his robe and straightening the white headcloth that covered his graying hair. "Father Gershom," she called, running to meet him and be swept into a hearty embrace.

"Alona, it is so good to see you," he exclaimed, peering over her shoulder. "I see you came by yourself again. What is that no-good son of mine up to this time?"

"You know Malchus." She grinned up at her father-in-law. "Always doing something important, always in a hurry." She gestured to her escort to follow her as they walked to the humble house in which her husband had been born. "He really did almost come this time, but his master cruelly snatched him away at the last moment."

Gershom lifted the mat hanging across the doorway, and Alona ducked under it. "Thank you, Father." She scanned the one-room house. "Hello, Mother. It's nice to see you again." With one hand Safiya shaped the loaves of bread for the noon meal as she had done for years, her crippled hand lying shriveled and useless in her lap. She looked up at the sound of her daughter-in-law's voice, and her eyes seemed to brighten just a little, but she said nothing. Alona knelt and embraced her, but made no move to help. She had long since learned that her mother-in-law did not welcome any assistance.

The servants sat respectfully outside to allow Alona some measure of privacy as she conversed with her husband's parents. After the formalities were out of the way, she said, "In a way I'm glad Malchus couldn't come today. There is so much that I want to tell you, but I don't want him to know."

Her father-in-law looked concerned. "Is something wrong? Is he treating you all right?"

"Oh, yes," she hastened to assure him, blushing. "In fact, our marriage is better than it has ever been. But something has happened, something important." She paused, Gershom and Safiya both listening intently. "Messiah is here."

Her dramatic announcement won a sniff of disbelief from Safiya and another concerned look from Gershom. "I have heard a great deal about the Teacher of Galilee," he said, "but I have a feeling this somehow concerns my son as well."

Alona looked steadily at him. "It does, and I fear he is in great danger." And starting with the incident at the cliffs of Nazareth, she told them all that had happened, leaving nothing out. When she finished, long minutes ticked by while Gershom stared off into space. Patiently she waited for him to speak.

At last he turned to Safiya. "Should we tell her?" he asked hoarsely, his voice barely audible. Safiya winced and covered her face with her hands, shaking her head in an emphatic no.

Hoping to relieve some of the tension she had unwittingly caused, Alona said, "Mother, I almost forgot. Malchus sent you a present. He brought it back from one of his travels." She drew out the bundle and handed it to her mother-in-law.

Safiya took it with her good hand and set it next to her, awkwardly unwrapping it. Alona and Gershom scooted closer, curious to see what it was. The younger woman cried out in delight when she saw the charming little doll, like none she had ever seen. Its face and hands were delicately carved and painted, and its clothing, though a bit faded, was royal purple, as if it were a tiny princess.

Safiya stared at the doll in shock. Soundless tears trickled down her cheeks as she hugged the doll fiercely, swaying back and forth in her grief. Gershom was much slower to recognize it, and when he did all the color drained from his face. His hand shook, and he ran his fingers through his beard, a dazed look on his face. "He knows," Gershom whispered. "Malchus already knows."

- - -

"Malchus, my boy, I wanted to see you," the high priest said, fingering a sheet of papyrus with a royal seal. "We are going to a party."

"Whose?" Malchus asked with genuine interest.

"It seems Herod Antipas is inviting all the most important people in his kingdom for a party in honor of his birthday, as well as whichever servants they select to attend them." Caiaphas paused. "I choose you."

"You do me great honor, Master," Malchus said smoothly, "but I trust you bear in mind the connection between Herod's former wife and your humble servant."

"Humble? Not even close, you rascal!" Caiaphas laughed until he wheezed, which made him cough. Recovering himself at last, he said, "Not that I blame you for being reluctant to go, but it will be fine. He will be too busy with his friends to notice a servant, even one as striking as you." Malchus bowed to acknowledge the compliment. "Besides, I have waited for an opportunity such as this for a long time. We must not offend him by refusing."

"As you wish," Malchus replied, secretly pleased. A bit of intrigue and danger was just what he had been hoping for.

"Finish your preparations by the ninth hour," Caiaphas continued. "Then you will accompany me on the journey to Machaerus."

"It will be my pleasure to serve you in this matter," Malchus said, and hastened home to pack.

"Where is Caiaphas sending you this time?" Alona's voice interrupted him as he finished fastening the strap on his saddlebag. He turned to see her standing in the connecting doorway of their chambers, her long hair spilling down her back.

"I have been invited to accompany Caiaphas to Herod's birthday celebration. It is a great honor."

A look of concern passed over his wife's face. "Caiaphas? At a party of Herod's? He is the high priest, and surely he does not set a good example by attending what will doubtless be a drunken brawl."

"It's not as bad as that," Malchus said patiently. "Besides, I think he would leave if it became too bad. Surely you can see that my master does not dare ignore this summons."

"I think your master should first answer his summons from Elohim," she commented. "I have heard nothing but bad reports of Herod's court, and I fear something bad will happen at this feast, too. I hear Malthace, his mother, is visiting just now. He will want to show off for her, to demonstrate his power. Where will the celebration be—Machaerus? Wherever it will be, it will certainly be a dangerous place." She dared not say more lest he guess that she knew his secret.

"Good," Malchus replied smugly, never suspecting that Alona had any inkling of how great the peril truly was.

Alona took a deep breath, let it out, and pictured Jesus as she had last seen Him, facing the madmen of Gergesa calm and unafraid. She would have to trust her husband to His care. Deliberately she crossed the room and touched Malchus' sleeve. "Just be careful—I love you," she told him, and kissed him on the cheek.

Malchus shook his head. Ordinarily she would have shouted or thrown something at him. Why hadn't she this time? Still, whatever the reason for the change, he was grateful. Seeking a safer subject, he said, "How are my parents?"

She hesitated a moment before answering. "They are as well as always. Your mother liked the doll, I think."

"Did she?" Malchus' gaze searched her face, and she forced her eyes to meet his. "It was hers when she was a child." He braced himself for an onslaught of questions.

"Yes, that's what your father said." If she wanted to ask more, she hid it well, sliding into his arms with customary farewell. "I love you," she whispered. "Go with Elohim."

— — —

Machaerus, southeast of the mouth of the Jordan, overlooked the eastern shore of the Dead Sea. Alexander Jannaeus had first fortified it, and later Herod the Great, Antipas' father, had rebuilt it into a citadel second in strength only to Jerusalem itself. After the death of Herod the Great, the Romans had assigned it to Antipas, who used it to escape the summer heat of his palace at Tiberius. Rumor had it that he had imprisoned Najiyah, his Nabataean wife, there when she learned of his infidelity. If that was true, it was little short of a miracle that she had escaped and returned to her father, the king.

The evening of the celebration Malchus awaited for Caiaphas to emerge from the guest quarters assigned him. Malchus offered his arm as they walked toward the banqueting hall, and Caiaphas leaned heavily upon it, also supporting himself with his staff. They joined the queue of those waiting to enter. Some of the other guests appeared to have imbibed even before arriving at the party, and tongues loosened by alcohol flowed freely.

"Bet this party will be better than anything Herod ever had while Queen Najiyah was here," one already half-drunk guest slurred.

"Hush, you fool," warned his friend. "Even to speak her name could be death. You know how Herodias hates her former rival. And now that King Aretas has captured part of our territory and destroyed Herod's armies, our king's hostility is just as black as that of our queen."

The inebriated man was not yet drunk enough to be oblivious to the danger. "Y'r right," Malchus heard him say. "Must not have been thinking too clearly. Long live Herod and Herodias!" He giggled, then shouted, "Long live the king!" A score of voices echoed, "Long live the king!"

The guards bowed to the high priest. Caiaphas nodded in return, holding up one hand in blessing. A vast square separated the gate and the entrance to the banqueting hall. Stone tiles paved the courtyard, and trees, flowers, and other plants dotted the landscaping. The center of the square boasted a fishpond with a three-tiered fountain rising from the middle.

Malchus settled his master on a reclining couch near the head of the second table before taking his own place far down the line. Both men lightly quenched their thirst with the sour wine that was the only beverage provided. The splendor of his surroundings could not fail to impress Malchus. The color scheme of the room was purple and white, with draperies the color of ripe grapes and pillars that gleamed like the snow of distant Mount Hermon. The guests were all men. The wives and other women were having their own banquet in an adjoining hall. Malchus smiled grimly to himself. The risk he took by his very presence in that place set his heart pounding, making every sense come alive.

At last Herod's arrival signaled the start of the feast. Endless servants carrying laden platters first served the king's table at the front of the room, then the two lower tables along the sides. Musicians performed in one corner of the banquet chamber. The center of the floor remained clear for the evening's entertainment, whatever that might be. The guests ate and became increasingly more drunk.

Suddenly the music stopped. As the silence gradually sank into their consciousness, the men hushed and glanced around expectantly. Herod raised higher on one elbow, craning his neck to see what might be in store. The giant double doors at the back of the room flew open with a bang. There, silhouetted by torchlight, stood a slim veiled figure. The flickering light caught in her long flowing hair.

The drums broke out again in a steady beat, faster this time. The other instruments joined with a crash. As if startled, the woman leaped into the air, and as she came down she flipped end over end to the center of the room. Her filmy robe whipped in the air as she whirled wildly around.

Up and down the rows of guests she flashed. The drums beat on, a solid wall of sound. As she passed Malchus, he realized that the dancer was just entering young womanhood. She made a quick motion to one of the musicians, and he tossed her a long-handled sistrum. Standing directly in front of the king, she swayed and bent, arms, legs, and belly weaving a sinuous pattern in the intricate dance. The sistrum threaded its own insistent rhythm through the pounding of the drums and the wail of the wind and string instruments. The music thundered back from the marble walls of the banquet hall and throbbed in the blood of the partygoers. The flickering torchlight and the heat of the room gave Malchus a headache. He pushed himself up into a sitting position, unable to keep his eyes off the dancer.

When her dance reached its feverish end, Herod Antipas leaned forward, eyes glittering. At the final, climactic chord the woman flung herself into the air, flipped around without touching the floor, and snatched the covering from her face as she landed, holding it aloft. Wisps of fabric clung to her arms, her body dewed with perspiration.

"Who was that?" Malchus heard someone whisper.

"The daughter of Herodias," another answered.

How strange, Malchus thought. *A ruler's daughter would not normally entertain her father's guests.* He wondered what had motivated the sensual display.

The young woman bowed in front of her stepfather. "Rise, Salome," Herod said hoarsely. "Where did you learn . . . ?" He glanced toward the doors leading to the women's banquet hall. "No, never mind, it must have been your mother, of course." He looked around the room, relishing the applause that greeted the dance in his honor. Wanting to display his generosity before his noble guests, he said grandly, "Name your reward, Salome, even to half my kingdom."

A gasp went up. Malchus knew that Antipas was only a client ruler. Only the Romans could give permission for such a rash promise. But Herod would have to honor it in some way. His honor stood at stake. Salome looked stunned and confused. "I beg a moment to choose this reward," she said finally. At her stepfather's nod she dashed from the room to the women's banquet hall.

Salome was not gone long. When she returned, her mother stood beside her. Herodias gestured her toward Antipas, but Salome hung back. Teeth clenched, her mother whispered fiercely to her, giving her a shove forward. Stiffly the young woman walked to the front of the room, her face now tight and scared. "I have chosen a reward, my lord," she said quietly.

"Don't be afraid, child; speak up." Herod tried to bring a light note back into an occasion that had inexplicably grown somber. "I said you could have anything you want. A necklace, perhaps, or a diadem covered with the jewels you women so love?" A strained laughter raced around the room, then faded away.

Salome fixed her eyes on her stepfather's face. "The reward I want," she said slowly, "is the head of John the Baptist on a platter."

CHAPTER 10

Herod choked on the mutton he had been chewing. Coughing violently, he seized his wine goblet and drained the contents, then dabbed at his face with a cloth. When he regained control, he found every eye in the room trained expectantly on him. "Surely my ears deceived me," he said with a pleading look. "Tell me I did not just hear you ask for the head of the Baptist."

Salome glanced fearfully to where her mother stood. The look Herodias gave her sent a chill through her. Slowly she turned to face Herod. "On a platter. John's head on a platter," she choked out.

Antipas stood and surveyed his guests. "And what of John?" he asked them, his arms spread wide. "Will none of you speak for him?" He waited for some protest, some reason to escape his foolish vow, but wine had numbed the senses of the guests, and they remained silent. Out of the corner of his eye Malchus noted a look of wicked joy on the face of his master.

Defeated, Herod threw up his hands. "Let it be done. You!" He pointed to one of his guards. "See to it!" The man ran from the room, his armor clanking with each step. Next the king turned to a shaking Salome, saying harshly, "As for you, I know who put you up to this. Well, you'll get just what you ask for. Sit over there until your reward arrives." The girl perched on a low seat over by the wall and burst into tears. Herodias, barely able to control her glee, swept from the room.

Herod was furious with himself for his weakness. Because of his own cowardice, he had condemned the prophet to death. He motioned to the court musicians to resume their playing and gestured for a servant to refill his plate and cup. Desperately he engaged the nobles at his table in conversation, unable to block from his mind the image of the executioner's ax finding its target.

Just as Malchus was beginning to relax again, a servant approached and spoke to him. "Herod wishes you to join him at his table."

"Me?" Malchus was incredulous. "You must have mistaken me for someone else."

"No, the king was most particular about it," the man insisted. "You are the one he asked for."

With a shrug Malchus got to his feet, following the servant to the front of the room. He automatically noted each exit, the clearest path to each one, and the number of guards who stood at each—too many! Caiaphas frowned warningly as he went past, but said nothing.

Bowing low to the ground in front of the king, Malchus asked, "How may I serve you, Your Majesty?"

"Come talk to me." Herod patted a cushion next to him. "I have been trying all evening to remember where I have seen you."

Always at his best when danger was near, Malchus replied, "My master is Caiaphas, the high priest. As Your Majesty is so faithful in the observances at the Temple, doubtless you have seen me there many times going about my master's business."

"I suppose," Herod replied, unconvinced.

"In serving my master, I also travel a great deal," Malchus supplied hopefully.

The tetrarch leaped gratefully at the topic. "Where is the most interesting place you have ever been?"

Malchus thought for a moment. "Probably the strangest would be Sidon, in the land of the Phoenicians. Their fleets travel throughout the earth and bring back such wonders as a person could hardly imagine."

"What sort of wonders? Would that I could see them for myself," Herod exclaimed. "Here, try some of this wine."

Not wanting to offend Antipas, Malchus drank deeply, then went on to describe some of the curiosities to be found in the great seaport. Every moment Herod's gaze remained intently fixed on his face. He knew he stood on the edge of a knife's blade, a whisper away from death, and that knowledge made him all the more witty and entertaining.

Many goblets of wine later, and midway through a description of a snake so large it could swallow someone whole, the wide doors of the banquet hall were again thrown open. A captain of the palace guard marched in, carrying a huge silver platter covered by a domed lid. He stopped before Herod, bowing as low as he could with his awkward burden. Malchus took advantage of the confusion to slip back to his seat.

The room was a flurry of excited whispering, and Herod went white around his taut lips. "Come, Salome," he snapped. The frightened girl approached him on trembling legs. "Remove the cover." At that, Salome began weeping again. Her cries were the only sound as a servant stepped forward and lifted the lid from the platter.

Aghast, Herod found himself staring into the sightless eyes of the Baptist, his head propped up by clusters of grapes, sitting in a bed of lettuce leaves. A supernatural fear possessed him, and in the horror of what he had done, Antipas became insanely angry. "Give it to her, I say," he exploded to the guard. "Give the wretched girl the reward she wanted."

Salome sank to her knees, wailing, holding both hands up as if to ward off a blow. "No, no, no! Please, no," she begged.

Herod rounded the table and snatched her up by the hair, forcing her to stare into the dead face of John. The girl shrieked, then cried until she hiccuped. Antipas was relentless. "Take it. Take it to her." Venom distorted his voice almost beyond recognition.

The girl had no need to question whom he meant. With desperate courage she grasped the handles of the platter and carried it toward her mother. It was heavier than she expected, and she was forced to brace it against her stomach while the tears ran unchecked down her cheeks.

Nearly to her goal she stumbled, but caught her balance. The head wobbled and tipped over. The sight undid her as nothing else could have, and Salome dropped to her knees, carefully set the silver dish on the floor beside her, and surrendered to the insistent heaving of her stomach.

Herodias sauntered casually forward. "Dear me." She shook her head at her retching daughter. "I think you dropped something of mine." She knelt, straightened the head on the platter, picked it up with ease, then held it up one-handed like a serving girl. "Thank you, my love. I hope your birthday was happy," she called over her shoulder.

"Drink, everyone. Have some more to drink," Herod called out, trying to erase the horror reflected in the faces of most of his party guests. All present, even Caiaphas, hurried to follow their host's command. Malchus tried to hide the shudders that raced through him.

Herod called for another round of wine, and another, and still another. Malchus tried to drink slowly, but even he was feeling a fog descend over his thinking by the time the tetrarch finally passed out in a stupor. Servants were dragging him off to bed when Malchus finally could make his unsteady way up to the couch where Caiaphas lay.

The high priest of Israel sprawled, giggling with delight, over his reclining seat and that of his neighbor's as well. His words were little more than gibberish, but plainly he was happy to have seen the end of the prophet who had infuriated him for so long. Malchus beckoned two servants to assist the intoxicated Caiaphas, who had just spilled a fresh shower of wine down the front of his linen robe.

Far too early the next day Malchus awakened to the news that he had a message from the high priest. He squinted blearily against the light, clutching his head as if it might fall off. Caiaphas, who normally wrote a fine hand, had apparently scrawled the note with his eyes mostly shut. "Malchus, my dear boy, sorry to have put you needlessly at risk. Safest if you leave Machaerus immediately. Take your pick of the donkeys. You have done enough walking for a while. Perhaps you could head north and personally oversee our project there for a short while. Do not delay." And then he had attempted to sign his name.

Malchus sighed, and the effort made him clutch his head again. "Don't feel like it," he muttered to himself, "but he's right. Herod noticed me. Must go. Not safe." He wiped his face with a shaking hand as a thought stabbed him. *What if the wine loosened my tongue? Could the servants have overheard anything?* Alona could not have been happy when he left without warning, and now he might not even be able to return to Jerusalem. That was one of the risks of being married to a servant of Caiaphas. His master often sent him anywhere at any time, though in this case it was for Malchus' own safety. He would have to send her a message, hoping that somehow she would understand. At least he thought his master might not mind if he stopped by his home in Jerusalem for a few hours before he left on his mission to the north.

— ~ —

Upon his return from Galilee Malchus went straight to the palace of the high priest. He wanted to deal with his business first before going home. No doubt Alona was extremely upset that his short trip to Machaerus had turned into an absence of more than two months. She might even blame him for what had happened to the Baptist. Perhaps he might be able to offset her wrath if he offered to go with her to visit his parents and actually accompanied her this time. Ah well, he would not have to deal with that for a few hours. In the meantime, the high priest was waiting for him.

Caiaphas waited in an outdoor courtyard in his own palace. The secluded garden was very small, very private, and just what he needed for clandestine meetings with Gentiles. Of course, he would never allow his home to be defiled by their uncleanness, but a man in his position did occasionally have to make concessions to speak with them. When Malchus arrived, a high-ranking Roman military officer had already joined Caiaphas. The soldier stood at attention, red helmet plume carefully arranged, his metal armor brightly polished. Caiaphas performed a brief introduction.

"Marcus, this is my servant Malchus ben-Gershom. Malchus, Centurion Marcus Aburius Geminus." When Malchus bowed to both men, he received a respectful nod from each in return.

"Marcus has heard a great deal about you, Malchus, mostly from me," Caiaphas said. "We want to talk to you about a certain project, a cooperative effort between the top levels of our governments. I hardly need tell you," he added, "it is of an extremely sensitive nature."

The corners of Malchus' mouth quirked up. "Isn't it always?" he murmured, sitting near his master. "How may I serve you?" he said more audibly. His eyes gleamed with interest.

Caiaphas, amused at his eagerness, nodded to the soldier. "Go ahead and tell him what you have in mind. And please, sit and make yourself comfortable."

The Roman clanked gingerly onto a bench. "Thank you." He set aside his shield with the emperor's symbol emblazoned on the front and laced his fingers together. "You see, Malchus, we have a mutual problem, your master and I." He looked intently into Malchus' face. "His name is Barabbas."

Surprised, Malchus sat up straight. "I know Barabbas has been nothing but trouble to you, but what does he have to do with my master? Most of my people see him as a hero. If word got out that Caiaphas caused him any harm, there is no telling what the consequences might be."

"Do you see him as a hero?"

"Who, me?" The Roman's question startled Malchus. "Not really," he said finally. "His reputation for cruelty is unparalleled, his ignorance is appalling, and his foolishness in pulling the tail feathers of the Roman eagle defies belief."

Marcus smiled. "I see. How refreshing to find an Israelite who supports Rome."

"Hardly," Malchus replied calmly. "It's just a matter of common sense. An immense enemy can be defeated only by an immense blow. Anything less will only anger one's opponent. And you can't deny that many innocent Jews have suffered a great deal because of Barabbas' conduct."

"No," Marcus said thoughtfully, "I can't." He turned to the high priest. "I can see why you recommended Malchus. Such fearless honesty is beyond price."

"You see, my boy," Caiaphas said, "if all Barabbas did was harass and murder Romans, this conversation would not be taking place. Sorry, Marcus, it's true. But the robberies that support him and his band of thieves have injured some very prominent men of Israel lately, and they have been secretly pressing me to act."

"So you understand, Malchus," the Roman officer continued, "it works for the benefit of both parties to have Barabbas cease to draw breath."

"Surely you have plenty of your own assassins," Malchus said coldly.

"I do indeed," Marcus replied matter-of-factly, "but that isn't what I had in mind. Barabbas is to be brought back alive. Caesar desires him to face trial. And that," he spread his hands, "is why we chose you. One of Barabbas' men has betrayed him to us. You are to infiltrate the camp and capture Barabbas, bringing him on foot as far as the En-gedi road. My men will meet you there and take charge of the prisoner. I am placing you in full command of this mission and will provide any and all resources you need. Here is a map of the location of the rebel camp. Destroy it before you leave this place."

He handed Malchus a crudely drawn map showing the Dead Sea, the En-gedi road, and an X scrawled off to the west at the edge of the desert. Malchus scanned it briefly and returned it. "Very good. I will begin preparations immediately, and when the time comes I will tell you what I need." He rose, bowed, and turned to leave.

"Just one moment, Malchus," Caiaphas called after him. "First, you are to include your cousin Othniel in this assignment. So far he has done fairly well on several limited assignments regarding Jesus of Galilee."

Malchus succeeded in keeping his face nearly expressionless, but Marcus was not so restrained. He rolled his eyes and sighed. "You Jews are always having one troublemaker after another claiming to be your much-anticipated Messiah. I don't know how you can stand it." He threw up his hands in disgust. "I can't even stand it!"

"We don't," Caiaphas commented. "At least not for long. Anyway, Malchus, the second thing is that I understand your donkey has returned to my stables. Take him with you when you go. Perhaps you misunderstood—he was not a loan. He was a gift."

Malchus' face fell. "Oh yes, Jori. Thank you, Master. Your generosity truly overwhelms me."

"You're welcome." Caiaphas smiled beatifically. "It's just a little reward for your faithful service. I want you to know how thankful I am."

"Truly, Master, your kind words are more than enough," Malchus answered, trying to keep all emotion out of his voice. "The only reward I want is the knowledge of a job well done."

"You may have all that and the donkey too," Caiaphas said expansively. "Now, don't keep trying to argue, or I will have to think you ungrateful."

Malchus' smile became rather fixed. "Never that," he said, teeth clenched. "Thank you again." And he wandered away in a daze, his mind filled with horrible visions of riding Jori at a fast trot up to the rebel camp, then running in circles through tent and campfire alike as he tried to dismount. He shuddered. It was a good thing Caiaphas didn't suspect his true feelings in the matter, or he would be quite offended.

━ ◆ ━

The aged priest laughed until he wheezed, pounding his knee, his whiskers bristling with glee. "Did you see his face?" he chortled,

coughing several times. "And he calls it Jori! I don't have to ask why."
A bit more restrained, the soldier chuckled with him. "Ah, the reports
I got of his adventures," the priest went on, wiping the tears from his
eyes. "It's hard to say which is more amazing—how he gets on that
donkey or how he gets off it."

CHAPTER 11

Some days Alona wondered if those pleasant weeks together had been
only a dream. Certainly it was hard to find any trace of the attentive
lover in the preoccupied, volatile man who now shared her roof.
Malchus' unpredictable behavior hurt her, but she tried to look past it
and keep sight of the real issue. Clearly he was involved in something
important, and that meant it was also dangerous.

For his part, Malchus was scarcely aware that anything had changed.
For months on end his every waking thought, and most of his sleeping
ones, he spent developing strategy. The hazardous part of his mission
would take place far from help or military intervention. Every detail
had to be in place. Disguised as a beggar, he even made several trips to
En-gedi, taking careful note of the terrain. Then, once he had charted
a plan of action, he had to select a handpicked group of seven men to
assist him in the raid. Grudgingly he wrote Othniel's name down along
with the other six.

When at last he thought everything was ready, Malchus locked
himself in his room for two full days. He fasted to clear his mind, drinking only water, and reviewed his plan in full, probing for any weak-
nesses. In the middle of the second night, satisfied that all was as
complete as humanly possible, he slipped several changes of clothing in
a bag and crept from the house.

The streets of Jerusalem were deserted as Malchus sped to the stables
of the high priest. The stableboy had been expecting him. Jori was
already bridled, and a sack of bread and dried fish hung by the door.
Malchus thanked the boy, slipped him a coin from the bulging bag at his

waist, and led Jori out into the night. Though cautious by nature, Malchus did not notice the curious shadows behind him. Barely darker than the night, they slid along walls, blended into doorways, and merged, only to separate again a moment later. Always they kept relentlessly just within sight of the man and his donkey.

He could sense them watching him. Gingerly he uncapped his water skin and tipped it back into his mouth. The jostling of the donkey's rough trot spilled water down his face to bead in his thick beard. He took care that his cloak fell back, revealing his fat money bag. Almost feeling the greed swelling out from behind the rocks and hills, Malchus rode bareheaded and undisguised, for no deception could remain in close contact with a desperate band of robbers without being found out.

A muffled whinny sounded ahead from a grove of trees, only to be quickly stifled. Behind several large boulders he could see the glint of metal. Malchus smiled grimly. His opponent was not exactly subtle. He rode on. Just as he passed by the trees they erupted on horses. Then the rocks disgorged several scores of warriors on foot. Each was armed with a stunning array of weapons, some clearly pilfered from dead Romans and others possibly manufactured from plowshares. Malchus feigned a start of surprise. "Wh-what do you want?" he inquired timidly, looking around in bewilderment. "Who are you?" Then he felt genuine amazement. Jori came to a halt all on his own.

One man nudged his horse forward, an arrow notched on his bow. His face was tanned from long hours in the desert sun. The midafternoon heat drenched his clothes with sweat, and bare flesh peeked through large rips in his tattered garment. Even so he sat like royalty, a robber king secure in his authority. "Get down from your animal," he said, lip curled in a sneer. "Give us your money. Your nice robes, too."

Malchus gulped. "M-my robes, too?" he stammered. "Don't you know I'm on an important mission for my master?" He pulled his robe more snugly around him, hiding his money from the many gleaming eyes. "Perhaps you have heard of him," he said pridefully. "His name is Caiaphas. You know, the high priest."

The regal-looking bandit laughed coarsely. "I don't care if you work for the emperor himself." His voice dropped low with menace. "Give us everything you have." He tightened his bowstring threateningly.

Cringing, Malchus started to slide off his donkey, only to pause halfway, one foot on the ground and the other sticking up awkwardly over the donkey's back. "What if I don't?"

The men's eyes widened at his audacity. "Then we kill you slowly instead of quickly," their leader replied calmly.

Malchus all but tripped and fell in his haste to finish dismounting. He straightened, his fingers fumbling at the ties of his pouch. "Are you—no, no, you couldn't possibly be. But maybe, well, *are* you Barabbas?"

The robber's face split in an unfriendly grin. "You've heard of me. I'm flattered."

"Of course I've heard of you," Malchus burst out excitedly. "I've always admired you, even wanted to be part of your band."

The man eyed him suspiciously. "How do I know you're not just saying that to save your own skin?"

"I am," Malchus admitted frankly, flashing a dazzling grin. "But why don't you give me a chance to show you what a city boy can do?" Sensing a glimmer of interest, he pressed on. "Look, there is only one of me, and"—he glanced around, lips moving silently as he counted—"at least 75 of you. Surely it would be as easy to let me join you as to kill me."

"Done," Barabbas shouted, and slid his arrow smoothly from bowstring to quiver. "But if the servant of the high priest wishes to become a member of my army, he must first pass the same test as everyone else—right, men?" The others gave a bloodthirsty cheer, holding their weapons aloft.

"There's always a catch, isn't there?" Malchus groaned. "All right, what do I have to do?"

Barabbas motioned to someone behind him. "Eben, you know what to do."

Malchus gaped as surely the largest individual he had ever seen in his life stepped forward. The man's head was bald, shaved so that no enemy might find an advantage by gripping his hair. He bulged with muscles from his ears to his ankles. A hairy garment belted at the thick waist covered his bulk. Eben was more than a head taller than anyone there, and the men roared with laughter at the comical dismay written all over Malchus' face. He clutched his chest. "Do I have to outrun him?" he asked, looking up.

"Here are the rules," Barabbas said. "You will fight Eben unarmed, man against man."

"And if I win you let me join," Malchus guessed.

"Close," the bandit leader smiled evilly. "If you *live* you may join."

Hearty laughter greeted his witticism, but Malchus said nothing, only stripping off his outer garments. His priceless dagger exposed to the light of day, he clutched its hilt defiantly for a moment, then shrugged. "Hold this for a moment," he said, strolling over to Barabbas and handing him the weapon. "I'll be back for it shortly."

Clearly pleased by the arrogance of his captive, Barabbas took the short sword and held it up admiringly. "Very nice. It will look good on me, don't you think?"

"I won't give it up lightly," Malchus warned him brazenly. He made sure Jori was tied, then turned to face his huge opponent. The men formed a ring around the two, clapping, cheering, and stamping their feet in anticipation of the fight.

Though Malchus stood in a relaxed stance, he watched Eben alertly. The bandit leered at him, opening and closing his massive fists, muscles rippling across his chest and back. With a roar of pure rage the giant launched himself across the circle toward Malchus. But when he pounced, Malchus was not there. He had stepped aside so quickly that it looked as if he hadn't moved at all. Eben shook the sweat out of his eyes, looking around in momentary puzzlement for his opponent. Then the fight began in earnest.

At least Eben was in earnest. Malchus seemed almost playful as he skipped and dodged the huge man, even showing off a bit for the crowd with flips and handsprings. Though perhaps the strongest man in Palestine, Eben was no match for the speed and agility of the younger man. Still, if he could grasp Malchus even for a moment, he would be able to pull him into his arms and crush his body like a bundle of dry straw.

Fully aware of the danger, Malchus nonetheless continued to bait Eben deliberately, hoping to anger him into making a mistake. The crowd cheered his daring, every man holding his breath involuntarily each time Malchus got close enough to make a strike. In a risky move, Malchus ducked low under the giant's arms and forced a blow into his solar plexus. If Eben had been any less padded with muscle and fat, the fight might have ended there, but with a bellow of pain he snatched Malchus up by the neck before he could leap away and held him, dangling, above the ground.

Malchus felt his strength slip away like sand through his outspread fingers, a dark haze swirling before his eyes and buzzing in his ears. Wondering if his life could be measured in moments just then, he tried to summon the will to continue fighting. With the last of his strength he curled his body and kicked, one foot against Eben's face and the other on his throat.

The sudden rush of blood from his neck into his head made Eben dizzy, and he groaned. His fingers relaxed, and Malchus fell to the ground, landing heavily on his side. He gasped for air, trying to bring his vision back into focus and force himself to rise from his hands and knees. Eben recovered faster and lunged. Still on his hands and knees, Malchus leaned down close to the ground and kicked upward, a powerful blow to Eben's chest. Faster than the strike of an asp his foot flashed lower, striking Eben in the knee. It didn't quite break, but the bandit would limp for some time to come.

Eben crouched on hands and knees, head bowed, as Malchus struggled to his feet. The smaller man staggered closer, grasped the wide skull in both hands, and smashed his knee into the broad, flaring nose. Now Eben would also breathe with discomfort for some time to come.

As his opponent slumped, quivering, on the hot, packed earth, spitting blood and saliva onto the parched surface, Malchus bowed with a flourish amid wild cheering. The men rushed forward, each wanting to be the first to congratulate the newest member of their band. Though breathing hard, Malchus accepted their exuberant praise, then pushed his way through to where Eben still lay on the ground.

Reaching under his arm, Malchus helped him to his feet, saying with a tone of admiration, "In all my life I've never fought anyone like you before."

Clutching one hand to his knee and the other to his nose, Eben replied in a muffled voice, "Be deeder."

"What did he say?" several of the men asked at once.

"Um, I think he said, 'Me neither,'" Malchus translated. Eben nodded his agreement, and Malchus clapped him on the back. Turning his attention to where Barabbas still sat easily on his mount, he said, "I believe you have something that belongs to me," and nonchalantly held out his hand for his prized dagger.

Barabbas caressed it one more time before holding it out, spoils for the victor. "Your talents would be wasted if I assigned you anywhere but as head of our security," Barabbas said, his expression warming a little. "Co-head, actually," he continued, "as you will work side by side with Eben. He will explain everything to you as we go. We have been in one spot far too long. Let's move, men."

The bandit leader turned his horse and led the way, the others following behind. Malchus smiled to himself. It had been so easy. Then he rethought his opinion as he fingered his neck gingerly, realizing the swollen flesh must already be discoloring. Maybe not *too* easy. A shadow fell across him, blocking the sun as Eben fell in step with him. "Do you really work for the high priest?" the larger man asked, puzzled. "I don't understand how someone like you could be a religious servant."

"Religious?" Malchus asked, laughing. "Not even close! And I could hardly describe my master—well, my former master—as religious either. You would be shocked if you knew all the things he has done to guarantee his position and power."

"But how did you end up working for him?" Eben seemed genuinely interested.

"My father's family has worked for the high priests for generations. Of course I had to carry on the tradition. I even married the daughter of a priest." For a moment Malchus fell silent as he thought of Alona.

Eben shook his head. "That's too bad. It will be a long time before you can see her or your children." Malchus winced but said nothing. "Even then, you will have to be very careful. Barabbas doesn't take chances." They marched doggedly on with the others through the scorching desert heat as they made their way to the next ambush.

— ◦ —

Long after dark, Malchus sat on a rock outside the cave entrance and leaned his back against the smooth stone face of the cliff. Less than an hour remained until the appointed hour for the raid. Taking a deep breath, he let it out slowly to calm his excitement. He scanned the group spread out before him, wondering who might be the traitor. Or patriot, depending on whose viewpoint you ascribed to. Malchus had expected the man to contact him sometime during the past three days, but whether due to extraordinary caution or mistrust, he had not. For perhaps the hundredth time, Malchus mentally reviewed each man in the band, trying to find his ally.

Of course there was Eben, the one man in all the camp that he almost trusted, but he seemed so loyal to Barabbas that it was hard to picture him giving his leader up to certain death, probably by crucifixion. Then there were Elan and Arnon, the brothers who stood at Barabbas' right hand, even to quartering with Barabbas in the best cave. Elan was a military genius, and Arnon was the treasurer. Many audacious traitors through history had held positions of highest trust, but Malchus didn't think that was too likely in this case. Nathaniel, the disgruntled scribe, was the one Malchus thought to be most likely, but if all went well it wouldn't matter at all.

"Barabbas! Barabbas! Barabbas!" the men chanted in unison. "Hail to the Messiah!" one man shouted, waving a length of fine linen in one hand and several strands of jewels in the other. "Death to the Roman dogs!" another yelled amid riotous laughter and tilted a skin of wine above his head, drinking till the wine overflowed his mouth and ran down his neck. Earlier that day Barabbas had made one of the most brilliant and daring robberies in his career, capturing a huge and well-guarded caravan laden with textiles, precious gems, and at least 30 goatskins of aged wine.

Malchus shook his head at the memory. Barabbas and his men had surrounded the train of camels like flies on carrion and ordered the men to throw down their weapons. The caravan master had drawn his sword in a vain attempt to protect his livelihood, so Barabbas had ordered every one of the men killed, their blood soaking into the rocky soil. A beardless youth still moaned pitifully when they left with their newly claimed riches. Barabbas paused just long enough to slash at the boy's abdomen, never looking back at his victim's desperate attempts to hold himself together as he died.

Some messiah he's turned out to be, Malchus thought. He stretched and yawned, pretending to be sleepy. *Good, they're almost all asleep, or just plain drunk. Any time now. . . .* The cry of a jackal broke into the growing stillness. An answering call followed closely on the other side of the canyon. Malchus' senses came alert. It was the signal. High above the camp the sentries at three different posts now lie gagged and bound. There would be no warning.

Malchus stood slowly and put a whole fig into his mouth, chewing quickly. No one was watching as he ducked into the cave that was Barabbas' chamber. The bandit leader looked up from the crude table on which he had spread the plans for the next month's attack on a Roman garrison. "Still sober, Malchus?" he asked. "Come take a look and tell me what you think." He bent back over the table. Malchus walked quietly up behind him and clubbed him on the back of the head with both fists. Barabbas slumped forward and was still.

Quickly Malchus carried him to the front of the cave and laid him on the skin that crossed the entrance. As soon as he stuck his head out of the entrance a faint slither sounded above him and a harness landed at his feet. He pulled the harness into the shadow, his hands moving deftly as he fastened it around the limp body of Barabbas, making sure special pads of lamb's wool were firm across the back to minimize any noise against the cliff. Two tugs on the rope, and Barabbas began to rise, his dangling legs silhouetted by the glow of the campfire.

A sharp intake of breath from behind him startled Malchus. He whipped around to see Elan standing there with red hair tousled wildly, his mouth hanging open in shock. His hand crept up to scratch the side of his head and he blinked groggily, obviously hoping he was only dreaming. He wasn't. In a blur Malchus rushed at him. He was unconscious before he had time to blink again.

Another sliding scrape, and the harness touched the ground again. Malchus looked down in dismay at this additional, unwanted limp body and swore under his breath. The whole mission was in jeopardy, and there was only one way to ensure its success. Malchus slipped his hand into his robe and closed around the hilt of his short sword and started to draw it out. Then with a muffled curse he shoved it back in and bent to pick up Elan.

A few minutes later, peering out the entrance of the cave, Malchus saw that everything was still quiet, but one man was sitting calmly by the fire looking right at him. His heart raced, but the man only nodded deliberately and turned away. That was it, then. Arnon must be Malchus' ally. He gulped and pulled twice on the rope. Elan began to slide up the cliff.

He was about halfway up when a shout rocked the camp. "Murder! Murder! Malchus has taken our leader!" Arnon ran from one drunken man to the next, shaking and shouting in their ears. Instantly Malchus knew he must act or face sure death. Skirting the cliff face to his right, he slipped into the dark cleft that served as a latrine. Here the cliff was steep but not sheer. Fitting his fingers into a crevice in the soft rock, Malchus began to climb. The uproar behind him meant that quite a few of the men were waking up, and they didn't sound too happy. Malchus pulled himself up faster.

They were waiting for him at the top. "What do you think you're doing?" a familiar voice whispered angrily. "The plan—your plan—clearly calls for only one person to be extracted. What were you thinking?"

"No time for that now, Othniel. We've been betrayed. Just grab them and run!" By this time the noise from below was deafening. Some of the men, Arnon among them, were already scaling the cliff, and the rest poured down the funnel of the canyon hoping to cut them off from the side. "Move!" Malchus barked. "Now!"

Malchus and the seven others each grabbed the nearest arm or leg of their captives and ran into the darkness, the sound of pursuit echoing closely behind them. They raced on and on until their lungs were bursting and the sounds faded. Only then did Malchus slow the men to a walk "There's not much time before they are on us again," he said softly. "We can no longer follow the most direct route. Instead we'll have to circle around from above to where the legions are waiting for us."

"How did they find out?" Othniel asked. "This plan was supposed to be foolproof."

"Almost foolproof," Malchus reminded him. "Our supposedly faithful contact turned double-traitor."

"Why would he do that?" Othniel asked bitterly.

Malchus grimaced into the darkness. "Because we have his brother."

The deadly game of chase continued throughout the night. Some of the time Malchus and his men ran, their feet crunching on the rough ground; other times they slid along silently, carefully placing their foot-steps between small bushes; and occasionally they crouched hidden, scarcely daring to breathe. When the sun began to brighten the hills Malchus sank down in dismay. Everywhere he looked on the hills to the north he saw Barabbas' men scouring the desert, barring the way to the rendevous. The bandits searched diligently and systematically. Malchus and his men were completely cut off from all possibility of help.

CHAPTER 12

Our only chance is to keep moving north and try to cross the road," Malchus whispered. "Maybe we can circle around behind them. We must hurry, though. Each moment of daylight increases their advantage. Just try to think of the reward when we bring in not only Barabbas but his military planner." He didn't sound very hopeful.

They pressed on with their heavy burdens. By now it had taken several additional blows to keep both prisoners unconscious. The men's shoulders ached and their arms were becoming numb. Othniel com-plained every time it was safe to speak in a whisper. "Just be quiet," Malchus finally snapped. "This is exactly why I didn't want to bring you in the first place. One more word, and I'll report you to Caiaphas when we get back." Surprised, Othniel gulped, but said nothing.

Just then shouts broke out to the rear. The bandits had spotted them. "Run!" Malchus shouted. Straining every muscle, they raced for the only spot where Malchus thought maybe, just maybe, they could hold them off until help arrived. They had not yet reached it when high on the cliffs above the road they heard the blare of a ram's horn trum-pet. As the echoes of its piercing blast died away they dashed beneath a sheltering overhang, dropped their limp burdens, and whirled into a coordinated position of defense.

Three archers crouched in front. Four swordsmen, Othniel among them, stood behind them with swords pointed outward, and Malchus knelt with the edge of his blade against Barabbas' throat. Sweat dripped from their bodies, and all were breathing hard as they waited.

The bandit army clustered briefly just out of arrow's range. Led by Arnon, they spread out into a semicircle in preparation for an over-whelming attack as Malchus and his men prepared to sell their lives at a high price. Then once again they heard the ram's horn, closer this time. Barabbas' men turned to look over their shoulders. Malchus simply raised his eyes. Across the road on a raised hillock sat the mysterious trumpeter on a sleek ebony horse. Again and again the call to attack was sounded.

Malchus had a fleeting sense that the horse was somehow familiar, but both it and rider were too far away to make out any details. Besides, he could see Arnon well enough, and the man had murder written plainly on his face. A round leather shield held in front of his body, the flaming-haired treasurer led the men in closer, scorning any concealment. Malchus' archers felled several of the men, but the rest came on steadily.

At first they thought it was thunder. The weird rumble seemed to come from everywhere and nowhere. Their backs against the rock, Malchus and his men could see nothing, but they watched with surprise as their enemies fled in terror, shedding armor and swords so they could escape unencumbered. Arnon looked behind him, enraged to see only receding backs. Without warning, he charged alone.

Othniel grabbed a second sword from the nearest man and stepped out calmly to meet him. With grudging admiration Malchus watched as his kinsman clashed with the bandit warrior. Arnon was a superb fighter, but his round leather shield was no match for the twin bolts of lightning in Othniel's hands. So intent was Malchus on the scene before him that he didn't even notice when the rumbling stopped, the stillness of the desert broken only by the metallic clanging of the deadly sword-song.

A ruthless slash sent Arnon to his knees, his sword arcing into the air and falling with a clatter on the ground some distance away. In defeat he bowed his head to await Othniel's death blow. The sound of applause and the deafening cheers of hundreds of voices startled them all. To his amazement, Malchus saw a full legion of the emperor's army arrayed along the road, Marcus Aburius Geminus at its head.

Sheathing his sword, Malchus nodded for two of his men to bring the prisoners and stepped forward. "You are indeed a welcome sight,

Centurion Marcus," he called. "Many thanks to whichever of your men alerted you to our little difficulty."

Marcus strode up to him and grasped his forearms. "It was none of my men, but I see you have succeeded in apprehending the rebel leader. Pontius Pilate and Caiaphas will both be pleased."

Malchus' eyes swept the now-empty hillock. He saw no sign of horse or rider. "Centurion Marcus," he said, "you will also be happy to hear that the others we have with Barabbas are his top two men, Elan and Arnon."

The Roman glanced at him in surprise. "Arnon? But he's the one who—"

"Yes, I know," Malchus interrupted grimly. "But he turned traitor yet again, betraying us to Barabbas' men. He nearly cost us all our lives."

The Roman officer walked to where Othniel still held Arnon at bay. "Who among you can testify to this?" he asked.

"We all can," Othniel said angrily. "Malchus was still inside the camp when this man raised the cry. Were it not for that, all would have gone smoothly." He glared at Malchus, but said no more.

Marcus motioned to several of his men, who stepped forward with hands full of plump goatskin bags. "The emperor wants to express his appreciation to each of you with 150 pieces of silver." The men accepted their payments with a sense of relief. "For Malchus and his brave cousin," the Roman officer went on, "there will be an additional bonus of 50 pieces of silver each for their part in the captures of Barabbas and his seconds-in-command. You men are welcome to our escort back to Jerusalem if you want it."

Othniel looked considerably more pleased. "Thank you, Centurion Marcus," Malchus said. "I think we will all accept your kind offer of an escort out of here." The men laughed shakily. "Did you want to take charge of the prisoners now?"

Marcus clapped his hands and his soldiers marched forward, engulfing Barabbas and his two men. Just then the rebel leader and self-proclaimed messiah awoke to find himself in the embrace of Rome. His shrieks rent the air as he fought tooth and claw to free himself, but to no avail.

"Now you," Marcus told Malchus loudly, ignoring the uproar, "had better get home to your lovely wife. She seems to place a much-higher-than-usual value on your tough old hide." With that he marched away, shouting orders and leaving Malchus to puzzle over the meaning of his remark.

⸺ ⸺ ⸺

Alona waited close to the door, impatient but not anxious. Oded had already arrived with the news that her husband had escaped almost certain death. Eager as she was for a full report, she sent him to stable Kivi as soon as she learned that once again Malchus had seen her mare. "How will I ever thank you, Oded?" she asked. "There is not money enough to purchase my husband's life, but anything I have is yours."

"Agreed," he called over his shoulder as he walked out the door to the impatient mare. "You must give me your maid, Erith."

As his brawny form receded into the distance, Alona began to shake with laughter. "Oded, you rascal," she chuckled, half to herself. Then she turned and saw Erith, her eyes mirthful and aglow with happiness.

"I was wondering if he would ever find the courage to speak," Erith said. "You know as well as I that he is a man of few words."

Her mistress ran and hugged her. "This is really what you want?" Erith nodded. "I am so happy for you," Alona squealed, hugging her friend again. "Do you think you can wait until after Passover, though? It would be hard to replace either of you before then."

"Of course," the servant woman assured her. "After all, we've waited this long. Another month or so won't make much difference."

A while later, when Malchus arrived home and swept Alona into his arms, she thought her cup of happiness would overflow. It seemed as if the long months of loneliness and frustration had never been. But it was just as well she didn't know how short would be the respite. Early the next morning the servants answered a pounding at the door and opened it to find Othniel. Alona had never cared for Malchus' arrogant young cousin and indeed pitied his neglected wife, but never did she dislike him so much as she did that moment.

⸺ ⸺ ⸺

Side by side they walked, two itinerant laborers deep in conversation as they skirted the edge of Gethsemane, an olive grove with a stone oil press built in a cave. "Our master turned my job over to you?" one of them asked, his voice rising indignantly. "And after I had spent months, even years, studying him and was only away on official business? Othniel, I swear if you weren't the son of my uncle I'd—"

"Josias. Call me Josias," hissed the other, equally indignant. "And he didn't give it to me. He gave it to Zarad. I was only following his orders, Malachi. You are Malachi this time, aren't you?"

Malchus smiled in spite of his very real anger at being replaced as the leader of the operatives assigned to combat the teacher. Othniel had always been a bit sensitive about his unusual name, and invariably changed it at the earliest opportunity when on an assignment. "Yes, Othniel, and I can see that what happened wasn't your fault," Malchus said, calming a little.

"Josias," Othniel mumbled rebelliously under his breath.

"Very well. Josias," Malchus smirked. "What are you going to do first, update me on my own case, or explain to me why you pried me out of bed my first morning home, still not having reached the second hour of the day?" His voice rose to a near shout on the last few words.

"How surly you are in the morning," Othniel sniped in return. "As ever, I am only following orders."

"Whose?" Malchus demanded. "Caiaphas', or Zarad's?"

"Both, actually. But I suppose I should start back at the Feast of Tabernacles. A few of us were called in to discuss our strategy with Caiaphas"—he hesitated, then continued—"and Zarad. They made it extremely clear that anything we thought of or did that led to the teacher's death would be richly rewarded."

"The Sanhedrin actually condemned a man to death without a hearing?" Malchus was incredulous.

"Not the Sanhedrin—not yet. So far it is strictly unofficial. But even you would not scruple at a reward of this size." He named a figure that made Malchus blink. "The money aside, I think one of our top agents may be a spy for that man."

"What do you mean? Who?"

"I don't know," Othniel said grimly, "but somehow the teacher knew that we were planning to kill him, and so he announced it to the whole crowd at the feast. Many of the people still support him, and for a moment I thought that they might turn on us."

"What did you do?" Malchus asked, a reluctant tinge of admiration in his voice. "Obviously you're still here and in one piece."

His cousin shook his head. "Barely. He was looking right at me. All I could do was turn the attention back on him. I said he must have an evil spirit in him that made him speak madness." Malchus sighed and shook his head. "It was all I could think of at the time," Othniel defended himself, "and in any case, it worked. But there's more."

"Isn't there always?"

Pretending not to hear, Othniel went on. "I won't bore you with the details of every little snare we laid, but suffice it to say he avoided them all." His tone was bitter. "In fact, the only progress we made the whole week was having the priests and rabbis preach all their sermons on the true nature of the Messiah, and how He will rule to the ends of the earth." He snorted contemptuously. "Whether it's true or not, our scrolls show a much different picture than a dusty wanderer who spends most of his time with the worst sort of sinners."

"If he was there every day teaching in the Temple, why didn't you try to arrest him then? That sounds like it was our best opportunity yet."

A long silence. At last Othniel said sourly, "We did try." Another lengthy pause. Malchus waited patiently. "All right, all right!" Othniel finally exploded. "We just didn't do it. Somehow he bewitched us, and we couldn't touch him!"

Malchus wisely refrained from commenting, remembering several occasions on which he had felt the same power restraining himself against his will. "I'm sure Caiaphas was unhappy," he said at last.

Othniel grinned in spite of himself. "You can only imagine. We couldn't even come up with a decent excuse. One of the Temple guards just blurted out, 'Nobody ever spoke like that man before.' I saved all of our hides by suggesting one last grand scheme. In all modesty, it was foolproof. Except that it wasn't . . . ."

"Whatever do you mean?"

Othniel beamed with pride. "I arranged circumstances so that Jesus would find himself caught between our laws and those of Rome. Whichever one he chose, the other group could be made angry enough to kill him."

"Which law?"

"The seventh. Commandment, that is." Malchus' eyes widened in the beginnings of comprehension. "We took to him a shameful woman who had been, er, caught in the very act of adultery. By our law she should have been stoned to death, but if Jesus condemned her, he would be usurping the authority of Rome, since they must sign any death warrants. It should have worked flawlessly." Here Othniel deflated a little.

"Who was the woman?" Malchus asked curiously. "Dare I ask how you knew she could be found committing adultery at that particular moment?"

Othniel flushed dark crimson, then curtly repeated a name.

"Ah" was all Malchus said, flushing a little himself. "At least *I* haven't done anything like that since I got married." Trying to change the subject, he said, "You didn't actually tell me how Jesus escaped your foolproof trap."

His cousin squirmed. "He bent over and wrote on the Temple pavement. Although he never used any names, I knew whom he meant. The first thing he wrote was 'Murdering your opponent to gain a position of power at the head of the people.' Caiaphas urgently remembered business elsewhere. Then he wrote, 'Stealing the priests' portion of the sacrifice from other priests.' That got rid of a couple more. There was 'Cheating a widow on the sale of her property three days ago.' I didn't see who that one was, and for me he wrote—"

"Never mind," Malchus grimaced. "I can guess. I'm just glad I wasn't there."

"One more interesting thing came out of all this," Othniel said thoughtfully. "We found that Jesus has more supporters than we had realized, even in the Sanhedrin. The council was just about to condemn him to death in their meeting when Nicodemus, of all people, spoke up in his defense, reminding the other rulers that they had never yet condemned a man without a trial. It shamed enough of the rest of them so that nothing happened."

"And that," Malchus remarked, "must bring us to the reason I am tramping across the Kidron Valley with you instead of being home in bed."

Seeing the anger in his cousin's face, Othniel hastened to explain. "Lazarus is sick."

That was all the explanation Malchus required. Lazarus was one of Jesus' closest friends, and nothing would be surer to summon Jesus to Bethany than an urgent message from the man's sisters. "How many of us are there?"

Othniel counted on his fingers. "A score or so. We will be the first ones to arrive, and the others will trickle in throughout the day. We will make sure everyone is spread out so that not even a fly can enter or leave the village without our noticing."

They saw a good many flies over the next several days, but no sign of Jesus or any members of His inner circle. Rumors indicated that Lazarus' condition was worsening. When family members began to arrive from all over, some leaving exalted positions in Jerusalem, Malchus and Othniel quietly slipped into the little town. They joined a small crowd of the poor who squatted on the street or leaned against the outside wall of the courtyard. The beggars waited patiently, fanning themselves in the heat, hoping that if Lazarus died they would be chosen to swell the ranks of the paid mourners.

Shortly before noon a wailing spread through the street, announcing that Martha's beloved brother no longer lived. Determined to give Lazarus the best funeral Bethany had ever had, she hired every would-be mourner on the spot. Malchus, Othniel, and six others of their agents were among those she led across the spacious court filled with hanging plants and into the large chamber where Lazarus now lay in state.

Malchus and Othniel both started a little when they saw the young woman who knelt, sobbing, at her brother's side. "The Magdalene," Othniel whispered, nodding his head in her direction. Malchus laid a warning hand on his cousin's arm.

Othniel's initial fear of being recognized waned as he saw that Mary never gave the mourners a glance. She lifted her eyes from her brother's gray face only long enough to watch the doorway. "If only Jesus had come, you wouldn't have died," she wailed. "I don't understand why He wasn't here when we needed Him most." A sudden clamor from the mourners drowned out anything else she might have said.

Martha interred Lazarus in the family's burial cave early the following morning. She would have delayed longer, hoping Jesus might still come, but already the odor of decay was becoming impossible to ignore.

The whole town was there, along with the grieving family and the hired mourners, all in torn robes and covered with ashes. Several men rolled back the covering stone. After Lazarus, now bound in strips of spice-soaked cloth to mask the stench, was laid to rest on the stony shelf just inside, the covering stone once more guarded the abode of the dead.

"How are we going to keep this up all week?" Othniel croaked to Malchus on the way back to the house. The mourning rituals would continue for several days.

"Quit complaining," Malchus answered. But he didn't see how they could last a full week of mourning either.

"If Jesus were going to return, He would have done it already," Othniel persisted hoarsely.

"We're not leaving at the moment," Malchus rasped painfully. "At least not until it gets dark, and maybe not for a day or two. Jesus may have been delayed."

Two days later Malchus paid little heed when a servant bent over Martha and spoke softly in her ear. The woman nodded, rose, and glided from the room. A short while later she was back and exchanged a few private words with Mary. The transformation in the exhausted woman was startling. Her face eager, she rushed from the room despite Martha's efforts to shush her. "He's here—let's go," Malchus whispered, pulling Othniel after him. The other mourners trailed behind, thinking they were following Mary to the tomb.

Oblivious to everything else, Mary ran to a quiet spot outside the town walls to throw herself down at Jesus' feet. "He and his followers are finally alone," Othniel whispered. "Let's signal the attack."

"No," Malchus cautioned. "There are still too many people around. Let's wait until tonight. Besides, I'm curious to see just what he will do."

Neither Malchus nor Othniel could hear what Jesus said, but found themselves once again part of a procession leading to the burial site. When they got there, the Teacher seemed to be bowed down by a great sorrow. He covered His face with His hands while He wept aloud. Malchus thought He wept for only Lazarus until Jesus' eyes singled him out of the crowd. It was as if Jesus laid bare Malchus' soul till he thought his very heart must break. One by one Jesus unerringly singled out Othniel and Caiaphas' other agents. *Who could have told him?* Malchus thought frantically. Never had he felt so exposed.

Then returning His attention to those immediately around Him, Jesus commanded in a loud voice, "Roll away the stone."

Martha's hands fluttered in horror to her mouth, then clasped and unclasped nervously. The village men looked to her for a decision. "But Lord," she ventured at last, "Lazarus has been dead four days already." She swallowed hard, trying unsuccessfully to think of a delicate way of phrasing her objection. "He—well, he stinks!" she finally blurted.

Jesus smiled gently at her. "Didn't I tell you that if you believed, you would see the glory of the Father?" And in a voice of such authority that no one else dared contradict Him, He ordered, "Roll away the stone!" Men scrambled to obey Him, and the scraping of stone testified to their efforts as they forced the stone along in the trough that held it against the opening of the cave. The light breeze touching their faces lifted the cloying odor of corruption and carried it through the crowd. Even some of the men gagged.

Malchus could plainly see through the opening that nothing had been touched. The swelling body of Lazarus strained at its bindings, the sweet smell of spices long since overpowered. Jesus' next words crackled through the air. "Lazarus, come out," He called.

Instantly the foul stench dissipated, and Malchus could actually see the body inside the tomb shrink to its normal size. Then, of all horrors, it twitched. Wiggling about, it struggled first to sit, then to stand. Malchus' bones turned to water and his legs trembled under him as the corpse shuffled blindly toward the opening, its head turning this way and that.

Jesus looked around and, seeing that no one had moved, He laughed. "What are you waiting for?" He squeezed Martha's arm. "Go let him out." With Mary at her side, Martha hurried to obey. Starting with the strips around their brother's head, they unwound downward, freeing his eyes and mouth and finally his limbs.

Malchus waited only long enough to be sure of the identity of the man being unwrapped. When he was positive that it was truly Lazarus, he fled as fast as his long legs could carry him. Gone was any thought of arresting Jesus, much less killing him. Malchus didn't even remember that he had left Othniel and his men behind until he was nearly into Jerusalem, so eager was he to escape the presence of the one who could command the dead.

— — —

The emergency meeting of the Sanhedrin lasted well into the night. Nicodemus and Joseph of Arimathea, both sympathetic to Jesus, did not receive any notification of it. Malchus and Othniel, standing side by side, testified to what they had seen and heard. If their hands trembled noticeably, it was not from nervousness at addressing the most august and learned body in all Israel.

Their report sent shock and disbelief ripping through the room, then scorching anger as the truth sank in. Even so, there were still a few willing to speak on Jesus' behalf. Many of the Sadducees, their belief that resurrection was an impossibility threatened at the root, still counseled caution. They feared lest the anger of Israel or of Rome should fall on them, robbing them of their power or position. Malchus leaned close to Othniel's ear. "Look at Zarad," he said softly. "He certainly seems to be enjoying himself." Though not a member of the Sanhedrin, Zarad occupied the place of honor at Caiaphas' right hand. He did seem pleased, arms folded in satisfaction and a smirk resting on his features.

"If you watch," Othniel whispered back, "you'll see how Caiaphas seems more and more the servant and Zarad more and more the master." Sure enough, when tempers had reached their highest and the debate its fiercest, Zarad leaned over and spoke to the high priest. Obediently Caiaphas rose to his feet, waited for silence, then began to speak.

"My fellow Israelites," he said, fingering the edge of his robe, "we are the children, the seed, of Abraham. Many times in our history we have been taken prisoner, scattered, and nearly obliterated from the earth. Today that is what we again face if we do nothing.

"Our wives, our sons, and our daughters depend on us to save them from this imminent and very real danger. This Galilean has stirred up the people to the point that many want to crown him king. The news of this latest magical working is even now racing across the land. Once Jesus' followers learn that his evil power can turn back the unrelenting tide of death, there will be no stopping them. And when they revolt,

Rome will do everything necessary to regain control. We will be killed, our sons sold as slaves, our women violated and forced to live in the homes of pagans." Nearly everyone began nodding their agreement.

"It is for us here, this day, to save our families, our Temple—yes, even the whole land of Israel. This Galilean who cares nothing for us or for our safety must be stopped." Caiaphas paused, then unveiled a most shocking plan.

"If Lazarus should be the bond that brings together this man's followers, then Lazarus must die first." The silence in the council was at first one of surprise, then contemplation. "Believe me, I have thought this through," the high priest continued. "My servant Othniel will see that it is done quietly, without involving any of us." He stared hard at Malchus' cousin, daring him to speak. "With Lazarus out of the way, it will be a simple matter to sway public opinion in our favor and arrest Jesus. After all, it is far better that one man should die than that a whole nation should perish."

Just like that it was decided. Malchus supposed he should feel some sense of triumph that the elite of the nation formally supported his campaign to remove Jesus, but he tasted only the bile of fear. He dreaded facing Jesus again.

Caiaphas motioned for Malchus and Othniel to approach. When Malchus was close enough to see his master's eyes, he noticed a subtle change. Though as bright and intelligent as ever, they somehow glittered with a strange new light, as of something hideous lurking just below the surface. Somewhere he had seen eyes like that before. A tug on his sleeve reminded him to bow beside his cousin.

"I am depending completely on you men," Caiaphas told them, apparently as friendly as ever. "You are the best that I have, and I know you will succeed."

Zarad towered above them, his high forehead gleaming with perspiration. "You have three weeks. See that it is done by Passover."

CHAPTER 13

Malchus fell in step with Caiaphas on the way to the evening sacrifice. It was the first day of Passover week, and the high priest would personally conduct the morning and evening sacrifices throughout the festivities. Malchus was relieved to be able to report that all the pieces now fit together in their plans to arrest and execute Jesus. "If he attends the feast," Malchus predicted, "we should see him arrive any time now. Our men are stationed at every gate. He can't get in without any warning this time. And from the moment he sets foot in the city scores of our agents will watch his every move, record his every word. Most important, we will somehow find out where he stays at night."

This was one of the most pressing points of their plan. For three and a half years Jesus had slipped into and out of Jerusalem, and they were still no nearer to discovering His place of shelter. "Where is he now?" Caiaphas asked.

"He stayed with Martha and Lazarus over the Sabbath." The high priest ground his teeth at the mention of the man Jesus had raised to life, but Malchus went on as though he did not notice. "At the last report, they all appeared to be getting ready to travel, so we should see him soon."

Caiaphas thought for a moment. "This could work out even better than I had hoped, if Lazarus also celebrates Passover here in the city. Whichever night we arrest Jesus, Lazarus must die. Tell Othniel to see that it gets accomplished."

Malchus was just opening his mouth to protest placing an inexperienced agent in charge of such a critical mission, but when he saw the Temple courtyard his mouth stayed open and no words came out. Priests readied the animals for the evening ceremonies, their garments crisp and clean. The lamplighters scurried around to the massive sconces in the marble walls, fire shooting up as they lit each torch. As the sun set, the artificial light would emblazon the whole of the Temple with its brightness, and the festive crowd would sing their songs of praise, their voices echoing off the neighboring hills and ascending even to the heavens. Except there was no crowd. No songs. Even the money-changers sat idle, drumming their fingers and absentmindedly stacking and restacking their coins.

The high priest pounced on an acolyte standing nervously nearby. "What is the meaning of this?" Caiaphas snarled, grasping the front of the young man's robe when he did not answer immediately.

The acolyte gaped for a moment, his eyes bulging wildly. "It's Jesus," he finally gasped. "The whole world has gone after Him!" Perhaps it was an exaggeration, but not much of one. A second glance at the nearly empty Temple showed that. With an unholy oath the high priest thrust his underling away from him, heedless of how the hapless man tumbled to the ground.

Caiaphas pulled off the blue turban of his office and clenched it in his fists. "Go," he said to Malchus when he could trust himself to speak. "Go and do whatever you can. We were prepared for anything. Anything!" Anything but this. Malchus raced down flight after flight of white marble stairs, slowing to a jog when he was sure he was out of sight of his master. Once more he found himself on the road to Bethany in search of Jesus.

He found him a mile or so beyond the city walls. At his first sight of the massive procession Malchus instinctively started to duck into the thick vegetation at the side of the road, but caught himself just in time. There was no point in hiding—he was now publicly allied with the enemies of the teacher. As Jesus approached closer, riding in royal estate on a donkey, Malchus was horrified to see Lazarus holding the rope at the animal's head. He shuddered in superstitious dread, lowering his eyes as the first part of the crowd passed by.

"Hosanna.* Hosanna to the Son of David!" sang little children and adults alike. Malchus recognized a fair number of the faces in the crowd. There with his parents was Taavi, the little boy Jesus had healed at the seventh hour, and Ornah, the widow of Nain, whose son had also been raised back to life. Malchus shivered again as he saw the young man, who had grown taller and was plainly in the best of health. Everywhere he looked he saw those who had been lame leap for joy, those who had been blind with their sight restored, and those who had been mute mingling their voices in their pleas for Jesus to save them. The triumphs of his evil power were everywhere. The people were begging him to save them as if he were God Himself.

We waited too long. They are going to crown him king tonight was Malchus' first thought. A horde of priests and rulers gave him a little hope as they confronted the procession head-on, bringing the entire proceeding to a standstill.

"Teacher, you must not allow your followers to demonstrate in this unseemly fashion," the self-appointed spokesman, a portly man with an orange-and-black robe, pompously announced. "This kind of noise is unlawful. Besides, the authorities will never allow it."

"If these people kept silent," Jesus said soberly, "the very stones would cry out." Anything further the religious leaders wished to say vanished in the renewed shouts of the glad crowd. The scowling men found themselves forced back, the flow of humanity surging past them. Malchus followed until the procession halted again on the very brow of the Mount of Olives.

This overlook of the Temple was the most famous view in all Israel, marred only by the Roman banners around the Temple complex. Israel's house of worship stood forth in all its snowy splendor, causing the heart of every true descendant of Abraham to swell with pride. Even from the mountaintop it was possible to see the massive wrought vine twined over the main gate into the Temple. Its green leaves, gold tendrils, and silver grapes represented the sweet vine of Israel. The throng hushed, caught up in the beauty as the setting sun caressed the smooth marble with its rosy light.

In the stillness Malchus heard the trumpets announce the start of the evening sacrifice. He knew the doomed lamb was even then being led through the Sheep Gate and up the stairs to the altar of sacrifice. There it would exchange its life for the sins of the people. Somehow he had always pitied the lamb as its life's blood drained away. The sound of a sob reached his ears—an agonized cry such as he had never before heard from a human throat. Jesus still sat on the young donkey, the coats of His inner circle serving as a cushion. His hands covered His face, and

He swayed back and forth as if He would collapse from grief.

No one there quite understood the source of the Teacher's pain, but all who heard it were somehow touched. Even Malchus, though he would have died rather than admit it. At last Jesus regained His composure and guided the donkey down the side of Olivet, a much-subdued crowd still following.

The road divided into three at the base of the hill, and Jesus chose the route that paralleled the Temple for a time. He seemed engrossed in the stunning edifice that towered above Him. Then the road turned in toward the city, and Jesus dismounted just inside the thick siege wall. Slowly, majestically, He walked into the Temple by way of the Sheep Gate, tracing the path followed by the sacrificial lamb.

— — —

Hand upraised to knock, Malchus stood with another man outside the high priest's chamber the next morning. The thick cedar doors did not entirely filter out the sounds of things crashing and breaking. Not sure what else to do, he lifted the latch and stepped into the room, closing the door quietly behind him. The guards on either side of the door glanced at each other and shrugged, accustomed to Malchus' fearless—some would say foolhardy—ways. The other man remained in the hallway, his hair neat and scented with expensive oils, his robes rich enough that he need not be ashamed of his appearance even in the presence of the high priest.

For once, Malchus realized as he glanced around the room, Zarad was nowhere in sight. But what he did see was even worse than the incident three years ago, the first time Jesus had driven out the merchants from the Temple. Now it had happened again, and this time Caiaphas had seized a bronze urn by the neck with both hands, using it to batter every article of furniture he could reach. Piles of splintered wood marked the location of each former chair and table. Even his imposing thronelike seat had several dents in it. And he was far from finished. He spotted Malchus and with a guttural roar lunged at him, urn held high.

Malchus could have sidestepped the older man. Instead he caught him by the wrists and restrained him. He pressed a spot on the high priest's wrist, and the urn fell to the floor with a metallic clang. Malchus did not release his master immediately. They stood, eyeball to eyeball, nostril to nostril, the high priest's teeth bared in a snarl. "I could have you killed," Caiaphas spat out.

Malchus smiled calmly. "I could have killed you already. Twice." He backed away and allowed his master to pull free. "Come now, tidy your robe," he said as to a child. "There is someone I want you to meet."

Sanity partially returning, Caiaphas looked around him with distaste. "This does not seem to be a very good time."

"Actually, the timing could not have been better." His servant smiled again. "As soon as this man introduced himself last night, I knew you would want to speak with him too." He opened the door, calling cordially, "Come in, come in."

The impatiently waiting man's eyes widened a little as he noticed the destruction in the chamber, but he recovered quickly and bowed respectfully to Caiaphas. Malchus tried to hide his gloating as he performed the introduction. "Master, this is Judas. Judas Iscariot."

— ◆ ◆ —

Alona did not like the change that had come over her husband in the days leading up to the Passover feast. True, he no longer slipped around in disguise, but as she saw him working hard to destroy the Messiah, she could hardly hold back the tears. Malchus and his colleagues were once again following Jesus at every turn, hoping to snare Him or at least somehow turn the tide of public opinion against Him. But where before they and the rabbis had tried to cloak their work with a mask of religious devotion, now their hatred of Jesus and His teachings showed in every word and action.

Still Alona sat close to Jesus' feet while He taught in the court of women, listening to His stories with new intensity. She didn't know how to put her fear into words, but somehow sensed that her time with the Man she believed with all her heart to be the Christ was nearly at an end. Though she paid little heed to the legal wrangling the priests and scribes tried to introduce into each discussion, her ears perked up whenever Jesus began a story or parable.

"Right under that part of the Temple wall," Jesus said, pointing to the farthest corner, "is a special stone called the chief cornerstone." His audience nodded. Most of them had learned the story early in their religious education. "When they were building the original foundation for the Temple, you will remember that they cut and shaped the rock in a quarry underneath the city, and then hauled it to the Temple site. That way the pounding and clinking of hammer and chisel would not desecrate the house of Elohim.

"One day the builders received the strangest stone from the quarry. It was huge"—He spread His hand wide amid general laughter—"and not very beautiful. They didn't know what to do with it, so they just set it off to the side and let it alone. But soon they found they had a problem. Every block they chose for the chief cornerstone crumbled under the weight of the other blocks. That is, until one day they tried the strange-looking stone. To their amazement, it fit perfectly and, most important of all, supported the weight of the whole building. Did you know that stone is still there till this day?"

Jesus laughed too, then, and shook His head at the blindness of the builders before growing solemn again. Carefully He emphasized each word. "The stone that the *builders* rejected," He said, "has become the chief cornerstone." Alona was quite sure that His audience realized that He was talking about Himself.

Malchus certainly understood, and the implications made him a touch uncomfortable, so he threw himself even deeper into preparations for the arrest, now planned for just after the evening meal on the eve of the Passover. Several times he met Othniel to oversee his plans for Lazarus' assassination, assuring himself that all was proceeding smoothly in that quarter. He avoided Alona almost completely, fearing that if she learned or guessed anything she would warn Jesus, and all his carefully laid plans would be for nothing.

At last the day came, and Malchus stopped at his home just long enough to bolt down his ceremonial meal of roasted lamb and unleavened bread. He scarcely had time to taste it, let alone contemplate the amazing rescue from Egypt it commemorated. As he rushed out the door he steeled himself against the hurt he noticed in his wife's eyes. This time he had not even allowed her to kiss him.

As planned, Malchus met with a mob of men in the center square of Caiaphas' palace, the Temple being crammed with worshipers.

Nearly adjacent to the outer wall of the Temple, the elegant sweep of its architecture and the tasteful design of each room contrasted harshly with the coarse, unruly crowd in Malchus' charge. Only the Temple guard standing at attention showed any semblance of order or restraint.

Malchus clapped his hands together, the sleeves of his white robe rippling. "May I have your attention?" he called loudly and to no avail. Seizing an ancient trumpet displayed on a nearby wall, Malchus blew a long blast. The men stopped and stared. "Listen to me, or you will not be paid," he snapped. That got their attention. "We need to review the plan for tonight," he went on. "There must be no mishaps. You have already been divided into three groups. The first will assemble at the Sheep Gate. The second, led by me, will gather at the gate leading to the Kidron Valley, and the third will meet at the Double Gate. Do not start until I give the signal."

A babble of noise started, and once again Malchus found himself forced to use the trumpet. "Remember what I said about pay," he said coldly. "You men there," he pointed to a smaller group huddled together like sheep, "don't forget that as the witnesses you are the most important part of the trial. Do you remember your testimony?" Mutely they nodded as one. Malchus was not reassured. "Meet me back here at this very spot as soon as we take Jesus to Annas. We'll go over your stories one more time to make sure you have them all straight."

One of them timidly raised his hand. "You may have noticed, Malchus, sir, that it is getting to be night. The Sanhedrin never meets at night. Are you sure you don't want to meet us in the morning?" His Adam's apple lurched up and down under a patchy beard.

"You fool! We went over this before. Yes, the Sanhedrin never meets at night." Malchus ground his palm into his forehead before exploding, "Except for tonight!" He sighed heavily. "This is an emergency, and you will testify."

The man looked far from convinced, but nodded his assent. Malchus couldn't blame him for being uneasy. For centuries the penalty for perjury was the same as whatever penalty was sought for the accused. In this case it was death. Even with the personal reassurances of the high priest that they could stand before the Sanhedrin and lie with impunity, they couldn't help being edgy. "It will be fine," Malchus reassured them once again. "Caiaphas himself has asked you to do this for the good of Israel. There is no braver or more patriotic duty, and I know you will do well." He hoped he sounded convincing.

"Just remember," he called as they began to resume their conversations, "seize the one who receives the kiss of friendship. Judas here"— he indicated Iscariot—"will show us the right man. Are all of you armed?" The men answered with a shout, holding up an odd assortment of weaponry: everything from swords and spears to sickles and pruning hooks. "Very good," Malchus said approvingly. "We will cross into the Temple as soon as the worshipers have gone."

As he surveyed the ragged bunch he found himself oddly reminded of Barabbas' army. When he thought of Barabbas, he remembered with surprise the execution of the rebel messiah and his men was scheduled for early the next day. "I doubt I'll get to go," he mused. "I'll probably still be busy with all this."

It was late when the Temple court had at last cleared enough for them to enter. The hired army continued to swell from the arrival of quite a number of the scribes, some of the priests, and even Caiaphas himself, all eager to watch the arrest of the man they so hated. As Malchus could have predicted, separating the mob into three parts created a fair amount of confusion, but he at last accomplished it with the aid of the Temple guard. Malchus delayed a few minutes, wondering why Zarad had not come to oversee the arrest. At last he shrugged. It was no concern of his, and perhaps if Caiaphas became disenchanted with the man, Malchus could resume his rightful place.

Beneath the archways on the outer wall of the city waited three contingents of Roman soldiers, dispatched to supervise the arrest of a man accused of plotting to overthrow the government. They took up positions along the outskirts of the mob. Judas, eyes bright with excitement, led the middle group out the Kidron Valley gate and into the night, Caiaphas right behind him.

"Where are we going?" the high priest asked irritably, still disliking Judas' smug insistence on personally leading the way to Jesus' secret hideaway.

Iscariot did not break his stride, replying only, "Just a short distance. It is only a little way."

Following the serpentine path into the valley, Malchus could see and hear plainly as the other groups marched along the other two branches diverging off the road to Bethany. Judas would tell them only that they would find Jesus on the western slope of Olivet. Malchus had decided to separate his men into three groups to ensure that their quarry didn't slip away on one segment of the road while they unsuspectingly took another. And of all the men in the mob, only he knew that the remainder of the Temple guard waited in the shadows over the crest of the mountain, blocking any escape in that direction as well. Malchus rubbed his hands together in satisfaction. He had not overlooked the least detail. Surely the reward for this night's work would be great.

On the slope of the hill the three divisions of the mob then merged into one. Unhesitatingly Judas led them a little farther and took a path leading to the olive grove and its olive press. In the daylight the place was a thing of beauty, but in the flickering light of torches and lanterns, full moon shining down from overhead, it was eerie.

Just at the entrance a volley of shouts rang out. A white ghostlike form rose off the ground, flailing madly, only to be followed by darker shapes, all scattering into the night. "Seize them!" Caiaphas ordered.

The white apparition staggered and stumbled as it tried to run. Not in the least afraid, Malchus darted after it, grabbing at its covering as it wavered in the air. Malchus heard fabric ripping, and a slender young man raced away naked. The guffaws of the momentarily distracted crowd speeded the panicked, headlong dash of the youth down into the Kidron Valley. Other members of Jesus' inner circle followed the naked disciple. Still holding the sheet in his hands, Malchus shouted, "Let them go. We didn't come here for them." He motioned Judas to proceed.

Expecting to have to search the olive grove, Judas was taken aback to see the figure of his former Master appear out of the darkness, walking steadily toward him. The brothers, James and John, together with Simon Peter, followed behind Jesus, their sleep-heavy eyes widening with shock as they saw the mob.

Malchus looked closely at Jesus. Here and there on his clothing were dark smudges that appeared to be either blood or dirt, but His face was calm, even serene. He looked levelly at the mob. "Whom are you looking for?" Though it was quiet, every ear heard His voice.

"Jesus of Nazareth," Caiaphas eagerly announced.

"I am He," the Teacher replied with dignity. As one the mob

surged forward to carry out the arrest, but suddenly a being as bright as the sun blocked their way.

Trying in vain to shield his eyes with his arms, Malchus cried out in terror. Powerless to flee, he slowly collapsed to the ground. He had no idea how much time had gone by when he came to himself. It was again dark. The torches had nearly gone out, but when their bearers recovered and held them aloft, the flames blazed with new life. The men picked up their weapons where they had fallen and stood once more, shaking and uncertain.

Once more Jesus asked, "Whom are you looking for?"

It was as if time had turned back and they had just arrived. Malchus braced himself for another dazzling display of might and, as Caiaphas was momentarily speechless, said, "Jesus of Nazareth."

"I already told you that I am He," Jesus said, taking a few more steps in their direction, "but let these others go free." He nodded at His three followers, who still held their ground. Malchus and the others shrank back, unsure of what the Teacher would do. Judas, afraid that he would lose his reward, pushed forward. Pretending to be separate from the unruly crowd, he boldly gripped Jesus by the shoulders and kissed each of His cheeks in turn.

"Greetings, Master," he said, tears of pretended pity in his voice.

Jesus was not fooled. "Where did you come from, Judas? Do you betray the Son of man with a kiss?" Judas stiffened. Abruptly he released his hold and pulled away, but his signal of betrayal had done its work. As the mob saw Judas touch Jesus without harm, its courage returned, and it again surged forward.

Jesus stepped forward to meet them, seeking to distance them from His disciples. Caiaphas motioned several of the Roman guard forward to tie the Teacher's hands, and Malchus was only too eager to help them. He blinked hard, spots still dancing before his eyes from the brightness of . . . whatever it had been.

Jesus held out his wrists to be bound, and Malchus began looping the rope securely around them. A shouted warning made him look up just in time to see a blade slashing in a downward arc. Peter's enraged face crossed his view. Only the years spent honing his reflexes kept the high priest's servant from being hacked in two.

The white-hot pain seared down the right side of his head, and instinctively he clapped his hand over the wound, reaching into his cloak with his left hand to awkwardly draw his dagger. The jewels twinkled in the hilt as he dropped to a low fighting stance, right hand still over the spurting wound that had been his ear. Even with his left hand, he was confident that he could quickly kill the untrained fisherman.

"Put your sword away." Somehow Jesus had pulled free of His captors, stepping between the two combatants. He was looking at Peter, but somehow Malchus felt that Jesus was speaking to him as well. As if in a trance, he slid his short sword back in its sheath, nicking the front of his robe as he did so. "Put away your sword," Jesus repeated. "Those who live by the sword will die by the sword."

Stooping to the ground, He picked up a piece of bloodied tissue and stood before Malchus. Gently removing the sheltering hand, Jesus put His own hand in its place. Malchus looked up into Jesus' eyes, as if seeing Him for the first time. In that sun-browned face filled with love he saw all the secrets of the universe. Face to face, Malchus stared into the eyes of God and trembled.

With the hint of a smile, Jesus reached for Malchus' hand, guiding it to the side of his head. His fingers closed over healthy, unscarred flesh. The chief servant of the high priest over all Israel stood gripping his right ear as if only that frail member could anchor him. He sank to the ground as Jesus walked back to the Roman soldiers, wrists held out to be retied.

When the last three members of Jesus' inner circle saw their leader submit to this humiliation, their last shred of control broke, and they fled. Caiaphas didn't waste so much as a glance in their direction. He could hardly take his eyes off the prize he had captured after so long.

Malchus was scarcely aware when the garden grew quiet, and the mob, its prey encircled in a ring of fire and iron, hurried Jesus away.

-----

* Literally, "save us." Derived from the Hebrew of Psalm 118:25 ("Save us, we pray"), the expression became a liturgical cry for divine mercy and later became associated with Jewish eschatological hopes.

CHAPTER 14

Othniel had discreetly watched Lazarus all day. It was going to be almost too easy. The man and his sisters had camped in the pilgrim tent city just outside the city wall. It would be a simple matter to wait until the tired worshipers had gone to sleep, then slip into the tent and complete his mission, with none the wiser till morning.

Now, many hours after sundown, it was silent, and Othniel carefully watched Lazarus' tent and the eastern wall of the city, both plainly visible from his hiding place. Then he saw it, the three clusters of light at the city gates. He couldn't quite make out his cousin, but he knew where he'd be: right at the front. That was the signal for him to act, and he crept soundlessly forward.

Once among the tents he slowed, hardly even breathing. All around him he heard the sounds of slumber. The cool evening air hung heavy with the smell of animals, for many of the travelers had brought their own offerings rather than pay the high prices at the Temple. Here it was—Lazarus' tent. Carefully Othniel loosened the stakes along one edge, any sound covered by the snoring from inside.

Just as he raised the side to slip under, one hand on the hilt of his knife, a bright beam of light cut through the moonlight, illuminating only the spot where he knelt. Othniel looked around in near panic, his deed exposed for any passerby to see. The shaft of light grew and swelled, shaping into what looked like a soldier made of flames. The being stretched out his sword with such easy strength that there was no doubt he was very capable of defending the man who had been raised from the dead. Suddenly Othniel turned and fled.

Making no attempt at concealment, he raced in the direction he had seen the torches follow. Feet pounding against the hard ground, he realized with clarity that he had been fighting not only against Jesus, but also against the living God. "Forgive me, Elohim," he gasped out. "Help me to warn my cousin before it's too late." Oddly, in spite of his headlong flight, he felt the stirrings of a peace he had never before known.

Hesitantly he followed the road leading toward Bethany, unable to tell even in the light of the full moon just which direction the mob had headed. Bent over, squinting at the dust to try to trace the footprints, he heard the sound of running feet. He had only enough time to straighten up before three fleeing men poured down the stairway at the left, the one in the lead crashing full into Othniel. Both men fell in a tangle, and Othniel caught just a glimpse of the other man's face. "Peter," he began. "Please, you must let me speak to your Master."

But the man leaped up and ran as if every foul spirit were on his heels, ignoring Othniel's call to wait. Slowly Othniel rose, dusted himself off, then hurried up the steps into the garden. The mob was not hard to find as it wended its triumphant way back to the city. Too late! Othniel tasted fear in his mouth as he pushed his way into the crowd, searching for his cousin. Somehow there might still be a chance, if he could only find Malchus and convince him that Jesus of Nazareth was really the Son of God.

━ ━ ━

Shocked to the core of his soul, Malchus sat trying to comprehend what had just happened. Every premise, the whole foundation of his entire life, had just been turned upside down and shaken. Tears ran unchecked down his cheeks, washing away years of bitterness and hatred. His apologies, confessions, and remorse poured out incoherently to Elohim, the God he had for so long denied. And though rambling, his first genuine prayer ascended as sacrificial incense to heaven.

It could have been hours that he sat there, but gradually he became aware that someone was calling his name. Hastily he brushed at his eyes and stood, thinking at first that one of his men had come looking for him. But no, it was a woman's voice. "Over here," he called unsteadily.

The lantern nearly broke in a headlong dash toward him. "Oh, Malchus, I've been so worried," Alona burst out, only to stop with a gasp when the light revealed her husband's bloody state. "What have they done to you? What's wrong?"

"I'm fine, truly," Malchus said, holding out his arms to her.

Gladly his wife stepped into them, only to draw back. "Then whose blood is it?" Her mouth took on a determined set.

"Well, it's mine, actually," he confessed, "but—"

"Malchus ben-Gershom, shame on you," she scolded, swiftly trying to find his injury. "Now, where are you injured?"

He trapped her hands in his own, and she tried to pull away. "There is so much I need to tell you. Yes, I was hurt. My ear was cut off." He raised his voice to stop her indignant outburst. "Jesus healed me."

She stopped struggling and looked up in amazement. "What?" One look at her husband's face convinced her that it was true.

"Jesus healed me," he repeated. "I was wrong about so many things. I'm sorry I wouldn't listen when you tried to tell me."

"There's no need to apologize," she said softly, tears glistening in her eyes.

"Yes, there is," he persisted. "I love you. I think I have always loved you, and I am sorry for not showing it."

Her tears overflowed, and she clung tightly to him. "I love you, too, and of course I forgive you." A few minutes later another question occurred to her. "Where is Jesus now?"

He almost dropped her. "I have to go," he said frantically. "There is to be a trial tonight. Caiaphas plans to have Him executed soon after sunrise."

"What?" Alona was aghast. "They can't do that. It violates every one of our laws."

"Much the high priest cares for legality at this point," he said cynically. "If I can't save Jesus, His blood will be on my hands." Hurriedly thinking of his options, he asked, "How did you get here?"

She lowered her gaze. "Um, I rode."

"Good. Where is your animal?" A sudden thought occurred to him. "Tell me it's not a donkey."

She shook her head. "It's a horse, and it's waiting just below in the valley."

Malchus took up the lantern and walked rapidly with Alona along the winding path. "Did you come alone?"

"No," she said. "My uncle's servant is with me."

"Good. It is too dangerous for you to be out by yourself on a night like this—" The words died in his throat as he caught sight of the familiar black horse, its bridle held in the capable hands of an unusually large man. "You!" he exclaimed.

The man raised his hand in greeting. "Hello, Malchus."

Malchus glanced at his wife, who looked sheepishly up at him. "You too?" She nodded. All the times he had thought he heard her voice rushed into his mind: at the shore of Galilee; at Nain when the boy was raised to life; the night of the storm. "You little wretch," he said admiringly. "I thought I was going mad." And without another thought: "So are you coming with me, or not?" One look at the happiness bursting onto her face, and there was no need to wait for a reply. Turning to the servant, he said, "Sorry to leave you on foot—um, whatever your name is."

"Oded," Alona supplied.

"Right, Oded. I know it's a sorry way to repay the man that saved my life, but somehow I have to undo the damage I've done tonight."

"Don't worry about it," the servant drawled good-naturedly as he boosted Alona onto her horse's back. "I can find my way back with no trouble. Besides, your wife was the one who lent me, most insistently, to Centurion Marcus. And it was her idea to have some of us follow you in the first place."

A smile flitted across Malchus' face. Obviously he had greatly underestimated the intelligence and daring of his wife. "Thank you, both of you." With great difficulty he clambered on behind Alona, quite content to let her guide the beast.

"Which way do we go?" she asked when they reached the divided road.

"Keep to the right," her husband answered. "We have to go to Annas' palace." Also near the Temple, in the wealthy upper city, the palace of the former high priest was certainly imposing. And quite empty.

"Where can they be?" Malchus asked in frustration. "Annas wanted to question Jesus first."

"You said there was to be a trial," she reminded him. "The Sanhedrin meets in the Hall of Hewn Stone. Could they have taken Him there already?"

"Of course." He smiled down at her. "What would I do without you?" But the Temple, too, was deserted and the Hall of Hewn Stone dark.

"Really, there is only one place left," she said thoughtfully, "and that is Caiaphas' palace."

The bustle of activity proved her right. Every torch in the compound was lit, and braziers had been set up at regular intervals around the square, as the waiting company warmed themselves against the cool early-spring air. Many of those present were women, so Alona was not overly conspicuous in her dark robes of coarse cloth. "Wait for me here," Malchus said softly, guiding her to one of the fires. "I'll try not to be long."

She gave him a brave smile. "Go ahead. I don't mind."

Looking around, Malchus saw the doors to Caiaphas' banqueting hall shut tight and Roman soldiers outside. That was it, then. He walked over prepared to batter those doors down if need be, but became distracted by the little cluster of men off to the side, still huddling together like frightened sheep. They were the false witnesses. His witnesses. "Have you already been inside?" he asked them. "What happened?"

Just then the doors flew open, almost slamming into one of the soldiers. Another of the witnesses, the man Malchus had spoken to earlier, flew out, wide-eyed and terrified. Caiaphas stood in the doorway, fists upraised, his lined face distorted in rage. "Get out!" he screamed. "You pack of idiots, you band of—" And then he caught sight of Malchus. His eyes narrowed. "This is your doing," he hissed. "I will deal with you later." The doors slammed with a bang.

"What happened?" Malchus again asked the witnesses, hardly daring to hope.

They shuffled their feet and hung their heads. One of them finally replied, "Our testimony didn't agree."

Malchus couldn't believe what he heard. "None of you?"

The man shook his head, shamefaced. "Not any two of us." He sighed, then added, "Will we still be paid?" But Malchus didn't hear him. Relief surged into his heart. He returned for Alona on light feet.

Surprised, she said, "That was fast. I see you have good news, though."

He pulled her off to the side to speak privately. "The best possible." The joy he had been trying to hold in broke through. "I may have condemned Jesus, but through the mercies of Elohim, I also saved Him."

She looked at him in puzzlement. "What do you mean?"

"Well, I was supposed to come straight back from the garden and make sure all of my master's witnesses had their stories in order, to ensure a quick and easy conviction."

"And?"

"And instead of reviewing their perjury with the witnesses, I was still in the garden, where you found me. Meantime, in front of the Sanhedrin, those morons, bless their hearts, couldn't agree on anything at all." Malchus grinned as he watched the comprehension dawn on his wife's face.

"And without at least two witnesses that agree in every detail, there can be no conviction," she finished. "Jesus must go free."

"That's right," he said with a laugh of relief.

"What do we do now?"

"Let's just wait right here until He is released. I want to see Him, to tell Him I'm sorry for all the things I've done to hurt Him, and to thank Him for saving my ear. It should only take a few minutes to proclaim Him innocent and set Him free." He took a deep breath. "And He can never be retried. This is the end of it."

But the hours dragged on, and still Jesus remained before the Sanhedrin. The nagging worry in Malchus' stomach grew into a stony knot of fear. Several times he reached inside his robe, the hilt of his dagger solid and comforting. But the words of Jesus kept coming back to him. "Those who live by the sword will die by the sword." If he was to obey, he must not use force.

About an hour before sunrise the guards escorted Jesus out onto the porch underneath a balcony. One of his cheeks was pale, the other with a red mark. His hands were still bound. Malchus ran his fingers through his hair. "What can they be thinking?"

Unafraid of the soldiers' presence, a large number of men crowded around Jesus, knocking Him to the ground and brutalizing Him. One pulled out a handful of the Teacher's beard. Then the crowd hid Him from view. Powerless to help, Malchus and Alona watched in horror.

"Look, there's Othniel," Alona said, her eyes fixed on the corner of the courtyard closest to Jesus. "Who's that man he's talking to?"

Malchus glanced in that direction. "It's Simon Peter, one of Jesus' disciples. Maybe he knows something we don't."

As he walked over he was surprised at his cousin's haggard appearance. And he and Peter seemed to be arguing too. Othniel put his hand on Peter's arm to detain him, saying desperately, "But I saw you in the garden. I know you were with Him!"

Angrily Peter shook Othniel's hand off. "I told you—I don't know that man." Then to emphasize his claim he poured forth such a stream of curses that even Malchus blinked, only to have his tirade interrupted. Awakened by the light and noise, and sensing the approach of dawn, a rooster perched on one of the walls let out a loud call. Peter stopped. The change in him was incredible. His face looked stricken, his mouth snapped shut over whatever epithet he had been about to spit out. Following the path of the fisherman's gaze, Malchus saw the mob part, leaving Jesus in full view for a moment. He was looking right at them, overwhelmed with sorrow. Turning, Peter ran out the nearest gate as fast as he could go.

"Malchus, you have to help me," Othniel said, his usually neat hair in total disarray. "We have been wrong about everything, and I don't know what to do. I tried to ask Peter, but he was no help at all."

"I know," Malchus said, "but what happened to you?"

Othniel didn't even notice that his cousin was liberally spattered with gore, but seemingly whole. "It doesn't matter right now. Jesus is all that matters."

"Yes," Malchus agreed quickly. "What can we do?"

But before they could do anything, more members of the Sanhedrin bustled into the courtroom, disorganized and hastily dressed. Caiaphas ordered Jesus brought back inside. "Wait!" Malchus shouted. "I must testify for the accused!" The high priest ignored him, slamming the doors in his face.

Then the guards blocked his path. Plainly they had orders to keep everyone out, even the servants of the high priest. Again Malchus fought the temptation to force his way in. Every time the thought came, he could still hear the quiet voice saying, "Put away your sword."

After only a few minutes he heard a commotion at the doors of Caiaphas' hall. Annas and Caiaphas now stood together in the doorway and Caiaphas shouted, "This man has been found guilty of blasphemy." The robe of his office had been torn, exposing his chest.

His words inflamed the crowd, who rushed into the room, intending to kill the prisoner then and there. Only the vigilance of the Roman guards prevented them from tearing the Teacher to pieces on the spot. Some of the guards looked disgusted at the undisguised blood-lust of the mob. Stunned beyond belief, Malchus clutched Othniel's shoulder for support. "Take care of Alona; she's right there" was all he said before striding up the steps and into the room to face the Sanhedrin.

The nation's judges had been sitting in their usual half circle, with the high priest at the center. Most of them were already on their feet, but cushions still dotted the floor. Malchus was a bit surprised to see Annas in the center seat. Apparently the former high priest still had more power than his son-in-law. The three scribes sat in front of Annas, their verdict sheets in hand. Even from a distance Malchus saw that the scribe on the priest's right, who counted the votes for acquittal, held a blank piece of paper.

"Fathers of Israel," he called loudly above the clamor, "I beg your leave to speak on behalf of the accused. My testimony is sufficient to clear His name and reverse the sentence of death." The members of the Sanhedrin looked venomously in his direction, but other than that they ignored him. He tried again at the top of his lungs. "Nicodemus! Where are you? Surely you did not agree to this miscarriage of justice." He faltered. "Or did you?" With growing uncertainty he looked around, but did not see the older man. Nicodemus' friend, Joseph, was also absent.

The slam of the wooden doors against the stone wall echoed sharply. Judas skidded into the room, his bag of silver held aloft. "Stop!" he called. "You have condemned an innocent man!" Instantly the hostile stares transferred from Malchus to Iscariot. "Please, take it back," Judas pleaded, holding out the money bag. "Here, you can have it. It's all still here."

"See to it yourself," Caiaphas sneered. "We have nothing more to do with it." Judas grasped the high priest's torn robes, pleading with him to release Jesus. Caiaphas pulled away contemptuously, ripping his garment further.

Judas pushed his way through the mob until he stood in front of Jesus. Out of breath, he gasped, "Master, save Yourself! I know You are the Son of God—make them let You go!"

Jesus looked sorrowfully at the flushed face of His betrayer. "This,"

He held out His bound hands, "is why I came into the world." Seeing that Jesus would work no miracle to spare Himself, Judas angrily threw the blood money into the center of the floor, the coins spilling and rolling across the stones. In a blur he ran from the room.

Caiaphas turned sternly to Malchus. "Because of your long years of faithful service, I choose not to have you killed." He drew himself up to his full height. "Leave my presence, and never return."

The priest's eyes flashed with a strange gleam, and Malchus felt a chill. Finally he realized where he had seen that look before. It had stared out from the faces of the demon-possessed men when they had tried to attack Jesus. Later he had observed it in Zarad. Now it appeared upon the features of the spiritual leader of Abraham's seed. When the change had happened Malchus wasn't sure, but he did know for certain Caiaphas was only a puppet, completely given to the control of demons. His heart breaking, he walked away with a crushing sense of finality. All the words in heaven and earth could not reach Caiaphas now.

Alona, Malchus, and Othniel trailed the mob to the Praetorium, the judgment hall of the Roman governor. Pontius Pilate was in residence for the duration of the Passover. Actually, he usually resided in Jerusalem during all the feasts, lest an uprising break out. Malchus suspected that Caiaphas now planned to call for a return of the favor he had done Pilate by aiding in the capture of Barabbas.

The Praetorium was in what had been Herod's palace. Pilate, freshly called from his bedchamber, appeared in the arched balcony outside the hall of judgment. In a distinctly unfriendly voice he asked, "Whom did you bring me this time, and why?"

The high priest pushed to the front of the mob. "A deceiver known as Jesus of Nazareth."

Pilate narrowed his eyes. "Yes, but what has he done?"

Caiaphas hesitated before answering. "Surely you know that if this man were not a criminal, we would never have bothered you with him."

Pilate had signed many death warrants for the priests. It was an unspoken understanding that they and he needed each other. The Roman governor required local leaders to implement the empire's interests, and the religious leaders needed Roman support to stay in power. But Pilate was always careful to make sure that the Jewish leadership clearly understood that *he* was the one ultimately in control. And he had to do it in a way that would not back them into a corner in which they felt that they had no choice but to resist him. Pilate needed their goodwill. Several times before, he had nearly provoked them to insurrection. "I will examine this man myself and determine if he has done anything worthy of death," he reminded them brusquely.

Malchus was pleased to note that Annas, Caiaphas, and the others were not at all happy at this unexpected order from the governor. In His private interview with Pilate, Jesus would have the opportunity to say whatever He chose, with none of His enemies present to give a rebuttal. A scuffle broke out as Caiaphas tried to pull free of his father-in-law's grip. Malchus edged closer so that he could hear. "I don't care; I'm going in there," the high priest said stubbornly.

"No, you're not," Annas replied with authority. "You are scheduled to perform the sacrifice this afternoon, and you can't if you are unclean from entering the house of a Gentile." With a grimace Caiaphas desisted and began to pace back and forth.

Returning to his wife and cousin, Malchus said, "All we can do is pray for Elohim to work on the heart of the governor. Perhaps Jesus can still be saved."

The three began to plead silently with the living God to intervene. Alona's eyes were wet when she raised her head. "I never thought I would see this day. Our Messiah is here, and instead of crowning Him, we are going to kill Him."

Malchus put his arm around her. "He's not dead yet. Maybe we still have a chance. It could be that Elohim is just testing our nation—and each one of us—to see what we will do with Jesus."

The murmurs of the crowd ceased as Pilate reemerged and held up his hands for silence, Jesus at his side. In a ringing voice the Roman official proclaimed, "I have questioned your prisoner and find no fault in him. He is innocent."

Alona sagged in relief, but Malchus tensed as the crowd exploded in wrath. Othniel glanced at him inquisitively, and Malchus nodded in the direction of the priests, who were nearly purple in their outrage.

Caiaphas was sputtering and yelling, shaking his fist. Annas tried unsuccessfully to calm his son-in-law until Pilate held up his hands once more. "Is there some additional accusation? If not, by law I have no choice but to free this man."

"I'll report you to Vitellius," the high priest shouted. "That man has stirred up the people from Gezer to Galilee! He has—"

"Galilee?" Pontius Pilate mused, stroking his chin. An idea struck him. "H'mmm. Very well, take him to Herod. He is here in Jerusalem for your Passover. " His tone brooked no argument. Grumbling, the priests waited for Jesus to stumble His way downstairs, accompanied by the Roman guards.

Joy spread over Malchus' face. "Maybe I was 'called to the kingdom' for such a time as this." He kissed Alona fervently and whispered, "I love you," clapped his cousin on the shoulder, and was gone.

Othniel was dumbfounded. "What is he doing? Does he really think Herod will listen to him?"

"Actually, yes," Alona replied quietly. "I suppose you will eventually find out anyway, but my husband is the nephew of the former queen, Najiyah."

Othniel reeled. "Herod will listen to him, all right," he exclaimed, "just before he chops his head off!" He could have bitten his hasty tongue when he saw the terrified look she gave him. "Come on," he said in an attempt to distract her from crying, "we might as well follow him. We can hardly get into more trouble than we're already in."

Taking his arm, she smiled wanly. "I wouldn't be too sure about that."

CHAPTER 15

Herod Antipas' guards gave Malchus no trouble when he pounded to a stop at the palace gates. In fact, they hardly questioned him as they led him to the tetrarch of Galilee. Malchus bowed low in the doorway, not rising until Herod motioned him closer. As the light illuminated Malchus, disheveled and covered with dried blood, Herod bridled in anger. "How dare you come before me looking like that? Guards, who let this man in?"

Boldly Malchus replied, "I am the grandson of your enemy, King Aretas. I have news that affects the safety of your kingdom, and there is not a moment to lose."

It seemed to take Antipas an eternity to digest this earthshaking series of pronouncements, with all its ramifications. At last he had a member of the Arabian royal family in his power, but, as Malchus had calculated, the desire to maintain his position won out over his lust for revenge. "Go on" was all he said.

"You have heard of Jesus of Nazareth," Malchus spoke quickly. "He is on His way here, the prisoner of Caiaphas. Pilate has sent Him to you for judgment."

"But Pilate hates me," Herod said. "Ever since that one incident with the—"

"He doesn't hate you anymore," Malchus interrupted. "But that is not the most important part. Jesus is innocent, and you must set Him free."

"You came here to tell me that? To order me as to what I should do in my own kingdom?" Herod lost his temper. "Guards, take this man away and kill him. Slowly."

But Malchus had one more surprise in store. "Jesus worked a miracle today. I saw it all."

His attention caught, Antipas demanded, "A miracle? What kind of miracle?"

Knowing he was one misstep from death, Malchus told his story. "I led the men who captured him, Caiaphas beside me." The tetrarch listened intently. "As I started to tie His hands, one of His followers rushed at me and slashed my ear off."

"I'll wager that's not what he was aiming for," Antipas commented grimly.

"I am sure you're right, but there my ear was, just lying on the ground." Suddenly Herod began to laugh, but Malchus persisted. "Jesus picked it up and stuck it right back on my head, and now you can't even tell the difference. He is the Son of the Most High, or He could never have done something like that."

Herod leaned close, minutely examining Malchus' unscarred ear, a rust-colored streak of dried blood now flaking off his neck, and the stiff, stained patches on the shoulder of his once-white tunic. "Have you seen any other miracles?" he asked at last.

"Lots of them," Malchus assured him. "I saw blind people made to see, the lame made to walk, and twice I saw those who were dead raised to life."

"You were there when he raised Lazarus?" Herod appeared impressed. "What I wouldn't give to see a miracle. I have always wanted to meet Jesus. Ah, I hear them bringing Him now."

Malchus bowed his way out of the room, and Antipas strode jubilantly out to meet Jesus. Equally jubilant, Malchus made his way outside, where he found Alona and Othniel waiting anxiously for him.

"He didn't kill you," Alona said wonderingly, stating the obvious.

"No, he didn't, and he won't kill Jesus, either. In fact, he seemed quite eager to meet Him."

"That's the first piece of good news I've heard in many hours," Othniel said, trying to stifle a yawn. "Now that this thing is all taken care of, maybe we can go home and get some rest."

"I, for one, won't rest easy until it's official," Alona said. "Remember, we're dealing with the same man who murdered the Baptist on the whim of his wife."

"That is very true," Malchus said with a shadow of concern. "I'll stay until the end. You two should go home, though. You both look exhausted."

"I'll stay," Alona volunteered. "I can sleep later."

"What is that noise?" Othniel jerked to attention. "The crowd doesn't sound very happy."

Malchus darted for the door, Othniel right behind him and Alona struggling to catch up. The usual guards were nowhere in sight, so Malchus swung the door open just in time for him to see Herod slap Jesus across the face, shouting furiously, "I have the power of life and death over you. If you work a miracle for me, I will set you free. If not," he shrugged, "maybe the soldiers will have better luck making you talk."

Taking the purple robe off his own back, he draped it around Jesus. "I'll give you one last chance. If you are the Son of God, work a miracle to prove it." Jesus remained silent. Antipas slapped him twice more, then shouted, "All of you come and worship your king!" Pandemonium broke loose as even the Roman soldiers joined in to brutalize the pale, silent man.

It was more than Malchus could stand, hearing the words he spoke in defense of Jesus being used as an excuse to torture Him. He drew his sword, planning to eliminate as many of the tormentors as he could before being struck down himself. Alona and Othniel, transfixed by the horror before them, did not see him prepare for a last battle.

As Malchus took his first step forward, two strong arms pinned him from behind in an unbreakable hold, and a deep voice said in his ear, "For the last time, put that sword away." Malchus felt himself being dragged backward, and the man spoke again. "Othniel, shut the door. All of you come with me—quickly."

As he obediently sheathed his short sword, Malchus turned. "Deron! I didn't even see you arrive. Why did you stop me?" He regarded his tall friend with a mixture of indignation and relief.

"The Messiah does not establish His kingdom by force," Deron said. "I know you feel as if you have to atone for what you did, but Jesus has already forgiven you," he added.

Malchus' eyes filled with tears. "It is my fault that an innocent person is suffering in that room. If He dies, I will be responsible, and I can't bear it." He choked back a sob.

Sympathy filled Deron's voice. "He will die. Nothing you do can change that. Your task now is to quietly witness His death and always remember the price He is even now paying for your sins."

As Malchus wiped his cheeks Alona pressed close to his side. "I don't know what to do," he said despairingly.

"Go back to Pilate," Deron instructed. "Jesus will soon be there."

"How can you know that for sure?" Malchus asked, but Deron had already walked swiftly away. "Let's go back, then," Malchus sighed. "I don't know what else to do."

The plaza was nearly deserted, and the three found a bench near the entrance and waited. It wasn't long before an angry murmur announced the return of the mob, who again filled the space below the Praetorium. For the first time so far during the proceedings Malchus caught a glimpse of Zarad. The mastermind of the plot against Jesus slipped quietly through the arches, followed by at least threescore men

Malchus had never seen before. They looked as if they could have been Zarad's brothers. All were tall and had the same striking features, but of course that idea was impossible. At an unseen signal they pushed their way into the crowd and mingled with the people. Only Zarad stayed inconspicuously to the rear.

Pilate appeared on the balcony, leaning on the banister in exasperation. "You have not proved a single charge against this man," he told the priests, "and I already told you I can find nothing wrong with him." He stretched out his arms. "Even Herod, a fellow Galilean, did not condemn him. I will have him scourged, and then release him."

Just then a messenger ran to the front of the crowd, waving something at Pilate as the guards led Jesus away. "This is not a good time, Valerius," Pilate said, turning to go back inside.

"It's from your wife," the messenger shouted. "She says it's urgent."

Pilate grimaced. "Very well, bring it up."

As he scanned his wife's note the governor became visibly agitated. He paced furiously, oblivious to the men who now circulated through the crowd, inflaming the people. Calling a guard to him, he gave an order in a low voice, and the armored soldier trotted away.

A few minutes later Pilate stood in the center of the arch with not one but two prisoners on display. One was Jesus, now barely able to stand, His lacerated body covered with blood. A circle of woven thorn branches clung tightly to His head, a cruel replica of a victor's crown. The other man was chained securely. His hair had grown even longer and shaggier during his stay in a Roman dungeon, and he struggled as fiercely as a wild animal with his bonds.

Malchus had averted his eyes and scarcely noticed the other man until Othniel elbowed him sharply. He looked up to see both of the men he had captured framed by columns of marble.

"Since it is the day of your feast," Pilate said genially, "I will release one prisoner. I will even allow you to choose which one. Today you must choose between Jesus," he held out his right hand, "and Barabbas." He indicated the man on his left.

A wall of sound overwhelmed the Roman official. "Barabbas! Barabbas! Barabbas! Barabbas!" The frenzied mob chanted the name, Zarad's men loudest of all. A few besides Malchus and Othniel shouted the name of Jesus, but they were drowned out by the roar of the crowd.

Pilate tried frantically to bring order. "What shall I do with Jesus?" he yelled.

"Crucify him!" shouted one of Zarad's men on the front row. The crowd took up the cry. Louder and louder it swelled. *Crucify him! Crucify him! Crucify him!"*

Disoriented by the noise and the sudden change in his fate, Barabbas walked down the steps and pushed his way into the seething mob. He turned for one more glance at the man who would take his place on the cross. The sight of Jesus' brutalized body stirred nothing more in him than bewilderment and relief.

Near the gate he caught sight of a familiar face and started toward him, hands spread like the outstretched talons of a hawk, and cold murder in his eyes.

Malchus started with surprise when he saw the man he had betrayed now approaching him. Shielding Alona with his body, he calmly faced Barabbas. The bandit leader paused as he belatedly remembered his surroundings. His eyes narrowed; he shook his finger at Malchus, mouthing, "When we meet again, I will kill you." Then he vanished into the crowd.

Pilate called for a bowl of water. As he dipped his hands in it, water spilled carelessly to the ground. "I am innocent of this man's blood," he said to the mob. "He is your responsibility."

The people shouted, "His blood be on us, and on our children." Turning to the guards, Pilate ordered, "Scourge him again."

The second flogging was even more brutal than the first. With each blow of the whip, bits of metal slashed into Jesus' back, ripping out chunks of flesh. Malchus pulled Alona away, but nothing could cover the sound of the cruel whipping. Through it all Jesus never cried out.

The crucifixion of Barabbas carried enough potential danger that Pilate had already assigned additional troops to conduct it. Malchus noted dully that Cenurion Marcus had been placed in charge. The Roman officer formed his troops into a perimeter to hold back the crowd, allowing the prisoners a space to walk. At the Tower Gate Arnon and Elan, each dragging their chains, joined the procession. Rough hands shoved heavy wooden beams on the shoulders of each prisoner.

A vast multitude of people joined the procession as it moved slowly along the streets of Jerusalem. The priests spread the word everywhere that Jesus' followers were safe from retribution now that they had the chief offender in their control. They hoped that those who witnessed the humiliation of their leader would abandon the movement, that it would then collapse of its own accord.

Though weakened by weeks in a tiny underground cell, Arnon and Elan managed to carry their crosses. But Malchus watched Jesus stumble under the weight of His, falling again and again. At the prodding of a Roman spear the Teacher struggled to regain His footing. The two brothers cursed the delay, but only halfheartedly, since it meant a few more moments without pain before their scheduled execution began.

Again Jesus fell, and Centurion Marcus could see that He would be unable to reach the city gate unaided, never mind carry the wooden beam all the way to Golgotha. He scanned the crowd. Spotting a face full of pity above a strong, dark torso, he ordered, "You there! Carry this man's cross."

The man obeyed instantly, not stopping to question. One did not argue with scores of spears, and if anything happened to him, what would become of his two sons? He bent and hoisted the wooden beam onto his own back and stepped away to allow Jesus to stand. No complaint passed his lips that this defilement would prevent him from joining in the Passover celebration he had traveled so far to experience.

Jesus tried several times, but could not rise on His own. Finally Marcus had to help him to his feet. A strange sympathy for his silent captive filled him. This prisoner was different than anyone he'd ever met before.

"They forgot the criers," Alona said, her first words in nearly an hour.

"What?" Her husband looked at her blankly.

"The criers," she repeated. "The ones who go out before the accused, begging for anyone who has any information at all that might clear the condemned person to please come forward."

"They didn't forget," Malchus said after a moment. "They were afraid that if they asked for evidence in Jesus' favor, they might get it."

"I don't understand," Othniel broke in. "How can Elohim stand by and do nothing? He should strike down all those who are abusing Jesus."

"I don't understand either," Malchus admitted, "but if He did, we would be struck down as well." He glanced down at the stone pavement of the street. "Look," he said softly, pointing with a shaking hand.

"We are walking in His footsteps." Still visible even after being trampled by scores of people, the bloody imprints told all too clearly a tale of suffering.

By the road outside the Damascus Gate a dead tree stabbed its branches high into the air. Wild dogs snarled and fought over a carcass at its base, and the procession was nearly abreast of it when those at the edge of the crowd saw what the pack was devouring. The face was unrecognizable, but there was no mistaking the clothing Judas had worn only a few hours before. As Malchus' gaze traveled up the tree, he saw the frayed end of rope dangling from an overhanging limb. Several men broke off from the rest to beat off the ravenous beasts and bury what remained of the body.

A little farther, to the west of the Damascus road, they wended their way to the execution site. Easily seen by anyone passing by on the busy thoroughfare, the spot was a favorite choice of the Romans for their crucifixions. As they neared it, the soldiers ripped off the garments of their prisoners, leaving them naked.

On a raised platform of sorts Roman guards slid their fingers into the grips of three square stones, lifting them to reveal cross-holes already carved into the rock. Setting the covers aside, they helped position the three crosses, one by each hole. A notice in Aramaic, Greek, and Latin had been nailed to the middle cross. The two brothers fought wildly as the soldiers held down their arms and legs, binding them with new rope. Their screams rent the air as guards nailed them in place.

Arnon was the loudest, shouting, "I shouldn't be here! Cenurion Marcus, tell them we had a deal. It wasn't supposed to happen this way! I don't deserve to be here." His voice trailed off in a sob. Then he turned on his brother. "It's all your fault I'm in this mess. If you weren't such a sheep-brained coward I wouldn't be here at all."

"You brought that traitor into our camp in the first place," Elan snapped, "but could you warn your own brother? Nooooo!" It was just a continuation of the argument that had raged throughout their imprisonment.

But Jesus, still silent, lay down and submissively stretched out His arms. He didn't cry out when spikes pierced His hands, though sweat poured down His face. A soldier bent His legs, aligning His feet with the front of the cross. Placing the spike on the outside of His heel, the burly soldier hammered it ruthlessly into place, pinning Him in a contorted position. Though excruciating, it gave the prisoners a footing upon which to push, allowing them to breathe. After all, the whole point of such a form of execution was to drag it out as long as possible.

Alona held Malchus' hand, and he squeezed it convulsively as the soldiers lifted the cross and dropped it abruptly into the deep hole, viciously jarring the condemned Man's feet and hands. He was close enough to hear Jesus moan, "Father, forgive them. They don't know what they're doing." Centurion Marcus looked up at the Man in astonishment. Nothing had prepared the centurion for the prisoner who had replaced Barabbas: a Man who, though dying naked in utter humiliation, could still ask forgiveness for those who were killing Him. The Roman tried to shake off a sense of worry and fear, but he couldn't help thinking that the inscription above the dying Man might be true. *Jesus of Nazareth, King of the Jews.*

Moved to offer what comfort he could, the Roman officer soaked a sponge in cheap soured wine that had been laced with something to deaden the pain. He held it up to Jesus' cracked lips. The Teacher took one swallow, then turned His head away, refusing to drink any more.

For the first time Zarad stepped to the front of the crowd, standing defiantly in full view of Jesus. Malchus was surprised to see a spark of recognition in Jesus' eyes, but no anger toward one of the men most responsible for His agony. "If you are truly the Son of God," Zarad sneered, "come down from that cross."

Caiaphas joined in with a malicious laugh. "He saved plenty of others, but he can't even save himself. I guess this messiah isn't as strong as he thought he was."

"Where is your God now?" Zarad taunted. "If you were really His Son, He would save you." The man edged closer. "Look around you. They all hate you. Even the ones you thought were yours couldn't get away from you fast enough." Then he lowered his voice. "You must have been mistaken. You only thought you were the Messiah. You're a deluded fool, Jesus!" he exploded, almost choking on the last word.

When Jesus didn't respond, Zarad lost his temper completely, screaming curses at Him while the priests added their own invectives. Zarad's men joined him openly in mocking the Man on the middle cross. Soon Jesus had difficulty breathing and had to push Himself laboriously up to inhale, putting His full weight on His nailed heels. The crowd showed no sympathy, only doubled and redoubled its mockery. Elan, with nothing better to do, joined them.

Arnon had very little to do either, but he had spent the past several hours thinking back over his failed life. For all that he said he didn't deserve to die, he had to admit that wasn't strictly true. Counting in his mind he came up with at least 37 additional crimes he had personally committed that would have earned him death had the Romans found out. He craned his neck to look at Jesus. A strange thought struck him: *No amount of suffering could ever erase the Teacher's nobility.* Suddenly Arnon wished he might be freed just long enough to bow down in front of Him and ask for His forgiveness.

At midday dark clouds rolled in to block the sun. Elan continued to rage against their fellow prisoner. "My brother, don't you have any respect for God?" Arnon said finally, unable to stand it any longer. "You know we both are getting what we deserve, but this Man is innocent." Elan's only reply was another oath.

On impulse Arnon leaned toward Jesus as much as he could. "Lord," he said hesitantly, "please remember me when You come into Your kingdom."

The sorrow lifted briefly from Jesus' haggard face. "Today, I give you My promise. You will be with Me in Paradise." The spreading darkness was pierced by a single beam of light that shone on the base of Golgotha for a moment before all turned to blackness.

CHAPTER 16

Malchus and Alona huddled together in the unnatural darkness, Othniel close beside them. The mocking of the crowd hushed, the only sound now the high-pitched wailing of fear. Lightning crackled across the sky close over their heads, giving them an occasional glimpse of the scene spread before them. The masses crouched on the ground in terror, and even the priests ceased their taunting. Centurion Marcus—it

could only be he—stood at attention at the base of the crosses, determined that if divine judgment fell on the world he would still be found
at his post of duty, and his soldiers soon followed his example. Only
Zarad and his men seemed unaffected, growing ever louder and more
hostile as they tormented Jesus.

During the next three hours many in the crowd tried to find their
way back to the city. Malchus shielded Alona the best he could as they
sat unmoving, their hearts torn by anguish, but still they were accidentally kicked many times, and several people fell over them.

In the middle of the afternoon the shadows began to lift, though
they continued to hide the dying Jesus. Lightning continued to strike
around the crosses. "See?" Caiaphas said, nodding his head sagely. "He
took the place of God, and now God is punishing him. He is doomed!"

Othniel gripped Malchus' arm and half-turned him. "Our people
are the ones who are doomed. Look behind you."

Malchus twisted about. Heavy darkness still covered the city of
Jerusalem. In a voice thick with tears, Alona quoted, "'For among my
people are found wicked men: they lay wait, as he that setteth snares;
they set a trap, they catch men. . . . Shall I not visit for these things?
saith the Lord: shall not my soul be avenged on a nation such as this?'"

Othniel pressed his clasped hands against his mouth. "I have to go
back there and find my wife." He bowed his head. "She must be terrified right now. And I have so many things to make right."

Malchus nodded. "I understand. If you need anything, I'll be right
here." Alona reached out to the cousin she had so disliked, clasping his
hand in wordless sympathy. They watched as Othniel made his way
down to the road and walked the short distance to the city gate, where
the blackness again engulfed him.

"My God, My God." The despairing cry seemed to erupt from the
foundations of the earth. "Why have You forsaken Me?" Malchus
sobbed openly as Alona tried vainly to comfort him. Zarad danced with
glee, spewing forth a fresh barrage of abuse. Then, in barely more than
a whisper, Jesus breathed, "I thirst."

Looking up, Marcus saw the battered face of his prisoner for the
first time in hours. Jesus was bruised and bloody, His swollen lips
cracked and dry. His ribs heaved convulsively, the bones showing
through some of the wounds on His sides. His legs shook with the ef-

fort of pushing up for each breath, while His mangled back scraped up and down the rough wood with each effort. Swallowing the unexpected lump that rose in his throat, the Roman again dipped the sponge in the mixture of wine and myrrh, holding it carefully aloft.

Jesus received the drink. Then gathering Himself, He pushed upward to draw a deep breath, then exclaimed, *"It is finished!"* Instantly He slumped, His head lolling lifelessly on His chest.

Bright light exploded from the sky and encircled the still form of Jesus. Malchus and Alona stood frozen, unable to speak.

"No!" The distorted scream was Zarad's. He shook his fists at the sky. "No!" he shrieked again, his fury boundless. Suddenly he vanished, a thunderclap lingering behind him. His men quietly faded away.

Malchus rubbed his eyes, sure they had deceived him. But no, Zarad was gone. "I talked to him," he stammered. "I worked for him." A moment's thought. "Caiaphas worked for him, was owned by him."

He did not hear his wife's reply as the darkness crashed in once more and a mighty earthquake shook the whole land. The people clung to the ground as great rocks broke loose and rolled down from the hillsides, leaving paths of destruction behind them. Graves opened up, tossing out the bodies they had concealed. The very bedrock of Calvary split asunder as the earth received the blood of its Creator.

In the Temple the massive curtain that hid the Most Holy Place ripped from top to bottom, exposing the table that had been placed there after the disappearance of the ark of the covenant just before the first Babylonian siege of Jerusalem. The priest who had taken Caiaphas' place for the evening sacrifice dropped his knife, and the startled Passover lamb fled, bleating its way across the Temple courtyard.

Then, as the darkness melted, the sun again shone and the birds sang. A balmy afternoon breeze lifted Alona's hair to tickle Malchus' face. Were it not for the graying body on the center cross it would have seemed like awakening from a terrifying dream.

Uneasily Annas and Caiaphas led the delegation of priests back to Pilate. Using as their excuse not wanting to violate the Sabbath, now only a few scant hours away, they asked to have Jesus' body removed, and for the other two criminals to have their legs broken so they would be dead before sundown. Pilate assented, having his own reasons for wanting Jesus taken off the cross as quickly as possible.

Annas, in poor health and exhausted by his exertions, returned home, but Caiaphas soon returned to the execution site to see Pilate's orders carried out. He walked right past where Malchus sat but did not acknowledge him.

Marcus nodded to one of his men to finish the grim task. Picking up a club, the soldier advanced on Arnon and swung the heavy weapon at the robber's shins. Through the dizzying haze of pain Arnon groaned, but said nothing, even in the face of the very priest who had turned him away from Jesus not long before. "Forgive him" was the prayer of his heart. "Please forgive Joseph Caiaphas."

Elan hoisted himself up as far as he could go and screamed obscenities as the soldier approached. A sickening crunch, and he hung there hardly able to breathe. Within minutes his head began to buzz and his vision to cloud. Still he continued to whisper epithets with his remaining breath.

When the soldier came to Jesus, it was obvious that He was already dead. Still, just to make sure, he forced his spear between the motionless ribs. A gush of straw-colored fluid poured out, and a thick cascade of clotting blood, both running into the deep crack in the rock. The Roman stepped back and nodded. "He's ready."

Centurion Marcus sighed. "I'd better go and tell Pilate myself. Leave Him there until I get back."

Tired and weak, Malchus and Alona edged closer to where a small group of Jesus' followers waited. Many of the inner circle were now there, looking lost and alone. John, the brother of James, held the grief-stricken mother of Jesus, supporting her in his arms. Stumbling on one of the rocks that littered the ground, Malchus bumped into a man, who started with fear and turned. It was Peter.

"I'm sorry," Malchus said, holding out his hand.

The man looked away, hesitating a moment before reaching out. "I'm sorry too." The tears spilled over. "I was one of His followers, you know."

Alona suspected Peter had told a good many people those words in the crushing aftermath of his denial. "I know," she said gently. "We both know."

Peter hid his face in his hands. In a muffled voice he answered, "It's too late to tell Him. It's too late to tell Jesus."

A Roman officer returned leading two wealthy men. Joseph of Arimathea walked by the soldier's side, and Nicodemus, heavily laden, followed behind. "John," Joseph called to the worried disciple, "don't worry about the burial. Pilate said we can use my tomb, and Nicodemus has the spices." Unwilling to delegate the task to a servant, Nicodemus himself carried the bag of myrrh and aloes, about the weight of a grown woman. Afraid to support Jesus openly during His life, the two members of the Sanhedrin now set aside their pride and status to be near Him in His death, completely ignoring Caiaphas' hostile stare.

Malchus stood at the back, watching solemnly as the two prestigious religious leaders laboriously removed the spikes and lowered the body of Jesus from the cross. Martha, who had procured long winding cloths for the burial, now hurriedly covered the broken body to restore some semblance of modesty.

"These two are both dead now, as well," a soldier called to Marcus. "What do I do with them?"

The Roman centurion examined the bodies. "Make sure they're dead, and throw them on that rubbish heap over there." He indicated a refuse pile on the other side of the road. The soldier hastened to obey, thrusting his spear into the chest of each man in turn. Then he and several others pulled the executed criminals down, dragged them off, and dumped them carelessly among the garbage. The rest of the men had dismantled the crosses, carefully setting the stones back in place to keep debris out of the postholes. The first group returned and picked up the hammer, nails, and pitcher of sour wine.

"All right, men," Marcus said briskly. "That's all. Let's go."

"Wait," Caiaphas screeched, "you can't just give the body to them like that." He pointed to where the disciples had just finished fashioning a rude hammock in which to carry their Master to His grave. "What if they steal it? They'll tell everyone He came back from the dead, and there will be rioting in the streets."

The Roman officer sighed. "Go and talk to Pilate. My men and I will wait here." Caiaphas bustled off, his beard waving in the breeze, a few of the priests still trailing behind.

Malchus and Peter stepped forward simultaneously to help bear Jesus' body to its resting place. Joseph took up the head, Malchus the middle, and Peter lovingly took the feet. Nicodemus, sweat running down his brow, still carried the heavy perfumes for embalming.

Fortunately Joseph's tomb was close at hand, carved into the rock. Alona gladly aided John in steadying the faltering steps of Mary, mother of Jesus. Outside the tomb opening they laid Jesus gently on the ground. Martha had planned for this, too, and knelt with a basin of water and a cloth.

"I'll do it," Peter said. Martha opened her mouth to refuse, but something in his face stopped her. Wordlessly she handed the cloth to him. Carefully he cleansed the dirt, dried spittle, and crusted blood from his Lord. As he came to the feet his shoulders shook. "When He was alive, I wouldn't wash His feet," Peter sobbed, overcome. "But He still washed mine as if He were a servant."

"We'd better hurry," Martha finally interrupted. "The sun is almost down, and it will be the Sabbath." The red orb of the Passover sun approached the horizon.

"What about the rest of the embalming?" Nicodemus asked. "We still have more spices."

"I'll tell you what we'll do," Martha said decidedly. "Let's wrap the body loosely, and we women will come at dawn on First Day to finish the embalming." No one had a better idea, so Martha divided the spices among the women who were going to help.

She wrapped the body in a simple pattern, its arms folded across the heart that had ceased to pulse. Joseph again took up the head, guiding the men into the tomb, helping them lay Jesus in a hollow chiseled into the wall of the chamber. Not knowing what else to do, they left the tomb with many a backward look.

A new squadron of troops arrived, Caiaphas accompanying them. The second centurion held the governor's seal to place over the door of the tomb. At his nod the soldiers marched to the heavy stone and rolled it along the trench to cover the door. On each side of the stone they hammered in a metal spike to keep it in place, then fastened the seal across the whole. The centurion dripped hot wax on each end, pressing in deep with the governor's insignia. At his order the soldiers spread, shoulder to shoulder, guarding the tomb from any tampering. Satisfied at last, Caiaphas left for home.

The little group of Jesus' followers gradually dispersed in twos and threes, some into the city and some, including Lazarus and his sisters, into the encampment of pilgrims. Malchus stumbled often, his red-rimmed eyes unable to focus on the stones in his path. Alona, though exhausted, did all she could to help him.

It was twilight when they at last reached their home. The servants were nowhere to be seen, but an oil lamp burned in the entry. Malchus leaned on a narrow stone table, head down, gathering the strength to walk to his bedchamber. A deep voice behind him startled him, and Alona looked up in surprise.

"I was beginning to think you two were never getting home," Gershom said cheerfully, lamp in hand. "I hope you don't mind us barging in without warning."

"Us?" Alona questioned. Malchus glanced up at his father, his face hidden in shadow.

Safiya peeped around the doorway, a shy smile on her lined face. Malchus, who had never seen his mother leave her yard in all the years since his birth, gaped in shock. "Surprise!" Gershom exclaimed. "I have been trying for months to convince her, and she finally listened. We are going to find Jesus and ask Him to heal her." Safiya nodded and smiled again.

Malchus reeled back, the light illuminating his ravaged face. Alona caught him from behind, straining to support him. Gershom sprang forward in fright, grabbing his son's arms to hold him up. "Malchus! Are you all right? What happened? Are you sick?"

His voice ragged, Malchus could say just one word. "Jesus."

"What's wrong?" Gershom asked, puzzled. He looked at Alona's pale face, but she only shook her head.

"He's dead," Malchus choked. "I killed Him."

— — —

Without any need for discussion, the family decided not to attend Temple services the next day. Instead they gathered to read for themselves the writings of the sacred scrolls regarding the Messiah. Alona chose the book of Isaiah, parts of which had always baffled her.

"Let's spend a moment in prayer first," Gershom suggested, so they silently bowed to ask Elohim to guide them and help them understand what had happened, and what they were to do next.

Alona shuffled nearly all the way through the scroll before finding the passage she sought. In her clear voice she read the ancient prophecy.

> "'Surely he hath borne our griefs, and carried our sorrows:
>> Yet we did esteem him stricken, smitten by God,
>>> and afflicted.
>> But he was wounded for our transgressions, he was
>>> bruised for our iniquities:
>> The chastisement of our peace was upon him; and with
>>> his stripes we are healed.'"

Her voice broke, but she struggled on.

> "'All we like sheep have gone astray; we have turned every
>> one to his own way;
>> And the Lord hath laid on him the iniquity of us all.
>> He was oppressed, and he was afflicted, yet he opened
>>> not his mouth:
>> He is brought as a lamb to the slaughter,
>> And as a sheep before her shearers is dumb, so he opened
>>> not his mouth. . . .
>> And he made his grave with the wicked, and with the
>>> rich in his death;
>> Because he had done no violence, neither was any deceit
>>> in his mouth.
>> Yet it pleased the Lord to bruise him; he hath put him
>>> to grief:
>> When thou shalt make his soul an offering for sin, he
>>> shall see his seed,
>> He shall prolong his days, and the pleasure of the Lord
>> Shall prosper in his hand.
>> He shall see the travail of his soul, and shall be satisfied:
>> By his knowledge shall my righteous servant justify many,
>> For he shall bear their iniquities.'"

They sat in silence for a long time. Finally Gershom said, "Jesus was our lamb, our Passover sacrifice." It was as if light had dawned over them all. It was not to overthrow the Romans, they realized, or to establish a new Israelite kingdom that Jesus had come, but to carry the sins of the people.

"That's what he told Judas," Malchus said. "At the trial, when Judas begged Him to set Himself free, He said, 'This is why I came into the world.' Could it be that He planned this from the beginning?" Malchus' overpowering sense of guilt eased a little. Even though his actions had caused the arrest and ultimately the death of Jesus, it helped to know that there might have been a larger plan at work. That Elohim had even those terrible events under His control and could use them in some way for good.

"I fear that our sacrifices are now useless," Alona said, cutting to the heart of the matter. "Everything about our system of worship pointed to Messiah's coming. Now He's already been here—and there's nothing left."

With that Malchus felt the cold lump in the pit of his stomach grow larger. "What do we do now?" he sighed.

— — —

A rooster's crow broke the early-morning hush on the first day of the new week. The guard detail at the tomb still stood at attention. That was no surprise—death was the penalty otherwise. Dawn was still afar off. Only a faint blush warmed the eastern horizon. Suddenly, as if the sun had fallen from the sky, a fiery bolt dropped down to land inside the circle of guards.

Pure white light brightened the landscape for miles. The soldiers dropped flat on the ground, trying to shield their eyes from the blinding rays, until they lost consciousness.

A dazzling being took shape. "Son of God!" His clarion call echoed like thunder. "Your Father calls You—*arise!*" The angel flung wide his arms, and the giant stone sailed through the air. The only evidences that it had ever covered the door were the dangling Roman seal and the metal spike, sheared off level with the face of the cliff.

Another glory, brighter still, shone from inside the tomb. The wrappings that had bound Jesus fell away, and He now stood, all the light of heaven in His face. Then He stooped, His hair falling forward, and picked up the graveclothes. Folding them neatly, He placed them at the foot of where He had lain. Then, radiating infinite joy, He stepped out to meet Gabriel, embracing His dear friend.

Jesus turned His face toward Jerusalem and held up His scarred hands. Each grave torn open during the great earthquake now stirred with life. Across the landscape they came, faithful witnesses of all ages. Some were giants, others were an ordinary size, but all were glorified even as Jesus was.

One last thing was left for Jesus to do. Facing the east, where the people of the city discarded their refuse, he found what was left of the two thieves. "Arnon," He called melodiously yet urgently. "Arnon, get up!"

The man sat up, looking around in wonder. The last thing he could remember was the cross, a searing pain in his legs, and being unable to breathe. He took a deep breath now, wiggling his fingers in amazement. There was no trace that he had ever been crucified! Excited, he jumped to his feet and saw Jesus surrounded by a band of newly resurrected men and women. Then he ran to join them as they bowed before their King.

"I have work for all of you to do," Jesus told them, laughing in sheerest delight. "Spread through the land and preach. There isn't much time before we go home." Embracing his cousin, he declared, "John, I have a special job for you." He held out his arms to Arnon, too. "You and Arnon will preach in Jerusalem."

CHAPTER 17

Well before dawn Safiya slipped quietly from her bed. She dressed herself with her one good arm and slipped out the door. The world outside looked large and threatening compared to her safe home, but she forced herself to walk out into it. More by instinct than anything else she found her way to the north gate.

Oddly enough, the gate was open and unguarded. She walked to the left along the city wall till she came to a beautiful garden. Inside was a hewn tomb, completely empty. Impulsively she went in.

Her heart ached as she thought of the things her son had told her and how Jesus had finally been laid to rest. Hoping to find the spot, just to be near Him, she wandered down the dim path past the grave. As she rounded a bush she saw a man that she at first judged to be very old. His hair was white, as were His clothes, but His face was smooth. Her gaze dropped to His hands. Red, puckered scars stood out vividly against the supple skin. His feet, just peeking from under His robe, showed similar scars. Safiya ran and mutely threw herself down at His feet.

"Hello, Safiya; I've been expecting you." His voice was so gentle and kind that she felt drawn to look up. The love she saw warmed and filled her. "Would you like to be made well?" She nodded emphatically. Jesus stretched out His arm, saying, "Give Me your hand."

Hesitantly Safiya held out her good hand. "Not that one," Jesus chuckled. "The other one."

Safiya looked down at the limp hand in her lap, willing it to move. Her fingers twitched, her arm jumped, and she jerkily reached her hand out to Jesus. "Master," she said through vocal cords rusty from long disuse. "Jesus."

Jesus cupped both her hands, and she could feel the scars on His palms. "Your little Josu is safe in My hands," He said quietly. "I am resurrection. I am life!"

Safiya broke down, her head bowed. "Please forgive me," she cried. "I should have trusted You."

"I forgive you," Jesus responded. "I always will." He pressed her hands one last time before releasing them. "There is someone else I must meet."

As she left through a different gate, Safiya could see a distraught woman enter the garden. When she saw the empty tomb, she wailed and collapsed on the ground. Jesus walked over to her. The woman looked up, her vision blurred from weeping, and Safiya heard her ask, "Sir, are you the gardener?"

— — —

Alona shook Malchus awake. "Where's Mother?" she asked frantically.

"Whose mother?" he mumbled sleepily.

Alona shook him again, harder for good measure. "My parents have been dead for years. Of course I mean your mother!"

Her husband sat up. "Did you already ask Father?"

"He's the one who asked me."

Wide awake now, Malchus threw on his clothes and made a quick search of the house. His worry mounting, he stepped outside and looked up and down the street. "Mother, where have you been?" he said to the woman hurrying toward him. She held out her arms to him. "Mother?"

"Oh, Malchus, I've seen Him. He's alive!" Never before had he heard her voice. And never before had he felt her arms around him. He clung to her, afraid to let go.

"Malchus?" his father called. "Oh, good, there she is. Safiya, we were so worried about you."

She pulled slowly away from her son. "I was with Jesus." Then she crossed to her husband and, with the arm that had been injured, reached up to touch his face.

He caught her hand and kissed it, staring with amazement at his suddenly youthful wife. "How can that be? Jesus is dead."

"Not anymore," Safiya said with conviction. "I saw Him, and I talked to Him."

"Don't stay out here on the street, Mother," Alona interrupted. "Come in and tell us what happened."

It was like a reunion. Safiya had so much to say, years and years of words stored up, waiting for their chance to be spoken. Malchus had to put his hand over her mouth just to ask her a question. "Why didn't you ever tell me about your family? They are my family, too."

"We thought it was too dangerous," his father interrupted. "Relations between Israel and Nabataea went from bad to worse, and we wanted to protect you."

Safiya plucked Malchus' hand away so she could talk. "Actually, we did tell you." Her eyes twinkled with mischief.

"I give up. How?" her son asked.

"Your name," she replied. "Malchus was a very important king of Nabataea. Even your name, Malchus, means 'king.'"

A pounding at the door startled them. Alona jumped up to answer it. "Malchus," she called, "it's for you. Caiaphas wants you—now."

Her husband went to the door. "I'm sorry," he said politely, "but you must have me mixed up with someone else. Caiaphas told me to go away and never come back."

The messenger wrung his hands. "He really did send me to you. He said to tell you it has to do with Jesus."

Malchus considered it for a moment. "Alona, my love," he bent and kissed her, "I suppose I'd better see what he wants."

"What if it's a trap?" she whispered, wide-eyed. "He did tell you not to come back."

"I'll risk it. Elohim will go with me," he reassured her.

Pandemonium reigned in the palace of the high priest. Pushing through the chaos and into the chamber where the trial had been held, Malchus found his former master huddled against the wall, tremors rocking his body from head to foot. It was not difficult to figure out why.

The other occupants of the room were the detachment of Roman soldiers. That was bad enough—it would take extensive ritual purifications to remove the defilement of having Gentiles under the same roof.

"Help me, Malchus, help me," the high priest blubbered. "The only way to salvage this is if these men say they were asleep and the members of the inner circle stole the body. Please make them do it—I don't dare leave, or I might meet him."

Malchus understood perfectly which "Him" Caiaphas meant. "You are asking the wrong person," he said calmly. "Perhaps you should be talking to Zarad."

"I can't find him anywhere. He has abandoned me—just when I needed him, too."

"Make that priest see reason," the centurion interrupted angrily. "Pilate will have us killed if he thinks we were sleeping on duty."

"No, he won't," Caiaphas said. "I will see to that. And I will pay you well for the risk. Whatever it takes, I will give you."

"Anything at all?" asked the centurion with interest.

The high priest nodded. "Anything!"

"I will not have anything to do with this vile lie," Malchus protested. "I'll tell as many people as I can about your foul conspiracy. I'll tell them how you broke every law of the Sanhedrin to find Jesus guilty. And I'll tell them that when Jesus came back to life you were so afraid of meeting Him that you hid in your palace and paid others to spread your lies for you."

"They'll never believe you," the infuriated man screamed after him as Malchus left the home of the high priest for the last time.

— — —

That was not the last of the strange events that occurred. Rumor swept the land that John the Baptist, as well as a host of others, had risen from the dead. Herod, especially, was frightened at that, but all of the main conspirators in the death of Jesus kept to their homes, behind locked doors. Even then they could not feel safe. Every time they closed their eyes they could picture that patient, suffering, godlike face, and see the man they condemned lighting up the sky with His glory.

And so it was that a few weeks later Jesus led the members of the inner circle up the slope of the Mount of Olives. Past Gethsemane, the scene of His arrest and betrayal, and up to the crest of the hill where Jerusalem spread before His view. Sensing that time was growing short, Malchus ran after Jesus, fearful that he would lose the opportunity to make amends.

Jesus heard the running footsteps and turned around to wait for Malchus. The man who had been a bitter enemy of the Messiah bowed at His feet and called Him Lord. At last he could say the words that had been on his heart for so long. "I'm so sorry, Jesus," he said humbly. "Please forgive me for all the things I did to hurt You. And thank You."

"You're welcome." Jesus pulled him to his feet and hugged him. "I forgave you a long time ago, Malchus." With a sparkle in His eyes He touched the side of Malchus' head. "He that has an ear, let him hear."

Malchus grinned. "I'm listening now, Master." He fell back with the multitude that was following at a distance and began searching for his wife and parents. Jesus continued on to the crest of the hill where He met a cluster of extraordinary humans. Malchus squinted into the sun at them. There was the Baptist, whom Malchus had seen preaching on the street corners of Jerusalem. But the man on Jesus' right hand looked like—no, it couldn't be.

"There's Arnon," Othniel said in his ear. "I saw him earlier in the city." Malchus was pleased to see his cousin now arm-in-arm with his wife, both looking happy. They must have worked through their differences and made a new start in their marriage.

The cloud of witnesses rose first. Jesus stayed as long as He could, but a powerful force drew Him upward until He was just a dark speck in the bright sky. Then a stray cloud blew by and hid Him from sight.

Malchus stood for the longest time, face upturned toward the heavens, straining to catch just one more glimpse of Jesus. "Why are you still looking up at the sky?" someone behind him asked. They all turned to look at the speaker.

"Jesus will come back just the way you saw Him leave," the tall stranger said, his curly black hair bobbing as he gestured emphatically. "So get busy and tell the world!"

"I've met you before," Gershom interjected. "Do you live around here?"

"I get around a lot," the man replied vaguely, turning to go.

"What is your name?" Malchus' father persisted.

The man lifted his hand in farewell, calling over his shoulder, "Gurion."

"Gurion. Gurion," Gershom muttered to himself. "I don't remember ever meeting anyone named Gurion. Oh well, it probably isn't important." Suddenly he straightened. "Wait, I remember. Come back!" But it was too late. Gurion had disappeared into the crowd.

Excitedly Gershom turned to Safiya. "Now I know where I met him. That is the man who saved your life on the day—um, on that terrible day."

"The day Josu died?" It was the first time in decades she had been able to say the child's name.

"Yes," her husband said. "He held your wound closed until I got there. Without him I would have lost you, too. And Malchus."

"Do you think he is an angel?"

It was the first time that thought had occurred to Gershom. "I'm not sure," he said slowly, "but that is twice now he's vanished. He could be . . ."

"I wonder if I've ever seen an angel?" Malchus asked. Somehow that made him think of his friend Deron, always turning up just in time to save him from danger. "Maybe I'll never know for sure, but Elohim has certainly taken care of me."

"Where do we go now?" Alona asked.

Malchus shrugged, but his mother blurted, "I've been thinking about that. Why don't we go and visit my sister? The last I heard she was living in Zoara. Besides, someone has to tell my people about Jesus."

— ◆ —

One Year Later

"Malchus, where are you? We have company." Safiya looked from one room to the next in the spacious house she and Gershom shared with Malchus and Alona. "I'm sorry; I don't know what he's done with himself. Oh, there you are! Come and say hello to your cousin, Malchus. His name is Husam, and his father is my half brother."

Fanning his face against the desert heat, Malchus entered the room. "Husam, I'm glad to meet you," he said, holding out his right hand in greeting.

"I also," Husam said, returning the gesture. Though not quite as tall as Malchus, the powerfully built man looked as if he could handle himself in battle.

"Do you have any word of my grandmother?" Malchus asked.

"Sitt Maryam is in good health, and she hopes to see you as soon as the infant is old enough to travel."

"Would you like a drink?" Safiya offered the men a cup of water fresh from the well.

"Thank you," Husam said, accepting it gratefully.

"Say hello to Abba, Simeon," Alona crooned, entering the room. The baby in her arms smiled and cooed when she handed him to his beloved abba. "He just woke up a few minutes ago, and I knew you'd want to see him."

Malchus managed to interrupt his patter of baby talk long enough to ask her, "Did you already meet our cousin, Husam?"

The man paid no attention, transfixed by an object hanging on the wall. "Where did you get this?" he asked strangely.

"My dagger?" Malchus laughed. "It's a long story."

Husam took the dagger down from the wall and stood looking at it for a great while. "Actually, it's my dagger. And I have plenty of time."

"You mean that was you? In the garden that night?" Malchus gasped.

Now it was Husam's turn to be surprised. "You? You were the one who took it from me?" He swallowed hard. "I guess we can both be thankful you didn't kill me."

Approaching Husam, Malchus put his hand on the man's shoulder. "Of course you must keep it, but tell me, aren't you even a little curious about what it's been doing without you the past four years or so?"

Husam clutched his long-lost weapon protectively against his chest. "Of course."

"It's a love story, the greatest love story of all time," Malchus said, beaming with joy, "and it started with a man named Jesus."